The Murder Queens 2

Michael Gallon

Lock Down Publications and Ca$h
Presents
The Murder Queens 2
A Novel by *Michael Gallon*

The Murder Queens 2

Lock Down Publications
Po Box 944
Stockbridge, Ga 30281

Visit our website @
www.lockdownpublications.com

Lock Down Publications
Like our page on Facebook: Lock Down Publications @
www.facebook.com/lockdownpublications.ldp
Book interior design by: **Shawn Walker**
Edited by: **Cassandra Barret-Sims**

Michael Gallon

Stay Connected with Us!

Submission Guideline.

Submit the first three chapters of your completed manuscript to ldpsubmissions@gmail.com, subject line: Your book's title. The manuscript must be in a .doc file and sent as an attachment. Document should be in Times New Roman, double spaced and in size 12 font. Also, provide your synopsis and full contact information. If sending multiple submissions, they must each be in a separate email.

Have a story but no way to send it electronically? You can still submit to LDP/Ca$h Presents. Send in the first three chapters, written or typed, of your completed manuscript to:

LDP: Submissions Dept
Po Box 944
Stockbridge, Ga 30281

DO NOT send original manuscript. Must be a duplicate.

Provide your synopsis and a cover letter containing your full contact information.

Thanks for considering LDP and Ca$h Presents.

Michael Gallon

PROLOGUE

"Alright, you busta-ass niggas. Take off your masks and keep your hands where I can see them," I demanded.

To my surprise, it was the niggas from the carwash. Lil Q, Ba-dass Mikey, and the pussy-eating-ass nigga who went by the name Goldmouth. I don't know why they even called him that, 'cause that nigga didn't have a gold tooth nowhere in his fuckin' nasty ass mouth.

The guy who was lying on the floor crying about his leg was called Skinny Pimp. First of all, his breath smelled like he had eaten two shit sandwiches for breakfast, and he had no teeth in his fuckin' stank ass mouth. I looked at him crying on the floor.

"Man, why they call you Skinny Pimp?" he turned over slightly, as he moaned in pain.

"Cause I used to pimp your mother, nigga!" he said back to me, as he held his broken jaw.

"Now you didn't have to go there," I said calmly. "Do you even know who my mother is?" Before he could respond to my question, Sexy Redd kicked him so fuckin' hard, he farted and passed out.

Strawberry threw his rusty piece of a gun at him while he lay there on the floor in a dead sleep.

"Why did you do that Strawberry?" Sexy Redd asked, with a surprised look on her face.

"Man, that wasn't a fuckin gun! That was some old ass piece of scrap iron made to look like a fuckin' gun!" Strawberry said, as she kicked Skinny Pimp in his back.

"So, you young cats were just gonna come up in here and rob a brother and his employees, huh?" I asked.

"Mike, you have to believe me when I tell you, it was some of your own dancers who set this fucked up idea in motion! They told us you always up in here flossing about how much money you be making, and how all the females be up in here walking around butt ass naked!"

"So, that gives you the right to come in my crib and slap one of my dancers in the face so hard she probably won't be able to dance for a whole fuckin' month? And then cause her to bleed all over my ten-thousand-dollar Persian rug? Not to mention, you tried to rob them of what they made over the weekend."

Sexy Redd was standing to the side of me with her chrome .45 pointed at them. "Not to mention, Mike, they were going to kill all of us after they robbed us!"

"Mike, that was them niggas and them silly ass hoes of yours," Badass Mikey said. "I told their dumb asses yesterday this was a bad idea. But, nah, they had to listen to them stupid ass bitches. Mike, man, just let me go, and I promise I won't say anything to nobody. I swear on my mama," he said.

I just looked at him and thought, *man, you must think I'm stupid or something?*

"Nah, Mike, this one wanted to fuck me in the ass," Nicole said, and kicked him right smack dab in his nuts, with her heels on.

"Baby, just let me do these clown ass niggas now and get it over with," Redd said. She pointed her gun at the leader of the group.

"Hold on, Redd, we can't just kill all four of them right now," I told her. "Hell, you don't want Detective Protho and his tall lanky ass partner to come hanging around here, do you?" I asked.

"Yeah, you right. So, what do we do with them then?"

"I tell you niggas what we're going to do. Bring me the females who helped you set this bullshit up. When you do that, we'll dead this and just forget it ever happened," I said.

"Hell, nah, Mike!" Mignon screamed, "if we let these fuck ass niggas leave, how sure are we they won't come back to finish us off?" The whole time she was standing there talking, the guy they called Lil Q had this shitty ass grin on his small ass face.

"Yo', lil' homie, why you all over there smiling and shit?" I yelled to him while Sexy Redd kept her pistol on all of them.

"Nah, it's like your lil' shorty right there is sexy as fuck. I just wanna fuck the shit out of her right here in front of everybody," he said, while standing there holding his dick in his hand, as if she had agreed to fuck him.

"Nigga, I don't do punk ass bitches who go around robbing people for a living!" Then, Mignon spat in his face too. He just wiped it off with his hand. Then, he licked it as he continued to smile at her.

"That's exactly what I like for a bitch to do. Spit on my dick while she choking on all this meat," he said and laughed out loud.

Mignon grabbed one of the guns that was off to the side of the countertop and pointed it straight at Lil Q's fuckin' head.

"Say something else, lil' ass nigga and I'll take your head clean off!" He laughed and tried to say something else.

Then, Skinny Pimp woke up. "Man, just shut the hell up before we all get killed. 'Cause if they shoot one of us, they gonna have to kill all of us!" Sexy Redd kicked that nigga right back to sleep. This time she kicked him so hard he shit all over himself.

"Damn, Redd, you do know someone is going to have to clean that nasty ass shit up, right?"

"Yeah, one of his fuck ass homies are gonna clean that shit up with they fuckin' shirt."

"Okay, this is how we're gonna do this, Goldmouth. Here is the number to call when you find me those bitches who crossed my girls and me. You have exactly one week to come up with those females. If not, Redd here will be paying each one of your mothers a fuckin' visit to leave them a black rose to remember you by.

"Nah, instead of paying them a visit, baby, I'm going to buy their mothers a black fuckin' dress so she can wear it to their funeral!"

Michael Gallon

CHAPTER ONE
THE BIG PAYBACK

After Goldmouth and his crew received their instructions, Sexy Redd escorted their broke, tired asses right out the front door. We kept their guns as we watched them pick Skinny Pimp up and carry him to the piece of automobile they called a car.

"That's why there wasn't no guard at the damn security gate," I looked at Sexy Redd and said, "they must have knocked him out or either tied his ass the fuck up. Then, them muthafuckas got in here without being noticed," I concluded.

"Mike, I don't trust some of these females that we allow up in here," she replied. "I wouldn't be surprised if it was one of the females in here who set us up," Sexy Redd said. She picked her things up from off the floor.

"Quiet, the girls will hear us talking," I said.

"Mike, do you want me to clean this mess up?" Strawberry asked as she came downstairs. She placed a rag and some ice over her lip. It was swollen four sizes bigger than its actual size.

"Damn, look at your fuckin' lip Strawberry," I said, as if I was Smokey in the movie "Friday".

"I know, Mike. You think I should go to the hospital?"

Nah, I gotcha, Strawberry, come with me," Sexy Redd said, as she whisked her away to help her with her three set of lips.

As they walked upstairs, there was one thing for sure. We couldn't let anybody know about what had taken place in the house that night.

Minutes later, Redd was coming down the stairs dressed in a pair of nice jean shorts and her cut-off Florida Hot Girl T-shirt.

"Baby, is everything all, right?" she asked.

"Yeah, but how her lips doing?" I asked.

"Funny, Mike. You know the girl was fucked up!"

"Yeah, you right. I'm sorry. Is she going to be alright?'

"Yeah, I gave her something to help with the swelling and something to put her to sleep. But I still think her eye is gonna be black and blue for a few days or so."

"Damn, I just got off the phone with the security gate guard. He said he had stepped out to check on one of the residents and that's why his punk ass wasn't in the damn guard shack!"

"Yeah, that was probably all the distraction they needed to get up in here," Sexy Redd said. She put some ice over her right hand.

"Okay, fine. Come with me to the pool house. There's something I need to show you."

We walked outside to the pool house, and upon emerging inside she looked and said, "Oh, my God! What is all this, Michael?" Her left hand covered her mouth since her right hand was wrapped in ice.

"Redd, this is the high-tech security equipment I had installed so I could monitor the house from out here. See, this right here will allow me to hear everything in every room. Did you notice how everybody was shaken except your girl Jasmine?" I quizzed her.

"Hell, yeah, I peeped that shit, Mike," Redd answered. "And how about they never touched her or said anything to her the whole time they were in the house?" Sexy Redd said. Her mouth hung open in surprise as she looked at all the high-tech equipment.

"Listen, tomorrow, take the girls to the mall, and I'll call Steve the security guy and have him install some more cameras. In the meantime, I'll figure out a way to get rid of our problem," I told her.

Meanwhile, Jasmine paced back in forth in her room wondering how Goldmouth and his crew of men had fucked up the plan. She decided to call her counterpart.

She answered on the first ring. "Hey, girl," Do-Dirty said, on the cheap ass mobile phone.

"What's up, chick?" Jasmine replied. "Do-Dirty, them fools done fucked up!"

"No, chick, what happened? Did they get the money?" Do-Dirty asked Jasmine, with fear in her voice.

"No, bitch! Them clowns got here and didn't make sure they had all of us downstairs. Sexy Redd came out of nowhere, and spoiled the whole plan, girl!"

"What, bitch? So, they didn't get nothing?" Do-dirty asked.

"No, bitch! Not one red cent. Then Goldmouth punk ass told

Mike it was some of his girls who set the whole thing up. So now Mike done told him to find the girls who set it all up and bring them back to him," Jasmine explained.

Do-Dirty listened and responded, "What are we gonna do now, girl. I really needed that bread so I could pay the bondsman for getting my baby daddy out of jail!"

"I needed it too, girl. I already had shit lined up. But don't worry. Let me think of something. We can probably still get paid. I gotta get this nigga before I quit the group," Jasmine said seriously. "It's entirely too much bread up in here and I gots to get mine," she said. She sat on the bed and daydreamed about how nice it would be to have me knocked off.

Sexy Redd knocked on the bedroom door while Jasmine was still on the phone. "Hold on, Dirty. Someone is at my bedroom door," she said and covered the mouthpiece of the phone with her hand. "Come in," she answered.

"Hey, Jasmine, I didn't catch you at a bad time, did I?" Sexy Redd asked her from the doorway.

"Nah, girl," Jasmine lied, "I'm just on the phone with my dude."

"Oh, okay. Since we just went through that ordeal, me and the other girls are going to the mall tomorrow to do some shopping. You wanna join us?" Redd offered.

"Nah, Redd," Jasmine replied, "I really need to get my hair done tomorrow."

"Okay, I'll have Preston take you around one tomorrow afternoon."

"That's perfect," Jasmine replied.

"Okay, I'll talk with you in the morning, chick," Sexy Redd said. *That's the bitch right there who set us the fuck up,* Redd thought to herself, as she backed out of the room.

Jasmine turned around to look out of her bedroom window. She put her phone back up to her mouth. "Hello?"

"Girl, that was Sexy Redd, wasn't it?" Dirty asked, before Jasmine could even get a word out.

"Yes, girl!"

"I can't stand her pretty ass," Dirty said told Jasmine, as she rolled her eyes on the other end of the phone. She chewed on a pickled pig's feet. Her mother kept at least four jars in the house due to the large household she had.

"Me neither, child. I told her I'm gonna get my hair done tomorrow. What in the hell are you chewing on, bitch? Jasmine asked Dirty. "The way you are smacking and shit, sounds like you sucking a big ass dick."

"Nah, bitch. You know how I like me some pickled ass pig feet, chick."

"Damn, it must be a good ass pig feet, your short, thick ass is chewing on 'cause you loud as a bitch in my ear."

"Sorry, chick, but what were you about to say?"

"Oh, be ready. I'm gonna have the limo pick you up and both of us can put together some type of plan for these fake ass bitches."

"What about them niggas who fucked up? And to think, I was gonna let Badass Mikey get some of this good ass pussy after we got that paper," Dirty said to Jasmine, as she thought about fuckin' Mikey.

"I'll call them when I get off the phone with you. They probably still at the hospital though. Sexy Redd fucked Skinny Pimp up so bad, they had to carry his bad-breath-smelling ass out of here."

Sexy Redd entered back inside the pool house with a disgusted look on her face. "Mike, she fell for it!"

"I know, I could hear everything on the intercom. How about that bitch been planning this shit ever since we let her in the fuckin' group!"

"No wonder whenever we went to the car wash she was always off to the side talking to them fake ass niggas," Redd Replied.

"Yeah, but I wonder why they decided to do it now and how they knew about my fuckin' safe. Only one person besides me and you knew about that safe. And that person is none other than Bernard Fats Walker, my first security guard. His ass is the one who helped me install it."

"Michael, not the Fats you caught eatin' Tiny's pussy the night of our first show?" Redd said.

"Yeah, Redd, that Fats!"

"Damn, that's so fucked up!"

"Tell me about it!" I uttered.

"So, what now?" Redd asked, as she stood there looking at me.

"Listen, it's getting late and I'm still somewhat baffled by the whole thing. I'm about to jump in the shower," I replied.

"Sounds like a good idea, baby. I think I'll join you so we can calm each other's nerves down," Redd said, as she followed me back inside the house.

We walked back through the kitchen and I turned to Redd. "Where, and when, did you get that damn gun? And do you even know how to use it?

"Like I told your black sexy ass in the beginning, there are a lot of things about me you don't know. And it's best that you don't know everything right now, Michael."

I shook my head and we made our way to the bedroom. *Damn, she sure as hell shut my black ass up,* I thought to myself. We then jumped in the shower and took care of each other's needs.

Forty minutes later, we were finished. We stepped out of the shower. She was drying my back off inside the bathroom when she whispered in my right ear, "You know I love you so much I would actually kill for you."

I quickly turned around and responded. "You just might have to for real, while you playing and bullshitting, thinking it's a joke."

We finished and she went downstairs to get us a glass of Chardonnay to help us fall asleep. After talking with her for like an hour or so, we fell asleep in each other's arms.

That night, I tossed and turned, wondering if Jasmine would try something while everyone was fast asleep. I woke up later that morning. I did a walk-through of the house and made sure everyone was safe and sound.

The first room I walked into was Strawberry's. She was laid out with the same rag still glued to her swollen lips. Next, I walked to the room where Entyce was sleeping. Her mouth was wide open and she had slobbered all over her Florida Hot Girl cutoff T-shirt.

I got to Mignon's room and found her sound asleep in a pair of tight-fitting boyshorts with half of her pussy lips hanging out. She, too, had on her Florida Hot Girl T-shirt. She was braless and those pretty ass, tantalizing titties of hers hung freely. She just didn't know how bad I had fantasized about making hot, passionate love to her.

By the time I made it to Nicole's room, my manhood had woken up to catch her lying there asleep with nothing on at all. She lay there looking so beautiful as the moon shone off her. She lay stretched out over that big ass bed, butt ass naked. The noise from outside her room must have startled her, and when she turned over in bed, she caught me looking at her.

"I see someone can't sleep, huh, Michael?" she asked me. She made sure I saw her nude body as she reached for the covers on the bed.

"Nah, I was just making sure everyone was safe and sound," I answered honestly.

"Thank you for being so concerned. Me and all this pretty ass nookie are safe and sound, Michael." She curled back over in her bed so I could see how fat her nookie was. "I'll see you in the morning, beautiful," I said.

I closed her door and thought. ... *Damn, that lil' female is fine as a muthafucker. If I didn't have Sexy Redd I would surely have her as my main chick.*

I walked to the room where Jasmine was fast asleep. A pair of sport's briefs covered her bottom, and a white wife beater T-shirt nestled over her beautiful full-grown breasts. *Why did you have to be so damn thirsty for money, that you had to try and rob me?*

Jasmine was a beautiful girl who stood around five foot seven and weighed one hundred thirty-five pounds. Her bra size was at least 36C. Her skin tone was a very bright-yellow, and she had an ass like a horse. I could still remember the first day I met her. I just couldn't figure out why she'd do me like that. I knew it couldn't have been that she was still mad at me for having my way with her the first day I met her. And it couldn't have been because I'd told her I'd promote her to being my assistant manager one day. Whatever the reason, I knew I would never be able to fuck her again. Or could I?

When I walked back to my bedroom, I eyed Sexy Redd lying there sleeping so peacefully. I couldn't help but stare at how beautiful she was. Her skin was so creamy and smooth, it looked as though she had fallen asleep with makeup on. Funny thing was, she didn't wear makeup. She had been born beautiful.

I finally feel asleep around three thirty that morning. I was back up around ten thirty. I made a call to Steve, the security guy who installed my high-tech security system. He informed me he would be out to the house around twelve that afternoon.

***

THE GIRLS WERE GETTING READY to go to the Mall. Jasmine was still lying in bed half asleep. Now the plan was for her and her girl, Do-Dirty, to get their hair done, but I would be one step ahead of them. With Redd and the other females about to leave, I placed a call to Goldmouth. He picked up the phone on the third ring.

"Hello."

"Goldmouth, it's Mike."

"Yeah, what's up, Mike?" We ain't even started looking for those girls yet 'cause my boy Skinny Pimp just got out of the hospital. The lil' homie had to get a damn cast on his broken leg."

"Damn, he was fucked up pretty bad, huh?"

"Yeah, man, but his ass will be alright," Goldmouth said.

"I was calling to let you know that there's been a slight change in plans."

"I'm listening, what's up?" Goldmouth asked. Knowing what I was about to say to him, I heard him smack his mouth and suck his teeth under his breath.

"Get your crew together and meet me at the old paper mill off Hwy 98 and Hubert Hurst Road, stall number eight," I told him.

"What time, my brother?"

"Let's say around three this afternoon," I answered. "And by the way, I'll get enough money for you guys to set y'all straight for at least a few weeks or so. That way, y'all don't have to be around here trying to rob people and shit."

"All right, Mike," he said. "We'll be there. So how much are you paying us off with," he asked, sounding all thirsty for money and shit.

"Around twenty bands for each one of you guys. I'm thinking about hiring y'all to be my personal bodyguards," I said.

As soon as I hung up the phone with him, I heard Jasmine's phone ring. My plan was in full effect. It was already around eleven thirty, and Redd and the girls were all dressed ready to go.

"Okay, bae, I'll see you later," Sexy Redd said just before she left the house, "have a nice day," she added, as she was walking down the stairs.

I looked at her outfit and stared at how nice she looked with it on. She had on some Gucci boots with a nice Baby Phat shirt over her nice pretty ass titties. A pair of tight, black Baby Phat jeans hugged that fine ass of hers. She looked like she'd just stepped out of an Ebony Magazine.

"Excuse me, Redd, but where in the hell did you get that nice ass outfit from?" I asked her.

"Oh, this little tight outfit here," she asked and pointed at herself, "the one I got on?"

"Girl, you know which one I'm talking about, stop playing." I displayed a crooked smile.

"It's nothing. Remember last weekend when you told me what's yours is mine?" she reminded me.

"Yeah, and what's the point, Redd?" I asked.

"Well, I used your credit card and purchased this outfit and ten more just like it. You should get the two-thousand-dollar bill in about two weeks." She smiled and showed all thirty-two of her pearly white teeth.

My eyebrows scrunched as I looked at her through tight eyes, and said, "You what?"

"Yeah, that's what I did since you decided to interview little Miss. Innocence last weekend in our hotel suite. Love you, see you soon," she said, and air-kissed me as she hurried out the door laughing. All I could do was smile and walk away. She was right about my little escapade with Innocence. All I could do was say to myself, *damn she looks even better mad.*

Just as her and the girls were getting inside of her black S600 series Mercedes Benz, Steve was walking inside the house to start on the install of more security cameras.

An hour later, Preston was pulling up in the limo to take Jasmine to get her hair done.

I opened the door to let him in. "Come on in, Preston," I greeted him.

"Hello, Michael, how you doing on this fine beautiful day?"

"I'm fine, Preston, give me about twenty more minutes. She should be ready by then."

"No problem Michael, I'll just sit here and admire how lovely your new home is."

He sat down in the living room and I dashed back upstairs to catch Jasmine as she was coming out of the bathroom with a towel wrapped around her naked body.

"You must like what you see since you keep staring at me," she said. She stopped in her tracks and stood in the doorway drying off her wet hair and sensual, naked body.

"It's all right," I said, as I leaned on the bedroom door.

"Whatever, Michael. You're probably thinking to yourself, 'boy how I would love to be fuckin' her right now'!"

"Damn, so you can read minds now, huh, Jasmine?"

"No, Mr. Mike. I can see the hard erection in your pants from over here," she said.

I looked down and realized my erection was protruding from my sweat pants. I was so embarrassed.

Minutes later, her long tongue was tied up with mine, as I pushed my erect manhood inside her soaking wet vagina.

"I knew you couldn't resist this good, tight ass pussy, Michael," she whispered. I could hear the lust in her raspy tone.

"Yeah, just like you couldn't resist this big ass, black, long dick I'm sticking all up in your fuckin' stomach. She let out a moan as I went deeper into her pelvis area. When I felt like I was at the bottom of her stomach, I placed her kneecaps up by her ear and started longdicking her ass. *Since this will be the last time I'll ever see her, I might as well enjoy it.*

Her facial expressions showed me just how much she was enjoying our sexual encounter at that very moment in time. She pulled me down on top of her, looked me directly in my eyes, and whispered in my ear, "Why can't you just leave that bitch and be with me, Michael?"

"It's not that easy, Jasmine. Why can't you just be patient and wait things out?" I let the question linger.

She began to cry but I continued to punish her vagina.

"I wish I could, Michael." She let out a few sniffles and groaned, "be quiet and just fuck me. That's all I am to you anyway—your little fuck thing," she said.

I pulled out of her and flipped her ass over and commenced to fuckin' her from the back. I happened to look up and saw Steve, my security guy, peeking through the door of the room, watching me fuck Jasmine. For a minute, I thought he was masturbating, but he quickly moved away when he realized I knew he was there.

Nosy red-headed pervert! I thought, with a half ass grin on my face. I maintained every stroke as though it would be my last time ever fuckin' her again.

Minutes later, Jasmine turned her head around and watched me fuckin' her from the back. "Michael, I'm sorry," she said, as I stroked her and perspired at the same time.

"Sorry for what, baby? I should be the one apologizing to you for punishing your pretty ass vagina like this."

We continued for about another thirty minutes before I finally exploded all over her back.

"No, please, don't pull out, Michael," she screamed. I tried not to mess up the sheets on the bed.

"Girl, I'm not trying to impregnate your tiny, pretty ass," I said. She grabbed my manhood as it exploded and pulled it inside her mouth. She slurped, nibbled, and gobbled. She sucked up all my fluids as though she knew it would be the last dick she would ever suck for the rest of her life. By now, I was standing up looking down on her as she tried to wrap her lips around the base of my manhood.

When I heard her choking, I quickly said, "All right now, Jasmine, you gonna hurt yourself."

"Whatever, Michael," she said with her mouth full. I'ma big girl, I can take it," she said.

The last bit of my fluids went deep inside her throat. She looked so beautiful to me as her thin lips wrapped around the head of my manhood. She grabbed it by the base and looked up at me with those pretty light brown eyes.

"All right, Mr., all clean and ready to go."

I pulled her up off her knees and kissed her on the cheek.

"You really don't know how much you really mean to me, do you?" I asked.

"Yes, I do, but you're the one who got the bitch from hell telling us what to do."

"Yeah, whatever, Jasmine."

I started to walk out of her room and I could hear her start to cry once again. I turned around to see her wiping her mouth and pretty ass brown eyes.

"Jasmine, what is really going on with you?"

"Never mind, Michael, you'll never understand. Just know this; you can't keep fuckin' these girls in your fuckin' group and think we're not gonna catch some type of feelings for your sexy black ass." She threw her rag at me and slammed her bedroom door in my face.

Damn, Sexy Redd had said the same thing to me over the weekend. And now one of my premier dancers had said it. I would find out later that she wasn't the only female in my group catching mad feelings for me.

At that moment, I realized I would have to control my actions before I destroyed myself and the world famous Florida Hot Girls.

Michael Gallon

CHAPTER TWO
I'M SORRY TO JASMINE

Now this is where the shit got muthafuckin' real for them fake ass niggas and bitches who tried to set me up. Now, remember when Jasmine and I were in a heated moment, and she looked into my eyes and said she was sorry? Well, I guess she was feeling guilty about trying to rob me and the females who had been at the house. No matter what the reason, it left me with no choice but to take matters into my own hands, and this is how it all went down. . . .

Preston, the limo driver came inside the house without Steve's nosy ass seeing him and went to one of my guest bedrooms. I told Steve if he needed me I would be inside my guest room watching some of my old football-highlight films. Jasmine got inside the limo and instructed the Jamaican limo driver to pick up Do-Dirty on 8th and Main. The limo driver did just as she asked.

"Excuse me, driver, there has been a slight change in plan," Jasmine told the driver, after Do-Dirty had been picked up, "drop us off at the carwash across from the Caribbean Beach Night Club." Again, the driver did as he'd been told. He dropped Jasmine and Do-Dirty off where Goldmouth and the rest of his crew were waiting for them.

It had been a minute since I'd last seen lil' fine ass Do-Dirty. Until just a few weekends prior, she had been a member of the group. However, once she was caught trying to steal from my girl, Nicole, she had to be terminated.

Now, here it was that her and pretty ass Jasmine were a part of Goldmouth's crew, and they were trying to rob me for everything I had. Now Dirty stood around four foot eleven and weighed around one hundred thirty pounds. A nice, thick, fat ass, gave her petite body that *WOW*-factor needed to set it off. Her skin complexion was a light-bright yellow. Her breasts looked to be at least a 32B. She always had a smile on her cute lil' face. There was just one problem—she always had a problem with telling the truth. No matter what it was, she always had to put a lie in whatever came out of her fucked up ass lil' mouth.

I guess she had been dealt a bad deck of cards throughout her confused, short-lived life. Especially considering she had five kids and not one of the children's fathers paid her any child support. Then to make matters worse, she lived in some apartments behind the local Winn Dixie, with her mother and the other children her mother was taking care of.

I met her when I worked as her Case Manager for the Wages program. If I had known what she was going through at the time, maybe the outcome of her life would have turned out differently; however, life had a funny way of getting rid of those who made other people's life a living hell.

As the driver pulled away from the car wash, he couldn't help but see them get in Goldmouth's black, 1994, Cadillac Escalade. He pulled out of the parking lot and headed straight toward the paper mill. It was around one forty-five pm.

The girls were at the Ocoee Mall shopping, or at least, that's what I thought. I would later find out that Nicole, Strawberry, Entyce, and Mignon were busy having lunch with another young lady. They had discussed starting up another group they would call the Queens or something.

Goldmouth and his crew got to the paper mill just in time to go over their plan of taking me out.

"Okay, listen guys, Mike called me earlier. He said we would meet him here. Now he don't have a fuckin' clue that we all here waiting on his cool, slick, muthafuckin' ass. He claimed he was bringing twenty bands apiece for each of us!"

"Twenty bands apiece? That ain't shit," Jasmine said. "He should be bringing us a fuckin' hundred grand or more. Why didn't you tell him we needed way more than that, fool?" Jasmine asked Goldmouth. Her face showed her disgust for the amount of money she would get.

"Listen, you thirsty ass bitch," Goldmouth said. Spittle flew from his mouth through the gaps where his teeth used to be before I'd knocked them out of his mouth.

Jasmine pulled out a small .22 automatic pistol from the knock-off Gucci purse she'd been carrying. She pointed it right between the small ass eyes of Goldmouth.

"Listen, bitch ass nigga," she said through gritted teeth, "you got one more time to call me out of my muthafuckin' name, and I'm gonna do what Sexy Redd should have done to your ugly muthafuckin' ass last night!"

"Damn, lil' mama, that's how you feel about me?" Goldmouth replied. A sly smile flashed across his face. He stared at her with fire in his eyes but the fear on his face was evident. His face was riddled with bad acne bumps from thirty-two years of taking showers in the dirty project water.

"Yeah, that's how I feel about any nigga who calls me out!" Jasmine said. Everyone else just stood around watching the two go at it. They hoped Jasmine wouldn't pull the trigger and take their leader out.

"Hold on, chick, he was only playing," Do-Dirty said, as she tried to get Jasmine to lower the gun pointed at Goldmouth's head.

"Nah, fuck that! This nigga almost got us killed last night by telling Mike it was some of his females who set his ass the fuck up. We don't need his dumb ass anyway! Hell, I can get us the money without him," Jasmine said. Everyone in the paper mill had given her their undivided attention.

"Damn, Jasmine, so you just gonna take the nigga out like that?" Skinny Pimp asked, as he tried to balance himself on the two crutches.

Jasmine looked over at Skinny Pimp. She turned toward Goldmouth and let off three shots to the front portion of his head. *Boom! Boom! Boom!* The shots rang out and his body fell to the floor. His small ass eyes were still open.

He lay there on the cold, hard, cement floor with three bullet holes in his head. A small portion of his brain oozed from his right ear. The rest of the crew jumped back in total shock as they witnessed his death right before their very eyes.

"What the fuck?" Lil Q screamed, as he watched his homie fall to the floor.

"Bitch, you just shot my dawg," Badass Mikey said. He checked to see if there was any life left inside of his homie's body.

He'd known him since he could wipe his own nasty, stankin' ass! "Muthafucker, you next!" Jasmine shouted. "Didn't I just tell that nigga laying there on the floor with holes in his big ass head about that fuckin' *bitch* word?" She pointed her pistol at Mikey's head.

"My bad, lil' mama," Badass Mikey said, with his scary ass. "I'm so sorry. I guess that leaves more money for us to split since my homie is dead and gone," he said. He stood up and wiped his hands after touching Goldmouth's dead body.

"Now everyone listen up. This is how we're going to do this to make sure we get enough money to set us straight for life. When Mike gets here, we're gonna kidnap his black ass and hold him for ransom," Jasmine told them.

"Who's gonna wanna pay for his black ass?" Skinny Pimp asked, as he accidentally fell off his crutches.

"I guess you don't know who his family is, huh?" Jasmine asked. She looked around and smiled at the rest of the crew of killers inside the paper mill.

"Nah, who?" Do-Dirty asked. A surprised looked etched across her face.

"The Valentino Family, fool. And not to mention, Sexy Redd's family is fuckin' loaded with money too,: she informed the crew. "Hell, she's the one who paid cash money for that damn house they all live in. And I heard her tell some of the girls her father is fuckin' made of money. So once Mike gets his black ass here, we're going to demand a cool million or his black ass is fuckin' dead," Jasmine said. She stared up at the ceiling of the old paper mill, dreaming of all the money she would have after kidnapping Mike's black ass.

"Hey, wait a minute," Do-Dirty said, "my first two daughters' father's last name is Valentino!" Her mind began to wonder.

"Oh, well, bitch, maybe they some kin. Have you ever checked?" Jasmine asked.

"I really hadn't paid any attention to it till now," Do-Dirty answered.

"Girl, you'sa silly whore ain't you? You might be entitled to some money and don't even know it."

"You know you might be right. I'm gonna ask Mike when his black ass gets here."

"Yeah, you do that. Meanwhile, let's get to the problem at hand," Jasmine said, as she walked around with her pistol. She scratched her temple with the butt of the gun.

"So, Jasmine, do you think Mike suspects I had anything to do with setting him up?" Do-Dirty asked. She pulled out a cigarette to calm down her frail nerves.

"He shouldn't, chick. He was too busy trying to get everyone out of his house to even think about who set him up," Jasmine said. Then she instructed Skinny Pimp and Lil Q to move Goldmouth's dead body.

"Hey, Jasmine, you sure Mike didn't hear you on the phone talking to me last night?" Do-Dirty asked, as she tried to light the cancer stick. She fumbled it around in her mouth because she couldn't seem to stop shaking.

"No, he didn't. I was in my room when I was on the phone with you."

Bitch, I mean, Jasmine," Skinny Pimp said, and quickly recanted the *bitch* word, "you're so fuckin' dumb! Don't you know he can still hear everything over his intercom system," Skinny Pimp tried to stand back up a second time.

Jasmine went over to him and kicked him down off his crutches. Then, she pointed her fire at his head. He threw his hands up over his head.

"Didn't I just tell your lil' dumb, stank-breath-ass about calling me out my name," she yelled. "Don't you see your dead ass homie over there with three small bullet holes in his big ass fuckin' head? You must don't want your half of the money."

"Yeah, I do want it, silly-ass girl. Just don't shoot me. I'm sorry, but my mouth gets like that from time to time," Skinny told her.

"That's your last warning, playa. The next time your half is all mine," Jasmine said, as she rubbed her pistol up against his head.

Lil Q pulled a tarp over the body of his fallen homie. He pulled his revolver out of his waistband. He contemplated taking Jasmine out in case she was having the same thought about him. He walked back over to join the rest of the crew of ruthless thugs who had been waiting on me to show up,

"Hey, Dirty, stand guard at the door and let us know when Mike gets here," Jasmine shouted.

She stood over by a table that held the items she was going to chain me up with.

Then, within a blink of an eye, from behind one of the open containers in the back, an assailant ran out blasting an array of weapons. First, a deadly 9mm tore off the top of Skinny Pimp's head as he fell lifeless to the cold pavement floor. They tell me he was dead before he even hit the floor.

Lil Q already had his weapon drawn, but because it was one of those cheap ass 380's he'd bought off the street from Crackhead Larry, it jammed on his black ass. He tried to fire and run at the same time. But to his dismay, all the exits were already blocked. He was shot twice in his stomach, and once right between his beady lil' eyes.

Jasmine got off a few shots from her small .22 pistol, but her weapon nor aim was a match for the skilled assailant. The assailant shot her two times in the left side of her skull. She fell to the floor before she could see who had given her a first-class ticket to her final resting place. It was a damn shame because if there was one thing good about Jasmine, it was that good ass sex game of hers. If she had just asked for some money the outcome would've been totally different, but she just had to do things her way, which in turn got her ass killed. Damn, Jasmine.

Now, I know you're saying what about Do-Dirty? I had to save the best for last. So, here we go...

Now, Lil Ms. Do-Dirty was lucky enough to run out of the building right into the arms of the Jamaican-looking limo driver who had dropped her and Jasmine off at the car wash. She thought to herself, *why is he here?,* as she ran full speed toward him, screaming for dear life.

As the Jamaican driver got out of the car to see what was going on, he was just as surprised as she was that he was even there.

"Help me, please, someone is shooting at me," she said, as she ran right into his arms. Her purse and personal items flew everywhere.

"Yeah, let me help you," the driver said. He pulled his semi-automatic weapon from behind the small of his back.

Boom! Boom! Two shots rang out. Poor lil Do-Dirty grabbed her chest, and it was lights out. Another bullet tore through the front of her skull and exited through the back of her head, leaving the shape of a Florida grapefruit.

They tell me before she closed her beautiful light-green eyes, she uttered the words, "I'm so sorry... I was only trying to feed my kids... please, tell them I will always love them," she said, as the last breath escaped from her lifeless body.

The limo driver placed his right hand over her open eyes and closed them for the last time before the grim reaper waited for her devilish ass soul to enter the next life.

They also tell me that the limo driver kissed her forehead and said a prayer for her departed soul. He had wiped a single tear from his right eye.

Brains were scattered everywhere as the assailant from inside the paper mill ran outside and saw Do-Dirty sprawled out over the hot, black asphalt.

"Help me pull her back inside of the mill," the driver said in his Jamaican accent. The assailant stood there, dressed in all black.

Once they had her inside with the rest of her crew, the assailant placed some drugs and prescription pills inside to make it look like a drug deal gone bad. The limo driver placed a bouquet of black roses at the foot of each individual's body then he closed the door of the old paper mill.

Minutes later, the limo driver asked the assailant, "Where to now?"

"To the mall, sir. There's a little shopping I need to do." The driver took his passenger straight to the mall.

As he drove through traffic, headed to the mall, the assailant used the time to change clothes in the back of the limo. The driver who was very attentive to his surroundings and couldn't help but peek at his passenger who was practically naked in the back of the limo. He noticed a small tattoo on her body that he'd never seen before. He tried to get a better look at the freshly-marked thigh of the beautiful passenger. However, she must've realized he was watching, so she quickly closed the partition, denying him the free peepshow.

The limo arrived at the mall ten minutes later.

"Is there a particular store you'd like to be dropped off to?" he asked the passenger.

"Yes, Macy's, please. I need to pick up a few dresses."

"Black, I presume," the driver said with an evil ass grin on his face.

"Yes, black is the color you wear when you go to a funeral in my native country," she answered.

"Have a nice day," the driver told the woman.

Just as the beautiful, caramel complexioned woman got out of the limo, she pulled her Gucci shades down over her beautiful face. She placed the blood-soiled clothing into a small, disposable bag. She climbed out of the limo threw the clothes into the nearest trash dispenser outside the mall. Then, she casually walked back inside Macy's department store as if nothing had ever happened.

As the driver drove away from the mall, he said to himself, "It's amazing that such a beautiful woman could be such a cold-blooded killer, and the most feared woman in the group, The Florida Hot Girls."

CHAPTER THREE
YANI

Once I was back at the house, I thought about how many individuals were really out to get me. I was still puzzled as to how they even knew I had a safe inside my house in the first place. I had decided not to tell anyone about the safe, so I wouldn't have to worry about someone breaking in trying to rob me.

The only other person who knew about the safe was Bernard "Fats" Walker, the ex-security guard, who I'd fired for always trying to eat out, or have sex with, the girls behind my back. He must have told Goldmouth about the safe. If so, then he was in on the robbery as well. Damn, I would have to get rid of his big black ass too, but how? I had already gotten Goldmouth and his crew taken care of. And I really didn't want too many people involved in what was going on. Hell, I didn't even want Sexy Redd to know I was the Jamaican limo driver who took out lil' ass Do-Dirty. There was only one person who came to my mind, and that was my girl, Yani.

Yani was an old, personal friend of mine who lived down in Lil Haiti, a small little town outside of Miami, Florida. She was a beautiful Haitian girl who lived with her mother and twin brothers. She was just the right girl for the job. She stood a mere five foot seven, weighed around one hundred thirty-five pounds, and had a nice, round ass. If she wasn't a part-time killer, she could have been a beautiful runway model for any magazine company in the Dade County area. Her breasts size was a nice 32B, and the sight of them made your mouth water whenever they came your way. I had met her and her family while I was attending college at Florida Memorial on a track scholarship, back in the day.

As I sat in total seclusion, inside of my den listening to Prince's "If I Was Your Girlfriend", I thought long and hard before calling her. She was the only solution to my problem.

So, I called her. She answered the phone in her Haitian accent. Just listening to her would turn anyone on. We talked for a few minutes before I finally told her about the job I needed her to do. She informed me that she needed some work and that she would do it for the right price.

I ran down the details and told her I would get back to her with her flight info. I was just about to hang up but she stopped me.

"Oh, by the way. my brotha, your Ms. Kitty is still here in the area. Do we still keep an eye out for you?" she asked.

"Yes, and once again, thanks for babysitting for me."

"No worries, young brotha."

After we'd hung up, I felt a whole lot better about my problem with Fats. It would only be a matter of time before he would be disposed of. Yani was a real expert at making people disappear for the right price.

I walked into the guest bedroom where Preston had fallen asleep. "Preston, Preston," I tried shaking him so he would wake up.

He jumped straight up. "Oh, I'm sorry, Mr. Valentino, I must have dozed off."

"Yes, you did, young man, you're okay. The limo is parked right out front. How did things go?" I asked him as I took off my Jamaican wig.

"Everything was okay. Steve never needed you for anything other than that, you're good."

"Thanks, Preston. Here's a little something for your troubles."

"Mr. Valentino, sir, you've already done enough for my family and me. There's no need for your continued kindness."

"Preston, trust me. No amount of money can compare to what you have done for my company and I."

Preston took the envelope I had placed in his hand and placed it in his pocket. He shook my hand and I walked him to his limo. I watched him drive off and down the road. I guess he must have opened it when he got halfway down the road, because the limo suddenly came to an abrupt halt in the middle of the road. For his showing up and assisting me with my issue, I had given him five thousand dollars. A mere fraction of the amount I'd told Goldmouth I was paying him before his untimely death. Preston quickly put the limo in reverse and came back. I met him on the front lawn, as he jumped out of the vehicle.

"Mr. Valentino, this is way too much money. I can't take all this."

"Nonsense, Preston. Use it for a small vacation since you haven't taken one since coming to our country."

He looked at me and started to cry and hugged me as if I had just signed the paperwork for him to be in the country.

See, I had been behind Preston ever since he and his family had arrived in Florida. The Valentino Family were the ones who loaned him the money to open his family's Caribbean Restaurant. We had also helped with his fast-growing limo service. He had turned both businesses into very lucrative businesses. So, Preston felt like I was doing entirely too much. He finally agreed to take the money and drove off.

Little did I know at the time, I would end up purchasing that particular limo later on down the road. As I walked back inside the house, nosy ass Steve was coming through the sliding kitchen door.

"There you are, sir. I thought you were still upstairs."

"Yeah, right. Still fucking Jasmine, right?" I said under a muffled breath. I walked towards his short, stocky, fat, redheaded ass.

"No, I was outside with my limo driver. Is everything okay?"

"Yes sir. I was just finishing up."

"Okay, how much is all the security work gonna cost me?"

"Whatever the cost is, sir, I'm pretty sure you can afford it, sir. Especially since you've got all those nice, expensive cars in your garage."

"Them old things, Steve? They're okay but I'm always looking for something a lil' bit different."

"Boy, aren't we being modest," he said. He rubbed his hands together, ready to collect on a nice payday.

"Nah, serious, Steve, those cars are old."

"Well, what about the house? I know it has to be worth around two hundred and fifty thousand dollars," he said. He stood and marveled at how beautiful my house looked.

"Nah, try three hundred thousand dollars, young man."

"Wow, whatever line of work you're in, Mr. Valentino, it must be nice."

"Just know it pays the bills, my fat, short, redheaded young man."

He handed me the high ass invoice. "Damn, Steve. I might have to finance this outrageous shit," I said. I cracked a half ass shitty smile.

"Oh, no problem, sir. We do have an affordable payment plan available," he said, as he smiled back at me, as if I couldn't pay the fuckin' bill.

"No problem, Steve. I'll pay for it now. Do you except cash?" I asked his nosy ass. I pulled out a stack of freshly printed hundred dollar bills. He smiled as I counted it off to him.

"My judgement of character was correct, Mr. Valentino. I see that you could afford the security work without a problem."

" Hell, I never said I couldn't cover the cost. It was the principal of me not wanting to pay the huge amount you were charging me." We both laughed and I walked him back to his truck. He then explained how the high security system worked. I thanked him and shook his hand.

"Hey. Mr. Valentino," he called out to me as I tuned to walk away, "why the upgrade on your security equipment? Did someone break in or something?"

I immediately turned to him and responded. "No, not really Steve. Why do you ask?"

"It's really nothing, sir. While I was putting some of the cameras up, I happened to notice some blood stains inside your living room area. I thought you might have had some intruders inside your lovely house. Customers usually want to upgrade their security system after someone tries to break in."

"Nah, Steve. It's just that I've had a lot of house guests throughout my home. One can never be too cautious with all the traffic that comes through here."

"I see. Well, you can never go wrong with extra security, sir. You have a nice day," he said. His redheaded ass got inside his truck and prepared to drive away.

"Oh, by the way, Steve, I noticed earlier while you were walking throughout my home, you happened to peek in on me and one of my house guest in a compromising position."

"Oh, Mr. Valentino, I didn't see anything, sir," he said. His face started to turn red and shame was written all over it.

"Thank you, let's keep it that way. Have yourself a nice day, Steve." He drove away with the sight of Jasmine and me still fresh on his perverted ass mind. I watched him bend the corner of my street and head towards the guard gate, trying to get his nosy ass out of Metro West.

***

SEXY REDD GOT BACK TO THE MALL and went straight into Macy's to purchase the black dresses for the families of the victims, as promised.

Nicole, Strawberry, Entyce, and Mignon came from behind the makeup counter.

"Girl, what are y'all doing in Macy's?" Sexy Redd asked them.

"Me, Mignon, and Entyce just had our facials done. Strawberry's shit is still too swollen for her to do anything to her fucked up mug. We wanted to step up our look for tomorrow night's show in Tampa," Nicole said to Sexy Redd.

"Damn, let me see your face, girl," Sexy Redd said to Strawberry as she looked at the size of her swollen lips.

"It looks like they going down a lil' bit, huh?" Strawberry asked Sexy Redd, hoping she'd answer 'yes'. She wanted badly to dance in Tampa the next day.

"Yeah, just a lil' bit, child. But I'm sure Mike will come up with something for you to do so you can still make you some money," Redd lied. Strawberry's face was so fucked up, it would take a miracle for her to dance the next night.

"So, what do you think about our facials, Redd?" Mignon asked her while smiling at her reflection in the mirror.

"Girl, y'all tripping. Them lame ass niggas in Tampa don't be throwing enough money for me," Sexy Redd said, as she looked through the makeup cabinet.

"I can't tell, Redd. Every time you dance at that small ass club, you bring home at least a rack or two," Mignon replied. She asked the clerk at the counter for a specific shade of makeup to match her skin color.

"You ladies can bring that much home too if y'all would do more dancing and less talking. The less you all be talking and flirting, the more you could be making," Redd told them, while trying to compare the shade against her face.

"So, Redd, why are you up in Macy's? I know damn well you don't be shopping up in here?" Strawberry said. She thought about, trying some lipstick on her swollen lips. But when she saw how swollen it still was she quickly thought twice and put it back in disgust.

"Aw nothing, just picking Michael up some sweaters for the cold nights out. I'm so tired of him wearing them damn suits all the time," Redd said.

"Girl, I don't know what you're complaining about. Mike be looking fly as hell with his suits on and shit. Especially when he puts on his matching Godfather hat on to set it off," Nicole said, smiling at her reflection in the mirror.

"Whatever, child, but please don't tell his ass that 'cause he already thinks he's Morris Day and shit." She laughed. "Hell, I don't even know who the fuck that is, come to think of it."

As they went to the counter to pay for their items, Redd pulled out some cash and dropped her wallet. She bent down to pick it up and noticed a red spot on her Gucci boots.

Damn, one of them bitches blood is all on my fuckin' brand new boots, she thought to herself. Discreetly, she tried to wipe the blood before one of the other girls could it. She quickly played it off.

As she swiped it away, Strawberry leaned her swollen lip ass over, and whispered in her ear, "I might not be the sharpest tool in the toolshed, but that looks like blood on your boots."

Redd turned to her and smiled. "You didn't see that, bitch." Sexy Redd winked at her. "Girl, let's go home. I'm tired, and hungry as a muthafucker."

The girls hugged one another and walked out of the mall laughing. Each had a hand full of bags and what nots as they headed to the parking lot.

Once in the parking lot, they piled all their bags in the trunk of Sexy Redd's brand-new, black S600.

The woman who had been working the counter inside the store ran outside with the bag of black dresses. "Excuse me, ma'am!" she called out to Redd, "you left your other bag," the lady said. She was breathless and nearly about to pass out from running to catch them.

Redd kindly took the bags. "Thank you, I forgot all about this one," she said. She smiled at the young lady and quickly put the bag in the trunk, out of eyesight of the other girls.

While the girls were on their way back, I was home, busy trying to make things seem as normal as could be. I was still somewhat distraught over what I'd had to do earlier that day. The thought of Do-Dirty was still on my confused mind. How could I have done something so harsh to someone, and make it seem as if I'd had nothing to do with it. Visions of her cute lil' face kept running through my head as I paced back and forth thinking of my next move.

While walking by my bedroom window, I could see the girls as they pulled up in the driveway. They looked excited about the day they'd had at the mall. With Do-Dirty's face still in my head, I could hear the girls talking amongst each other as they entered the house.

"Hey, Strawberry, did you get the acid wash jeans you wanted?" Nicole asked her. She threw her bags on one of the living room chairs

"Nicole, you know I didn't get them," Strawberry replied. "I only had like three hundred dollars to shop with."

"Damn, girl, where all the money you be making and shit?'

"Nicole, I really don't be making that much since I really don't know how to dance that well. I just be lounging around the club," she told her. "I wish Mike would just let us do VIP, or let us leave the club with the guys so I can make some real money."

"Hell, I don't know what you talking about. I make really good money when I'm dancing," Sexy Redd told Strawberry.

"Me too," Mignon quickly replied.

"Yeah, I do pretty damn good to Berry, so what's the fuckin' problem?" Nicole asked. She sat down, ready to hear what Berry had to say in response.

"Y'all no damn well what I'm tryingto say," Strawberry said. She sat on one of the barstools looking all sad and shit.

"What did Mike say about you not being able to dance?" Mignon asked her, while opening a box with brand-new Prada shoes inside of it.

"He told me he was gonna get Sexy Redd or Lil Kitty to teach me how to shake what my mamma gave me."

Now while all that was going on between Strawberry and Mignon, Entyce had leaned over the counter in the kitchen to listen. She sipped on the apple juice she'd gotten out of the fridge.

"Damn, whatever she gave you, she must have kept the rest of it for herself," Nicole said, laughing.

"Shut up, Nicole, everybody ain't blessed with a beautiful face and banging body like you."

"Strawberry, listen, boo. You're a cute girl. You just don't know how to use what you got to get what you want. First of all, you're gonna have to start buying something that fits your wide, flat ass. Then you're gonna have to *wear it*, instead of letting it *wear you*. And your hair is so long and silky like Indian hair. It's beautiful," Nicole complimented her. "Are you part Indian?" she wondered aloud.

"No, Nicole. I'm half black half Puerto Rican. My mom said I might have a little white in me too."

"Can't be, chick, 'cause I'm half Black and Puerto Rican," Sexy Redd said, as she headed toward the stairs.

"Excuse me for being mixed with all kinds of flavors of the month, Sexy Redd," Strawberry yelled to her with a smirk on her swollen face.

"Now, that's where that white girl mess comes from," Mignon said, laughing.

"Thanks, Mignon."

"You're welcome, Strawberry, if you really wanna know, girl, I heard if you let your man fuck you in the ass, your ass will get fat."

"Nah, Mignon," Strawberry said. She shook her head from side to side. "Who told you that dumb ass shit?" she asked, as she tried to hold her smile back.

"Some nigga who probably wanted to fuck her in her ass," Nicole said. She sat down and laughed at what she had just said to everyone.

"For real, I heard if you let him fuck you in the ass every now and then, your ass will start getting bigger and bigger."

"Okay. So, Strawberry, I'm about to go upstairs and get my dildo so I can fuck you in your flat ass," Entyce said. She pretended as if she were about to run up the stairs to retrieve her dildo.

"No the hell you ain't! Ain't nobody about to get in my flat ass! If that's how you get a big ass, I guess I won't get one," Strawberry said. She burst out laughing.

"So, is that how your ass got fat, Nicole? By letting guys fuck you in the ass?" Strawberry asked her. She held a piece of ice on her swollen lips.

"Nah, chick. I was born with a nice, fat, juicy ass, smart mouth," Nicole replied.

Strawberry stood up to admire how nice Nicole's ass looked in her Baby Phat Jeans.

You see, Nicole was the girl in the group who made sure she was always on point. Her game was official just like her clothes, which she'd only wear once. You'd never catch her with the same outfit on twice. And to make her appearance even more stunning, she always made sure her hair and nails were done the same color as the outfits she wore. And she'd change at least twice a day. Even her bra and panties matched what she had on. Besides Sexy Redd, she was the girl who stood out the most.

Like I always said, if I didn't have Sexy Redd as my ride-or-die chick, it would've been Nicole, hands down. It's funny that I felt that way about her, because as the time went by, she had started feeling a certain way about me, and I didn't even see it. All I was seeing was the ever-changing growth of the group known as the Florida Hot Girls.

Michael Gallon

CHAPTER FOUR
THE 'BOUT IT-'BOUT IT GIRLS

Since the girls had been back home, I could hear portions of their conversations. I sat in my den still seeing images of Do- Dirty as she'd lain dead on that hot, black, asphalt. My mind was in a spiral.

"Boy, I can't wait 'til Mike sees these new outfits I bought," Redd said, as she proceeded to open all kinds of shopping bags.

"Hell, you go shopping every other day, Redd. So, I'm sure he sees enough of you and your new outfits all the time," Entyce said, still sipping on the glass of apple juice.

"Damn, Entyce, I didn't know you felt like that, home girl," Redd said with widened eyes.

"I'm just saying, Redd, you and the whole group knows Mike don't see nobody but your fine ass. In his eyes, you're his everything."

"I guess you got a point there, Entyce. So y'all see that in him too?" Redd asked. She looked around and waited for the girls to answer.

"Girl, ever since the day we came back from Miami, all he thinks about is you. He even puts you before the group, so consider yourself lucky. You have what we all wish we had."

"And what's that, Mignon?" Redd probed further.

"A good fuckin' man, Mignon answered. She looked at the faces of the other girls.

"Nah, I think you're wrong in regards to the group, Mignon, he always tells me the Florida Hot Girls are his heart and soul. He said it himself, 'without the group, he wouldn't have shit'. Ever since he lost his job as a Case Manager, this all he knows how to do, besides cook," Redd said. She stood up to open another one of her boxes.

While the girls were still talking, I walked down stairs and headed for the fridge. I said hello to everyone. Redd slid in the kitchen right behind me. I poured myself something to drink, and when I turned around, she was staring at me as though she'd seen a ghost. It dawned on me as I was drinking my juice, that I hadn't changed my entire outfit. My dumb ass had taken off the wig which made me look like I had dreads, but I still had on the rest of the attire I'd worn earlier that day at the paper mill.

Fuck! I was trying to be so fuckin' careful and smart about how I would take them fools out, I slipped up when it came to removing all the clothes like Sexy Redd had removed hers earlier in the back of the limo. As I placed the glass down, she looked at me in total shock.

What the fuck? Is what she wanted to say, but no words came out. I quickly dashed back upstairs and she ran right behind me. The girls just thought she was just glad to see me.

As soon as I hit my room door she yanked me by the arm. "Michael, that was you the whole time driving the fuckin' limo and your black sneaky ass had me thinking it was somebody else all that time?" she said, with shock written all over her face.

I held my head down for a brief moment be- fore I answered her question. "Yes, Redd. That was me the whole entire time," I said. I sat down on the edge of our bed.

"Nigga, you had me thinking it was one of the limo drivers and your slick ass was the driver all along. Why didn't you want me to know?"

I took her by the arm and sat her next to me in the bed. I sighed and began explaining my reasoning for trying to be so obsolete.

"Listen, bae, the less people know about a crime, the less you have to worry about anyone being able to tell on the culprit of the crime. For instance, you don't want the girls down stairs knowing you were the one who took them fools out today, do you?"

"No, I don't, bae. But check this shit out. How about I didn't even have to take out Goldmouth."

I looked at her with a surprised look on my face, as I stood up from the bed. "What? Is he still alive?"

"Nah, your girl Jasmine shot that black ass nigga right between the eyes!"

By now, I was standing by the window looking at the traffic of people who were getting off from work that time of the evening.

"Why?"

"You're not going to believe this. The black ass nigga called her a fuckin' bitch, so she got mad and took him out. Right in front of everybody, bae. She even threatened to shoot Skinny Pimp for calling her a bitch too."

"Damn, she was a real piece of work, huh?" I asked.

"You could say that. I'll tell you one thing though ... your girl had her eyes on kidnapping your black ass. She was gonna ask your family, and mine, for a million dollars.

"Damn, that's it? Hell, I would've thought she wanted more money for my black ass!"

"Whatever, Mike," Redd said and laughed.

"So, you telling me you wouldn't have paid that much for me, Redd?"

She looked at me with her light-brown, beautiful eyes and said, "Mike, I would have paid whatever it took to have you back. But not to that group of crooked individuals. My uncles and my entire family would've gone to war to rescue you!"

"Damn, so you telling me I mean that much to you?" I smiled.

"Boy, stop acting like you don't know. Now let's go clean up that nasty ass room Jasmine left looking like the fuckin' projects."

"I already took care of it, sweetheart."

She looked at me and smiled. Then, she went back downstairs to retrieve the items she'd bought from the mall.

As I sat there contemplating with my hand over my forehead, I still saw Do-Dirty's face in my mind. I could still see the way she looked at me before she took her last breath. What was she trying to say to me? And were things that bad that I had to have them all taken out? Whatever the case, it was all too late to think about it now. They were all gone, every single one of them.

I should have thought about my actions before I made the decision. Now, I had to live with the afterthought of what happened. The decisions I'd made would alter the future for a lot of people, not just me, but their individual families as well.

Not only was Do-Dirty someone's child, but she was also a mother of five beautiful, innocent children. Now, her kids would grow up without their mother in their lives due to my fear of being robbed. It would be up to her own mother now, to raise her five children along with whoever else's children she was raising.

Damn, what was I becoming? Was this the life I really wanted? Or was this something that was supposed to have taken place? It was the life they led. And in the end, you live by the sword, you die by the sword. In their case, it was by the gun that caused them to leave everyone else behind.

As I continued to sit there in total darkness, I couldn't help but think of all the crazy things that were happening within the group. A month prior, I had hired a group of girls who called themselves the Bout It-Bout It Girls. It seemed as though the guys were wanting to do more than just throw dollar bills at the Florida Hot Girls. They also wanted to fuck something, and that something was my beautiful Florida Hot Girls.

Now, the Bout It-Bout It Girls consisted of five off-the-chain-ass females who would do just about anything for a damn dollar.

One night the ladies were complaining about not being able to do VIP'S. I had to step in and give one of the dreaded speeches they had grown to hate whenever they were in the wrong about something concerning the group.

"Ladies, I thought I had explained to you all in the beginning that there would be no sexual activities while working as a Florida Hot Girl, period. And if any females are caught involved in any sexual situations, she's to be fired immediately."

You see, this was law, and there were no exceptions—I didn't care who you were in the group. It wasn't happening until one night while at the Caribbean Beach Night club.

I had overheard one of the ladies' conversation with one of her customers.

"Mike doesn't allow us to indulge in anything sexual with the customer,"

"So, in other words, he's cuffing the pussy and stopping you all from making real money," the young guy said to hot ass Lil Kitty.

That night was the first night my authority over the rules were ever challenged. Now, while the girls were busy counting their money that night, Lil Kitty's hot ass spoke up.

"Mike, I have a question?"

*"Go ahead, Lil Kitty, I know I got an answer for your question,"
I said with a smile on my face.*

"I had a customer tonight who wanted to pay me like five hundred dollars to go home with him. I couldn't go because of the no-sex rules," she said. She had the attention of every other girl in the room.

"First of all, Lil Kitty, that dude was not gonna pay your ass that much fuckin' money for a piece of ass. That's just game, Lil Kitty. Now before you ladies all got hired, I explained to your ass that there was no sex. I am not going down because some of you ladies wanna sell ass for a lil' bit of cash!"

"So how about if we wanna leave with someone after we finish the show?" J.K. asked in her squeaky ass voice.

"That's entirely up to you all if that's how you want to put it!"

"But, Mike, what if they wanna go into the VIP while we're dancing?" Strawberry asked. She pulled her panties up over her wide, flat ass. I was between a rock and a hard place at that moment. Until one of the new chicks spoke up.

"Mike, me and my crew can handle that. That's why we called the Bout It-Bout It Girls. We'll do just about anything for that cash." At that very moment, I agreed to let them do what they did.

"Mike, if it's a nice price that my customer is offering me, I'm doing me," Tiny said. She held up her money bag so I could see how swollen it was due to all the ones she'd made that evening.

"It's not fuckin' fair if them hoes can make their money and ours too. Hell, we the ones getting them niggas dick all hard and shit. But them hoes are the ones who is fuckin' them and then making our fuckin' money," Lil Kitty screamed out, as if she was going to take control of my fuckin' group.

My decision to let them do them eventually got out of hands a few weeks later, so I was forced to boot them out of the group and let my girls do what they wanted to do. A decision I would regret later down the road.

I figured letting them go their separate ways was for the best since they were so outgoing and forward. They were doing things at some of the shows that I just didn't feel comfortable with. Months later, as I thought back to when they were with the group, I wouldn't put it past them as the ones who killed them four cowboy-looking-ass-niggas that night, and then made it look like the Florida Hot Girls had done it.

It didn't matter now, here I was with the death of six people on my mind and I just couldn't shake it. But as they say in show business, the show must go on. I walked back downstairs while the ladies were still talking amongst each other.

"Excuse me, ladies, earlier, I overheard you guys talking about how I felt about Sexy Redd and this group."

"Oh, you heard us, bae?"

"Yes, Redd, I did, and to assure you all of how I feel about you, please, let me explain. You see, without you there is no me, and there is no me without you. So, please, understand all of you females play an important role in the survival of this group." As I was explaining their roles, every one of those females was looking at me as though I were a preacher and it was Sunday morning service.

You see, Redd, you are my right-hand man, and Nicole, you are my left-hand man, the group is my back bone, and together, we make a very strong team! They started smiling at each other as I continued telling them how important they were to our success.

"Now, don't get me wrong. Some of the ladies on the team are full of shit, and that's why we must weed out the bad ones in order to make this thing we have work. You females that live here with Sexy Redd and me are my strongest females, and that's why you all are here. Now, could we all get dressed so I can take you all out to dinner?"

"So, Mike you're paying for it, right?" Strawberry asked. One side of her mouth was still swollen the fuck up.

"Yes, Strawberry, because I know you don't have any money!" Everyone burst into laughter, including Strawberry. She ran upstairs with everyone else to get dressed. When her flat ass got to the top of the stairs, she turned around and looked right at me. I was still laughing.

"That shit ain't funny, Mike!"

"Girl, he is only playing with you," Sexy Redd said. We walked off to our separate bedrooms so we could get dressed.

"Okay, Mr. Funny Man, since you're paying for it, we wanna go to Lobster Fest and fuck up some seafood," Nicole said ,as she strutted her lil' fine ass into her bedroom.

"Lobster Fest it is ladies," I shouted down the hallway to.

***

WHILE DRIVING DOWN ORANGE BLOSSOM TRAIL headed to Lobster Fest, the ladies were excited about going to Tampa the upcoming Tuesday. They couldn't wait to get back to club Apollo South.

"Excuse me, ladies not to jump in you guys' conversation, but once we get through eating we can do a little shopping next door at the Florida Mall."

"Oh no, Mike, we've been at the mall all day. After we finish eating, it's back to the house so we can all get some needed rest for tomorrow night's show," Mignon said. The rest of the ladies agreed as they looked out of the back-seat passenger window.

"Oh, my bad. You are so right, young lady. You all were at the mall all day."

When we pulled up in the parking lot, Redd was the first one to say, "Baby look, this place is packed and we're not going to be able to get a good seat."

"Don't worry, boo, I got this," I said, "you just make sure you can eat forty dollars' worth of food."

"That's right, Mike, you did say you were paying for dinner."

"Strawberry for the last time, it's on me. I just hope y'all are hungry enough to eat. Because forty dollars a person is a lot for some damn lobster and crabs."

"Mike, believe me when I tell you, I'm so hungry, I can eat your black ass right now, and then spit you back up and eat you again."

"Hold on, Strawberry, the only person eating him is me, so hold your horses," Sexy Redd said. Strawberry laughed at her own joke.

"Girl, I'm just playing. I don't won't to eat his black ass!"

"Whatever, y'all. Can we just go inside and eat? I'm hungry for real," Nicole said, as she stepped out of my black Yukon Denali sitting some fat ass 24-inch chrome wheels.

After being there for a few hours, it wasn't until around ten thirty that night that we finally got back home. Everyone was so full and tired, we said good night and went off to bed. I checked the home security system, and then made sure the house was secured.

I crawled into bed while Sexy Redd was in the mirror doing her hair. I lay there on the bed watching her until I pulled out my two-way pager and checked it for any messages. I had one missed message that went as followed:

⌀ Family, I received your message about the incident that went down in your spot. Your problem has been solved. Fireworks went off earlier, and you may want to catch the late news so you can witness something beautiful.
Your brother a.k.a. Firstborn. ⌀

I rolled over and retrieved the remote off the night stand and flipped from ESPN to channel five news, just as they were showing the news clip:

"This was the scene earlier this afternoon at the old paper mill off Griffin Road. The local fire department believes that the explosion might have been caused by some type of chemicals used to manufacture drugs. There were also six badly burned bodies found inside the fire as well. We will keep you posted on this, and other stories, on your morning news at day break."

Redd casually walked over to her side of the bed and got on her knees and said her prayers. I quickly followed suit and did the same thing.

"Bae, we need to start going to Church more often," she said, while crawling up into bed.

"You're so right, boo. But when we come home, it's always on Sunday afternoons," I said. I pulled the covers up to my bare chest.

"Well, I guess we'll just have to go to church in whatever town we're in," she said, as she kissed me on the lips. I agreed with her and hit the lights so we could go to sleep.

"Oh, by the way, Michael, where is my two-way pager?"

I rolled over so that my back was facing her and replied, "Under your pillow, ma."

"So, when did you buy me a two-way pager? These things are quite expensive," she said, as she pulled the pager from underneath her pillow in sheer excitement.

"Yeah, that they are. Somewhere around about three hundred fifty dollars or so. Don't worry though, remember when you said what's yours is mine?" I laughed sneakily.

"Michael, no you didn't?" She kicked me lightly under the covers.

"Redd, yes I did, good night."

"Michael, I'm gonna get you," she said. She tried to pull me over to face her in the bed.

"Nah, I'm gonna get you first. Now, pull off them panties so I can get me."

"I'm not wearing any, papi, it's all yours," she said. I rolled over with a full erection and inserted all ten and a half inches of my rock-hard manhood inside her warm, wet, tight vagina.

Thinking back to that beautiful, warm, summer night, I think we must 've made love for two hours straight before we passed out. But, it was just another day in the life of the Florida Hot Girls.

Michael Gallon

CHAPTER FIVE
THE DAY AFTER

That Tuesday morning, Redd and I decided to sleep in since we'd been through such a long day the day before. Besides, she was still tired from the previous night's activities.

It was around twelve thirty in the afternoon before I finally rolled out of bed. I looked over at my beautiful, Puerto Rican Princess who was still laying in one of the positions I had left her in the night before. At first, I thought about partaking in part two of our love making festival. But due to the way Redd was stretched out, I figured she'd had enough of me and John Boy the night before.

As I climbed out of bed, I once again noticed the new art work she had on the upper portion of her inner thigh. I tried to get closer to see what it said, but she must've felt my presence, because she quickly closed her legs and rolled over.

I thought nothing of it as I got up and did the usual things one does when they wake up. You know, brush your teeth, wash your face, and if your ass is dirty, take a shower.

As soon as I finished, I headed down stairs to prepare some lunch for the girls and me. While in the kitchen, my phone rang. I quickly checked the caller ID and saw that it was no one other than Suga Bear.

Now, Suga Bear was the little sister of your girl, Chazz. She stood five foot six and weighed around one hundred thirty-five pounds. She had a nice, chunky, fat ass, and her skin tone was a beautiful dark-yellow complexion. Her beautiful titties were probably a nice 32B. She always had this laugh about her that made you laugh right along with her. In other words, you could say she was the loud type, right along with her sidekick, Peekachu. Suga Bear had a nice smile about her that made her look even more attractive.

The one thing that separated Chazz from her younger sister was that Stephanie's ass was a bit more rounded than hers. Not to mention, Chazz was brown skin and Step was light skinned. Now, her crazy ass partner, Peekachu, stood around five-five and weighed around one hundred twenty-five pounds, and she was bright as hell.

She had an admirable breast size of 32A. She had a small but, somewhat, round butt, and she always walked around with it stuck out. She, too, had a certain laugh that made you want to say 'damn, do you have to laugh like that?'

Either way, they were both two girls who gave the team that upbeat attitude. Whenever Step, or should I say Suga Bear, made a comment, you could best believe Peekachu was right behind her with a smart- mouth comment as well.

"What's up, Step?"

"Hey, Mike?"

"Yes, Step."

"Hey, listen, I got a new girl who wants to dance tonight. Can I bring her?"

"You need to call Redd and see how many girls are going tonight."

"Man, you know how she be acting, Mike. She always seem like she be mad and shit."

"It's not that, Step," I tried to explain as best I could, "she just knows that half of the girls in the group be trying to give me some play behind her back. So, she doesn't trust a lot of girls."

"She don't have to worry about that with me, 'cause if I want you to have some of this good ass shaky pudding, your black ass is gonna get it. Like it or not, she might as well get over it."

"Step, you crazy." My mouth twisted in a half grin. "What's the new chick's name and how does she look?"

"Her name is Henrietta, and she probably weighs about one hundred forty-five pounds. She got big ass titties and her skin complexion is a little darker than mine. She's nice, and cute in the face as well. She really needs a job, Mike. She lives with her mother for right now. She claims her mother told her she gonna have to move out in a few months. So, she really needs to make some cash real fast."

"Is she eighteen?"

"Yes, Mike."

"Okay, she can come, but she needs to have gas money upfront and you're gonna be responsible for her."

"Man, I got her, Mike. What time y'all coming through to pick us up?"

"'Round eight thirty, so tell Lovely and Chazz to be ready."

"Lovely already over here and so is my girl Peekachu."

"I hope your girl Peekachu got her money for that fat ass fine she owes."

"Yeah, Mike, my girl got her shit right tonight."

"Oh, and let her Bobby Brown-looking-ass know, there won't be no more doing drugs for her hot ass. If she wants to do drugs, she can stay her crackhead-having-ass the fuck home."

"Mike, she said she not doing pills no more."

"I hope not, Step. And sure as hell not the ones you gave her."

Step recalled the night Peekachu tripped out on the X pill. She started laughing and tried to tell me what really happened.

"Mike, I didn't give her no pills. All I gave her was some good ass fuckin' weed I had got from my sister."

" I know that's right, 'cause your damn sister be having that fuckin' shit they call gas weed, whatever that shit is." We both started laughing.

"Step, let me go, I'm cooking lunch for me and the girls."

"Lovely said to ask you if we can come over and eat lunch with you guys?"

"I don't think that Sexy Redd wants all y'all over here right now. And besides, she's still upstairs getting her beauty rest."

"Nah, I'm right here, Michael. Who are you talking to?" Redd questioned me. Then, she snatched the phone out of my hand.

"Hello, and who might this be?"

"This Step, Redd."

Redd's face scrunched up and her mouth poked out. "Who?" she asked with more attitude.

I just stood there and thought, *wow*. That's what we do now? Just snatch the phone out of my hand."

"Suga Bear, Redd."

"Oh, hey, Suga Bear." Redd moved the phone away from her mouth and mouthed the words *Suga Bear.* She laughed.

"I was just asking Mike how many girls were going tonight

'cause I got a friend who wants to dance tonight."

"No problem, girl, you know you could've called me. What did Mike say?"

"He said it was cool."

"Okay, Step. I guess we'll see you guys later tonight. Oh, and make sure Peekachu has her money for that fine she still owes,"

"Yeah, she got it."

"No problem, here's Mike. I'll see you tonight."

"Mike, see how your girl be on that serious tip shit?" Suga Bear said, as soon as I placed the phone back to my ear.

"Well, I told you she runs the group so everything goes through her."

"Man, I'll see you tonight, Mike. Peace," she said, with sarcasm in her voice. She hung up.

As soon as I got off the phone with Suga Bear, Redd was right there leaning over the kitchen counter, wearing one of my Dallas Cowboys Jersey's with a pair of red thongs underneath it. She looked like she wanted to make love again.

"I hope your lil' friend didn't get mad, Mike, but I'm not dim-witted."

"What are you talking about now, Sexy Redd?"

"Mike, I see how her and a few more of these lil' pissy ass females in the group be looking at your handsome, sexy, black ass. If I didn't keep my eye on them, they'd be in here trying get up in my bed with you," she said.

"Now what makes you think something like that? Like I keep telling you, Redd, all I see is you, and all I do is you. So, stop letting your mind think anything else. Now give me a kiss and get ready to eat." She puckered up and kissed me, and I could still smell the scent of the spearmint mouthwash on her breath.

"It smells so good, what did you cook?" she asked. Standing there in the jersey, her fat ass twat-twat seemed to be staring back at John Boy. I could feel the inside of my pants start to transform back into the Incredible Hulk.

"You know what it is. It's your favorite: smothered cube steak, rice, cabbage, macaroni and cheese, and sweet cornbread.

"Damn, Mike, you really trying to get me fat, so you can get rid of me."

"Redd, please, I'm only trying to feed my lady and the rest of the girls inside the house."

She pressed the intercom button.

"Okay, ladies, lunch is ready. So, please come and eat."

I fixed Redd's plate and we sat down and ate as we watched the news.

"Do we fix our own plates, Mike?"

"Yes, Strawberry. I'm not the fuckin' maid. They don't come back until next week," I told her.

"Thanks, smart ass."

"I heard that, Strawberry. That's a twenty-dollar fine," I said to her while chewing on my nice, tender piece of smothered cube steak.

"I'm just playing, Mike. You know how slick my mouth can be."

"Whatever. Y'all eat as much as you like. I made sure I made enough for at least seven people."

Redd and I continued eating and watching the news. A minute later, my two-way pager went off. I pulled it out to see who it was and saw it was DJ Grand Evil from the club.

I read the message out loud:

Yo Mike, it's yo' boy Grand Evil. When you get to the club tonight, someone would like to speak with you about bringing your girls to their club on Tuesdays. See you soon.

"So, what are you going to do, baby?" Redd asked, as she wiped some brown gravy from her sexy ass lips.

"I guess I'll speak with him when we get to the club tonight. Right now, I'm about to fuck up the rest of this cube steak and rice."

"Boy, you are so fuckin' crazy. Wait until I cook you up one of my favorite meals," she said, as she gulped down some of her strawberry Kool-Aid.

"And what would that be, babygirl?"

"Oxtails, rice and peas, cabbage, plantains, and maybe some homemade sweet skillet cornbread."

"Damn, if you gonna put down like that, then do the damn thang, and you better make sure the oxtails are good and tender." As we sat eating, neither of us realized it was getting late.

***

THE FIRST FEMALE WE PICKED UP that night was a new crazy chick who went by the name Mercedes. After that, we shot over to Eatonville to pick up Stephanie and her crew of girls. When we got to her house, she had four other girls with her. All of them were ready to make some cash. By the time I picked up J.K. and her crew of girls, we we're full.

"Hey, did y'all hear what happened at the old paper mill yesterday?" Lil Kitty said as soon as she got inside the truck.

Redd looked over at me, and Chyna answered Kitty's question. "Yeah, they said the building exploded. It was all over the news yesterday and last night."

"Yeah, I heard on the news this morning somebody had some type of lab in there and they were cooking up drugs when it exploded," J.K. chimed in.

"Damn, that shit just blew up like that?" I said, as I merged onto Interstate 4 headed to Tampa.

"Yep, that's what it looked like," Kizzy said, as she tried to position her fat ass into her seat.

Now, everybody inside the damn truck was talking about what happened, asking each other if any people were inside the mill when it exploded.

Then nosy ass Lil Kitty said, "They found some bodies inside the fire. But that they were so badly burned up, they're gonna have to go through their dental records to positively identify them."

The ladies talked about the incident all the way to Tampa, while Redd and I just sat there listening to what was said.

When we finally got to Apollo South, all the ladies stepped out looking like brand-new money. There was a rule that whenever we went to a show, they had to be looking their very best. It didn't matter if it was a bachelor party or club. Whatever it was, they always had to step out of whatever vehicle we were in looking like new money.

Ms. Innocence was looking like a fuckin' model as she walked through the club with the rest of the girls behind her as though she was the leader of the group. I told Redd she wouldn't be dancing that night since I had to meet with someone about the ladies dancing at another club. Of course, she didn't have a problem being candy on my arm.

As all the ladies walked into a full house of people, the anticipation was overwhelming. The guys knew the Florida Hot Girls had just entered the building, and DJ Don Juan was about to let the ones know who didn't know, by making an announcement over the speaker system. The girls were off in the dressing room getting ready for their grand entrance.

"Let me have your attention, please! Fresh off the plane and straight from Tampa International Airport via heavy police escort, the Florida Hot Girls have just entered the building from their around-the-world tour. So, get your ones together, and get ready for one of the hottest female dance groups in Florida. They don't just turn heads, these females are so damn fine, they break necks!" he said to the crowd, as he started playing "Looking For A Hot Girl" by Cash Money.

Fifteen minutes later, the DJ shouted over the speaker system a second time. "Ladies and gentlemen, club Apollo South proudly presents the World-Famous Florida Hot Girls!"

The ladies came out of the dressing room looking like they were really some badass females who had just come from around the world. Ms. Small ass Kitty came out first with her thong up her narrow lil' ass sideways. Behind her, was big head ass Peekachu, with a yellow thong pulled so far up the crack of her ass, you couldn't tell if she had on anything or not. Then came your girl Chyna who came out looking like a fuckin' baby doll. She was looking so cute that night, and them big ass titties were calling my name. Step and

Lovely along with Henrietta, all came out like they were fuckin' sisters and shit. Suga Bear stepped out with a black and mild hanging from her thin ass lips like she was fuckin' grown and shit.

J.K. and her crew of bandits slid their asses right on out and headed straight to some young looking dope boys' table. They had spotted them as soon as they walked in the club. As Strawberry walked out of the dressing room, she bumped into a guy and he spilled his drink all over Tiny's back. Tiny turned around and gave Strawberry an angry ass look that just sent chills up her spine. Carmen and White Chocolate walked right on by them and kept it moving like they hadn't even see them in front of them.

By now, the girls who hadn't gone up on stage were off to someone's table dancing.

Mercedes had her crazy, but cute ass, over in the comer dancing on some old ass man who looked like he should've been home sleep in somebody's bed. Lovely was wrapped up with an up-and-coming local Rapper by the name of Rated R. Mignon was returning to the club where she first started at, but no one could tell. She had changed since she'd left with the Hot Girls that night. She was looking like brand-new money as she danced on stage with Innocence by her side.

People were throwing money at them before they could even get on stage. Entyce was over in the corner with some local DJ by the name of Shadow. I remembered him from a few years back, and he was the same nigga who used to fuck one of my baby's mother. *Slick ass nigga.*

Now, your girl Chazz was over at the bar between some nigga's leg with her back facing him and one of her arms was wrapped around his neck. She was smoking a blunt with her other hand. That damn Chazz was something else. No matter where we went, she always found her a blunt to wrap her skinny, black ass lips around.

Strawberry was inside the DJ booth dancing for free, as usual, until I said something to Sexy Redd about it.

"Hey, baby, go over there and tell Strawberry to make sure her friend isn't tipping or she's gonna have to walk back to Orlando tonight. I'm so tired of her not getting her money!"

"I gotcha, baby. I'll be right back," Redd said, as she walked away to the DJ booth. Half of the club watched her fine Puerto Rican ass. That's when I looked over to see Peekachu and Suga Bear over in a dark ass corner just moving their ass up and down on two niggas who looked like they were too young to even be up in the club.

"Hey, you two, I sure hope them two young ass niggas tipping y'all short fuckin' asses," I shouted over the loud music.

Suga Bear pulled the black and mild from her mouth and yelled, "Don't worry about this tight ass pussy over here, my nigga! We good."

Peekachu, as usual, also had something to say. "Yeah, nigga! We got enough money between the both of us to buy your black ass so pretend your last name is Jackson and beat it!" They burst out laughing.

I tried to come back at them with something but only came up with, "Oh so y'all got jokes tonight? Well that means you two shouldn't have a problem with paying the tip out fee for your girl Henrietta, 'cause it don't look like she gonna make nothing tonight!" They looked over and saw her sitting at the bar trying to buy her ass a drink. That's when I heard Peekachu say the smartest thing I've ever heard her say in her fuckin' life. "Oh, hell nah, that chick better get her double-wide-trailer-having ass out there and get that money!" They ran over to the bar to get her up and dancing.

"Oh, and by the way, the tip out fee tonight is forty dollars apiece," I told them, as they passed by me.

I laughed as they looked at each other. They looked like two females in a horror movie, and the monster was right behind them.

They sat down beside poor Henrietta and looked at her and said, "Girl, you better get up off that wide, big ass booty of yours and get that cash, 'cause we're not paying your tip out fee. Hell, we trying to take our money straight to the weed man and start selling some good ass Kush.

Damn, it was just another wild and crazy night with them muthafuckin' Florida Hot Girls.

Michael Gallon

CHAPTER SIX
THE DEAL IS DONE

Sexy Redd came back from the DJ booth and told me that Don Juan wanted to speak with me. So, together, we walked back to the booth while the girls kept doing their thing. As I walked by Suga Bear and Peekachu, you could still see the look of horror in their eyes, as their girl sat at the bar as if she couldn't get up.

As soon as I entered the DJ booth, Don Juan made his request. "Damn, Mike, I need one of them girls with me tonight. Sheeit, I'll take two if I can."

"Don Juan you're a fool, man. How in the hell are you?"

"Man, I'm doing fine now that you and them fine ass dancers are here."

"Hello, Ms. Sexy Redd, and how are you doing tonight?" he asked. "I already know you're fine, so you don't need to tell me that."

"Don Juan, you're so crazy. So if I'm already fine, I guess I'm good then," Sexy Redd replied. She looked sexy and sophisticated in the pair of tight, red Sergio Jeans and the white, silk, see-through shirt she's paired them with. A pair of white Prada shoes, she'd picked up at the mall, set the outfit off.

As she stood there talking, I stared at her from the side and couldn't help but see her striking resemblance of Sharon. And not to mention, her and Sharon both loved them some Prada shoes. The more I thought about it, the more I thought they could damn near be sisters. I quickly erased the notion out of my head but continued to stare at her. Her skin was glowing as she stood there with her fat ass pushed back against my dick while she and Don Juan shoot-the-breeze.

I whispered in her ear, "Alright now, keep pushing back on all this meat if you want to. He gonna burst right through these black ass silk slacks and slip right inside that tight ass booty hole of yours."

She turned around and giggled playfully. "Boy, shut up. I'ma go check on the girls," she said.

"Yeah, you do that before I put a damn baby up inside you right here in the club."

"Mike, man, she has to be the finest Puerto Rican chick I've ever seen in a long fuckin' time," Don Juan said, as he watched her walk away. Look how all them niggas staring at her. Why she ain't dancing tonight anyway?" he asked.

"Because I was supposed to meet Grand Evil tonight. He said somebody from another club wanted to speak with me about doing their club on Tuesday nights also."

"Yeah, that's probably that club near Howard and Armenia called Hollywood Nights. It used to be a regular club but business been kind of slow lately. So, they trying to do something different on Tuesday's nights by incorporating strippers," he informed me, "you know niggas gonna always come out if they see some half-naked asses," he added.

After about ten minutes, Sexy Redd came back with Ms. Innocence. I had heard the crowd oohing and ahhing but didn't know why until Sexy Redd walked her into the DJ booth.

"Well, I'll be John Brown!" Don Juan said loudly, just as soon as he lay eyes on her. "Man, she's as fine as fine wine!" Innocence smiled from ear to ear as she let the compliment marinate. The print of her pussy was perfectly defined through the outfit she'd worn.

Damn, I would love to just fuck the shit out of her one more damn time, right here inside this small ass DJ booth, I thought.

"Well, Mike, how does she look?" Redd asked. All I could do was stand there and stare at the same thing Don Juan was staring at.

Now, don't get me wrong, Sexy Redd was all that and a bag of chips, but Innocence was just as beautiful standing there with a red two-piece outfit on that showcased her stomach, which was as flat as a washboard.

Her legs were nice and lean and they seemed to flow right up to her nicely proportioned ass. It made the average nigga melt from just looking at her. Her breasts sat on her beautiful chest just begging for attention. Not to mention, how beautiful she was on top of everything else.

"She looks good, Redd," I finally answered. I held my head

down due to being embarrassed that I couldn't seem to control my manhood from wanting to enlarge inside my black slacks.

"Hell, she looks good enough to eat, Mike," Don Juan said, as he fumbled around for the next song to throw on. Mike, where is she from?"

"I met her in Jacksonville one weekend. After I gave her a quick interview she was ready to leave with us and join the group."

"Okay, and you call her Innocence, right?"

"Yes, and if you're lucky enough to get her fine red ass in bed, you'll see why I call her Innocence."

I knew she had to be nice if Don Juan wanted her. Don Juan was never the type of guy to sweat the girls. You had to have your game tight if he wanted to get with you. He was just that type of fellow.

As I walked out of the booth, I walked to the back of the club so I could get a nice table for me and Sexy Redd, away from the huge crowd that had gathered up in the club to see the world-famous Florida Hot Girls.

Now I know there's gonna be some people who are gonna say, 'aww, man, they weren't all that', and my reply to that would always be the same. "You might as well stop hating because those were some badass bitches who were a part of the original Florida Hot Girls. The sad thing about it is that they didn't know how bad and how beautiful they were at the time.

I would eventually take the name and talent to one of the highest levels of wealth, fortune, and fame that they would have ever imagined.

While Don Juan had the club rocking to some Trick Daddy, Redd and I continued watching all the niggas inside The Club throwing dollars at my girls. The environment was like none other I had experienced before. By now, every one of my girls were somewhere in the club making mad fuckin' money. And me, well, I was enjoying every minute of it.

Sitting back in the rear of the club, I was clad in a black and white ensemble that had all the brothers saying, 'that nigga has to be the coolest pimp in muthafuckin' Florida'—a title I never wanted to have. But as long as I had those badass females with me, it was a name I would just have to get used to.

By now, the official crew of Hot Girls had on their official Florida Hot Girl necklace that your girl Chazz had designed. As they walked around the club with their chains hanging from their necks, they created such a buzz, every female wanted to be a Florida Hot Girl, and the niggas wanted to fuck one.

While Redd and I sat over at our nice table in the back of the club, away from the crowd of bystanders in attendance, I really wanted to believe they were there to witness one of the beautiful wonders of the world, which to me, was them mutha- fuckin' Florida Hot Girls. Now, I usually don't drink, and I sure as hell didn't smoke, so I just sat there trying to look like I had everything under control. No one really knew how nervous I really was. I had fifteen girls in the club with me that night, and money was coming in from every direction. On top of that, there was very limited security watching my back.

"Bae, there's no need to worry," Sexy Redd said, as she leaned over closer. "I'm all the security you need." She showed me the loaded .45 she always kept close at hand. Then, she showed me a loaded .380 nestled inside her Louis Vuitton purse. My eyes grew wide after she showed me her weapons of choice.

"And besides, Michael, you see them two Puerto Rican dudes over by the bathroom? Those are my cousins, Javier and Sanchez. from Belle Glade, Florida. I also had the club make sure they had extra security for us at the front door."

"You are really a piece of work. What would I do without you?"

"I don't know, and I don't want to find out. Now let's enjoy tonight and get something to drink," she said, while placing her hand on my inner thigh, trying to wake up John Boy.

By now, the club was thicker than it was before. It seemed like people had called their friends who then called their friends. All I know is girl after girl turned in ones as though they were tipping too.

While sitting there scanning the club for my girls, I saw Lil Kitty and Nicole's fine ass on top of one of the pool tables with guys gathered all around them. They took off all their clothes and got butt naked. Your girl, Chazz, was still over on the same guy still smoking and drinking as though she had become his girlfriend in the short time we'd been there.

While Lovely was still star struck by Rated R, who had stopped tipping her two hours prior, Mignon and Entyce were over by the entrance of the club dancing on two guys who I think played for the Buc's. J.K. and her crew of girls were still with the same dope boys from earlier. I would find out later that those guys made mad money by traveling to small towns and robbing banks for a living. Strawberry was over by the side entrance chit-chatting with some nigga who was throwing nothing but tens at her apple headed ass. She saw me look over in her direction and smiled, as she pointed down to the floor at all the money between her legs. Even though she was still somewhat of a sight to see due to her swollen lip. Tiny and Carmen were off to the back of the club doing tricks on the floor. Each one demanded attention and that's exactly what they were getting, from two old ass niggas who looked like they had just broken out of a nursing home.

Now Innocence had just got off stage with Chyna who was all in her ass like she was her mother or something.

"Hey, Redd, Chyna seems to be really hanging with poor lil' Innocence like they're sisters or something. I don't know if you noticed it or not, but it seems like Chyna likes girls too."

"Mike, I don't know where in the hell you've been for the last few days, but she does like girls!"

"So, you telling me Chyna likes girls?"

"What are you a fuckin' parrot or something, Michael? Yes, the bitch is fuckin' bisexual," Sexy Redd said, as I laughed at her calling me a damn parrot.

"Damn, Redd, why do I have to be fuckin' parrot?"

"You're not, baby. I'm sorry, I just can't believe you didn't already know that about her red ass. Hell, she came at me a couple of times. But you know I don't get down like that!"

"Excuse me, Mike." J.K. approached me.

"Yes, J.K."

"I need to speak with you."

"Damn, J.K., what is it now?"

"Darn, Mike, do you have to act like that? I haven't did anything to your lil' black sexy ass," she said, as I stood up from the table so Redd wouldn't hear our conversation.

"Nah J.K., it's not you. I'm just trying to chill and watch y'all make your money. And if I'm so fuckin' sexy, why ain't let me knock the stuffing off that Egg McMuffin yet?"

"Shut up, boy, you so fuckin' crazy."

"Damn," is all I could say. We laughed at my joke.

"It's really not that big of a problem, Mike. It's just that there are a few guys who want to take a few of us girls home with them after the club."

That's entirely up to you, and whichever girl wants to go. I don't have nothing to do with it. You know how I feel about y'all leaving the club with guys after the club closes."

"I understand, Mike. But he said him and his boys want to check out the girls and decide from there which ones they wanna take."

"Like I said, J.K., that's on y'all. I'm not coming back down here tomorrow to pick y'all up!"

"No, he's gonna take us back in the morning. We not about to miss dancing at the Caribbean."

"Yep, because if y'all do, I'ma suspend your ass for two weeks!"

"Mike, you tripping. Why two weeks?"

"So, y'all will know what's more important. One night with a total stranger, or making money for two weeks straight. Now, can I please go back to my table and join my girl, before she comes over here and checks the both of us?"

"I guess, Mike. Why she be actin' like that anyway? Don't nobody in this group want you like that?"

"Well, you try telling her that. She claims she knows of about five girls in this group she doesn't trust at all when it comes to me."

J.K. shook her head and was about to walk away and head back to her table. She looked me dead in the eyes and said, "By the way, old sexy ass black nigga, if I let you hit this Egg McMuffin, your black ass would have to move in with me. I ain't nobody's side chick, baby!" She walked away twisting her big round ass from side to side.

Now while walking back over to my table, I was approached by this lil' short guy.

"Excuse me."

"Yeah, what's up?" I replied.

"You Mike, right?" he inquired.

"Yeah, what's on your mind?"

"I'm the guy who wanted to speak with you about the girls coming to our spot on Tuesdays.· He introduced himself to me, and I did likewise. He started telling me about his club and how he and his partners wanted the Florida Hot Girls at their spot so they could draw in the crowd. He explained to me how the crowd in Tampa was following the Florida Hot Girls and going wherever they danced. They felt if my girls went to their spot it would be good for us and them.

I agreed to give it a shot, but I couldn't leave Apollo bone and dry like that. Especially since they'd been the first club in Tampa to give the Florida Hot Girls their big break.

So, I would take half of the girls to Apollo South, and the other half would go to Hollywood Nights. The deal was done and it was settled. Now we could dance on Sunday, be off on Monday, dance at Hollywood and Apollo on Tuesday, do Caribbean on Wednesday, take Thursday off, and then do Jacksonville on the weekend, if we didn't have a bachelor party or club to do on that weekend. It couldn't get any better than that. We would be in full demand almost every day of the week.

After speaking with the guy from the club, I walked back over to my table. Upon getting back at the table, Sexy Redd was nowhere to be found. I looked over the club for her and spotted her up by the stage area. She was making sure the ladies were getting their money. I walked up behind her and wrapped my arms around her waist.

"So, I leave you for a few minutes, and look where I find your lil' red ass!"

"Now, Michael, if it would have been for a few minutes, I

would have still been sitting there, but you and I both know it was more like forty-five minutes."

"So, damn, you were timing me while I was gone?"

"Not really. I was making sure the girls were alright, and checking on you at the same time."

We continued talking and Entyce came up to us. "Excuse me, Mike. Those guys over there at that table want to speak with you about some of the girls."

"You didn't find out what they wanted, Entyce?"

"Nah, they said they wanted to speak with the manager or the owner of the group."

Redd turned around and said, "Mike, are you cool? Do you want me to speak with them?"

"Yeah, I'm good. You go ahead and talk with them, Redd. Hell, you're the manager. I'm just the guy who gets the girls to the shows."

"Okay, watch how your girl handles this situation."

Now while she was taking care of that, J.K. was busy talking with the same guys from earlier. Chyna and Innocence were busy over by the pool tables collecting money and phone numbers. The others were busy dressing back in their regular clothes.

Redd stepped back to me. "Bae, they wanna do a bachelor party sometime around the middle of the month. They want at least seven girls, all cute, and at least two white girls. I told them you usually don't do white girls because it brings too much attention to the group."

"Did you quote them a price?"

"Yes, I told them that it's gonna cost them around fifteen hundred."

"Damn, why so much?"

"First, for them wasting my damn time and making me listen to the tall one brag about how much money he be making. And second, for the number of girls he wants. He already gave me a deposit to lock it in."

"Damn, you did it like that?"

"Yep, here's your deposit and the five hundred dollars is for them clowns wasting my fuckin' time!"

Damn, I'm glad I'm dating you 'cause you can be very expensive."

"It's called high maintenance, baby. And, oh, here's a hundred dollars for Entyce for hooking the show up."

"Okay, beautiful, make sure the girls are getting dressed so we can get ready to go."

As soon as Redd left my side for one minute, J.K. came running up to me. "Mike, they want like eight girls with them."

As soon as she uttered the number of girls in my ear, Shitty Smitty was in my other ear. "Hey, Mike, please bring the girls down to Lou Doc's tonight. We legit now, and besides, you owe me, nigga. Yo' black ass fucked the only dancer I had and then you took her and put her on your team!"

Smitty, that's the way the game is played. Hell, I didn't choose her, she chose me, pimp. Never hate the playa, pimp, hate the nature of the game." I patted his shoulder as if he were a student and I was the teacher telling him 'good job.' I smiled as though I had really done something.

"Okay, Mike, whatever. I promise you, we're straight legit now. We have security and we have a nice ass VIP room along with a full liquor bar. We just need your badass girls!"

J.K. came right back at him in her squeaky ass voice. "Mike, we don't want to go to no damn Lou Doc's after what happened to us the last fuckin' time. I got some guys over there who wanna take eight of us home with them, and they're going to pay our tip out fee along with our fine for leaving the club with them!"

Redd then walked back up behind me with her sexy ass. "Bae, I got this. Go handle Shitty Smitty!" I smiled as I walked away with Shitty Smitty still talking one hundred miles per hour, about nothing.

"Listen, Smitty, the last time we did something together in your club, the damn place got raided. Then my precious lil' Strawberry ended up with scratch marks all over her leg due to her being dragged halfway down the road by our limo!"

"Mike, it's not my fault the bitch couldn't outrun a limo. You should have left her ass down here with us. She would have been alright until you got back to get her."

"Yeah, I know. You and your boys would have fucked the shit out of her ass and then dropped her ass off somewhere in the middle of nowhere!"

"Damn, Mike. we would have at least fed her before we would have done her like that."

"That's a damn shame, Smitty. See, that's why I can't be fuckin' with you, man.

You don't care about these chicks. You just wanna make you a few dollars and you good."

"C'mon, Mike, man. You got a whole truckload of bitches, plus you took my girl Tarshay. Can I have at least a couple of them so I can make me some money tonight?"

"Hold on, man. Let me see what Redd is talking about."

"Mike, that's who I want right there. The one they call Sexy Redd," he said, rubbing his dick. His ass was so drunk, he stumbled backwards and looked like the younger version of Fred Sanford.

"Excuse me, Shitty Smitty. I'm not for sale, boo. I'm with Mike, so you don't have to ask him about me. The only dick going up in me is his."

"Damn, boy. You got her trained well."

"No, that's just the way she is. She's a very loyal, sexy ass bitch."

By now, Sexy Redd was whispering in my ear again. "Okay, Mike, listen. They want eight of the fifteen girls, including Innocence."

"Nah, nah, they can't have her, she's new."

"Bae, I know, but Chyna said she'll be responsible for her.

"But Chyna ain't even going with them so how in the hell she gonna be responsible for her.

"I know, I kept asking her that, but she claimed she got everything under control."

"Chyna, come here for one minute, please!"

How is she going to be responsible for one of the girls and her ass ain't even gonna be there with her to watch her? I kept thinking to myself. She walked over to me with a smile on her beautiful face.

Man, she had just tried me and one of the muthafuckin' Florida Hot Girls.

Michael Gallon

CHAPTER SEVEN
THAT DAMN CHYNA

"Yeah, what's up, Mike?" she asked. She stood in front of me and Sexy Redd with a dirty ass unit over her face. The rest of the girls were getting inside the truck, ready to go.

"Please, explain to me how in the hell are you going to be responsible for someone if you're not there with them?"

"First off, Mike, the girl is grown. She can handle herself. And besides that, she said she hasn't made enough money and she needs to make some more. So, just chill and let her go get some more paper."

As the rest of the girls were getting in the other vehicles so they could leave, Chyna turned around and said the wrong damn thing. "Besides, Mike, you don't want her to go 'cause you don't want anyone else fuckin' her." Everyone standing around just froze as the statement rolled out of Chyna's small fuckin' ass mouth. She was right. I had acquired some type of feelings for Innocence and I didn't want anyone all up inside of her. Hell, she was a beautiful young lady and I didn't want her being taken advantage of. I guess you can say, I had fallen for her just that fast. In the end, I really wanted the best for every female I'd ever come across. But for some strange reason, some of them didn't see it that way. But to this very same day, some fifteen years later, I still feel some type of way about every single female who ever had the chance to be called a true, loyal Florida Hot Girl.

While I stood there in a daze watching Innocence get into that guy's car, Sexy Redd screamed my name from inside the truck.

"Mike, Mike, what are you going to do? The rest of us ladies are ready to go!"

As I went to get back inside my truck, Shitty Smitty pulled me by the arm.

"Damn, Mike, you let them leave with them niggas. So can I at least have the ones he didn't take?"

"Let me handle this, Mike!" Sexy Redd said, as she placed her hand on my lap so she could say something to Shitty Smitty.

"Smitty."

"Yes, beautiful? Hell, Mike can leave you here with me, and I'll marry your fine cute ass in the morning," Smitty said, while stumbling backwards when Sexy Redd yanked her arm from his grasp.

"How nice, Smitty. Now listen real close, my nigga. Them niggas just put two stacks in my damn hand to take those beautiful women with them. All we get if we come to your club is a hard time and a club full of broke ass niggas. Now you do the math and tell me what would you have done? Good night, Shitty Smitty. We'll see your ass next week!"

As we drove away, I could see Smitty in my rearview mirror cussing me out. I couldn't actually hear what he was saying until I rolled my window down. I could of sworn I heard him say something like, 'you pretty wanna-be-pimp-ass nigga!' Damn, Shitty Smitty.

The ride back home was quiet, since most of the ladies had decided to stay down in Tampa. When I made a right onto Hillsborough headed to Interstate 4, it gave me time to speak to loudmouth-ass Chyna. Honestly, she looked like she was more upset that Innocence had left than I was. I guess because she had gotten so use to having Innocence next to her while she slept. I explained to her why I never liked the idea of the girls leaving the club with the guys after a show. That's why I started having the girls pay a fine so they wouldn't leave. But smart ass J.K. changed that when she came up with the idea of having the guy just pay the fine. Hell, if whoever it was taking one of them home, wanted the female that bad, what was a few more dollars to pay. No matter what I imposed on them, they always found a way to go around whatever I came up with. I couldn't fight them about it. Hell, it was money, and it was what they wanted to do. I had never forced a girl to go with a guy if she didn't want to. Most of the time, they would lie to me so they could leave with them anyway.

Wednesday morning had come too soon. That awful, dreaded day, I had woken up around ten thirty that morning. Something was wrong and I just didn't know what it was. As I lay there looking off into space, I couldn't help but look over at Redd. She lay in bed fast asleep, as though she didn't have a care in the world.

And why should she? It was me who started the group, so whatever problems that came along with it, I had to man up and deal with them.

By now, it was around eleven thirty in the morning. At first, I laid my hand over Redd's nice, thick ass and thought of waking her up to make passionate love to her. Then, I thought about Sharon and how I had been putting her off for the last few weeks. I hadn't seen her since moving into the new home. Damn, I knew it wouldn't be long before she tracked me down and really put my black ass on blast.

Then, there was the murder of Do-Dirty and the images of her face that still crept through my head. I had lain down after we got in earlier that morning, but before I dozed off, I thought I saw her standing inside my bedroom with a bullet hole lodged inside her skull, waiting on me. With all those mad thoughts running through my head, I felt like I was about to lose my mind. My phone rang from inside the pants I'd taken off earlier. Upon answering it, I would soon find out why I'd felt something was wrong.

"Damn, now who in the hell could this be?" I said to myself, as I rolled over to retrieve my phone. I hadn't bothered to look at the caller ID because I didn't want to wake Redd. I grabbed it and answered it while walking towards the bathroom.

"Hello," I answered in a groggy tone.

"Mike?"

Damn. It's muthafuckin' Chyna. Now what in the hell does she want? I thought and exhaled deeply. "Yes, Chyna?"

"You up?" she asked.

"I am now, Chyna. What's up?"

"Mike, before you get mad, are you sitting down?" she asked.

"Chyna, what the fuck is it?" I asked nervously.

"Innocence's sister just called and asked to speak with her."

"Okay, let her speak to her ass," I told her, somewhat irritated.

"Mike, she isn't here!"

"Yeah, thanks to you, Chyna. Remember, 'let her go Mike, let her go'," I said, reminding her of her words.

"Man, her sister said her father is in the Air Force and he's about to call the police and have them put out a missing person report on her ass!"

"What?" I was shocked and confused.

"Yes, her father is really tripping."

"Hell, I thought she was fuckin' grown."

"Her sister said she lives with her parents and they haven't seen her since last Saturday."

By now, I had walked back to the bedroom. I was sitting on the edge of my bed with my head in my hand. *What in the hell was I thinking? No wonder her lil' ass didn't wanna go home and pick up no clothes.*

"Well, on top of that, she's not back from Tampa yet, Mike."

"Hell, I know that, Chyna. If she was, she would have at least talked to her sister." I shook my head, worried. "Why hasn't the guy brought her back yet?" I asked.

I stood up and looked out of my bedroom window. I was totally confused and wondered what I should do next.

"He never brought them back," Chyna answered. "They came back on the Greyhound Bus."

"What about her, Chyna?"

"Apparently, the guy she hooked up with had a girlfriend at home and when she called him to tell his ass she had to go to work, he had to go home to take her. He left poor ole Innocence in the hotel room and never went back to get her."

"Aww, shit, where's she at right now, Chyna? Stuck somewhere in a hotel in Tampa?"

"Nah, Mike, she's at some hotel in Saint Petersburg (St. Pete)."

"St. Pete!" I shouted.

"Yep, St. Pete. Mike you have to go get her and bring her back."

"Why me, Chyna? You were the one who was supposed to be responsible for her young ass!" I said angrily.

"Yeah, but you were the one who brought her down here so she could dance and make money. So, she's your responsibility, Mike!"

My head hung low as I stood with my hand on my waist. I was

disgusted at what I was hearing. I had only myself to blame for leaving her down there. Chyna was right. I had brought her, and I was the one who should've been responsible for her. I shouldn't have ever listened to Chyna in the first place. I let her big titty ass talk me into letting her lil' fast ass go. After that day, as far as I was concerned, Chyna's days in the group had been cut muthafuckin' short.

By now, Sexy Redd had woken up. She sat up and listened to the whole conversation with a unit on her face.

Now, I had to really get rid of Chyna. Not just for that fuckup, but for the one a few weeks prior to that incident.

One weekend we had gone to Jacksonville and she decided to bring a new hood chick who she'd introduced as her fucking cousin. She vouched for the chick by telling me the damn girl was eighteen and fully grown. As soon as we got to Jacksonville, we went to the Flea Market, and the lil' hood chick Chyna had brought had gotten caught shoplifting. She tried to say some guy told her to just pick out an outfit and walk her dumb ass right out the fuckin' front door of the Flea Market, 'cause he was going to pay for it. You stupid lil' hood bitch. The guy was nowhere to be found when the cops came and put them silver bracelets on her wrists. She shed big ass crocodile tears. My dumb wanna-save-a-bitch ass told the store owner I'd pay him eight times what the outfit was worth so she wouldn't get in any trouble.

The skinny ass Chinese man looked down at me from his perched high ass countertop and said, "Buck dat shit, I'm tied of deese lil' bitches tealin' out of my damn stoe, her black ass is going to dail."

What in the fuck did he just fuckin' say? I didn't understand a damn thing that came out of his rotten teeth mouth having ass, I had thought to myself.

As the cop was marching her thieving ass to the back of the mall, she looked over at me and said, "Mike, please, do something!" Tears ran down her face.

Yeah, I'm about to do something alright. Hell. I got three warrants on my black ass, I'm gone!

The cop came back from the office, where they had her black ass sitting. "Hey, Mr.-Want-to-Bring-Young-Bitches-in-The-Mall-to-Steal, do you know how old this lil' young thief is?"

I just stood there looking at him with the dumbest look a nigga with three warrants on his black ass could have. That's when the slave in me came out and I replied to him sounding as if my name was Toby from the movie Roots.

"No, sir, I bees not der knowing of her age, sir!"

"Nigga, that der girl is only fifteen der, dumb ass nigga. Get yo' dumb ass out of here and don't come back," he said, mimicking what I'd done. I turned around and hauled ass like he'd told me I was a free slave. He didn't have to tell me twice. Man. I told all them girls to get their things head straight to the truck. Whatever girl wasn't there by the time I got there, her ass was about to get left right there at that fuckin' mall.

As I bent a right headed for the interstate, Chyna was sitting in the back seat talking about, "That lil' bitch told me she was eighteen."

"Yeah, right, Chyna," I said, as I drove like a bat out of hell trying to get to our hotel. The police called the girl's mother and she had to come all the way from Orlando to pick her lil' young thieving ass up.

Two weeks later, the Chinese store owner moved his store out of the Flea Market, due to people not wanting to shop in there anymore. I really think Sexy Redd had something to do with it 'cause before he left, he claimed he had been threatened by some Puerto Rican dudes who didn't like his attitude.

Chyna was still on the phone talking about how sorry she was for convincing me to let Innocence stay down in Tampa with the rest of the girls. As I reminisced, the sound of her voice brought me back to the present.

"Mike, are you listening to me?" she asked, noticing my slow response.

"Yeah, I'm here," I told her. "Do you know what hotel she's at, Chyna?" I asked.

"No, I'm about to call the number she called me from earlier.

I'll call you right back. But you going to get her right, Mike?"

"Yeah, I ain't got no other choice. She's *my* responsibility, re-member?" I said, repeating what she'd said minutes earlier. I hung up without ending the conversation.

Now, I had to hear what Redd had to say.

"Michael please, don't tell me they left Innocence's lil' grown ass down there by herself."

"Yes, Redd, she's somewhere in St. Pete by herself, probably scared half to death."

"So, are we going to get her?" she asked.

"Yeah, ma, get dressed."

Redd jumped straight up and headed for the shower. I remained seated on the edge of the bed. Even though my mind was boggled, I still couldn't stop myself from watching her ass as it switched from side to side. Just the mere color of her caramel complexioned skin turned me on. She seemed to glide to the bathroom. Just as she reached the door, she turned her naked body around and looked at me.

"Bae, everything will work itself out," she assured me. "So just chill. No matter what, I got your back."

I sighed heavily. "I hear you, bae."

As soon as she closed the bathroom door, my phone started ringing once again. It was Chyna calling me back.

"Hello."

"Mike, she's at the downtown Hyatt Regency," she said.

"What room number?"

"219."

"Thanks, Chyna."

"Mike, can I ride down there with you to pick her up, please?" she asked.

"No, don't you think you've done enough, Chyna? Just call her back and tell her to stay put. We're on the way," I told her.

"I'm sorry, Mike," Chyna sounded as if she suddenly realized the trouble she'd caused.

"Yeah, well, I just hope we get there in time."

"Oh, Mike, Innocence said she's hungry and a little scared.

"Well tell her to order room service. And just make sure you let her know we're on our way and we'll be there soon. I'll talk with you when we get back." I ended the call and prepared for whatever lie ahead.

I placed a call to Preston to ask him if he could take us over to St. Pete. Unfortunately, he informed me he was the only one working in his restaurant so he couldn't leave. He let me know he'd send Triston to pick us up immediately.

By the time I'd hung up with him with Preston, the other females who had also left that night, were walking through the door with all types of shopping bags in their hands.

"Mike, we had so much fun!" one of the girls said, as they nearly ran right into me, as I made my way down the stairs.

"Did everyone make it back safely?" Nicole asked. She brushed her ass up against my leg as she slid past me. She could tell something was wrong with me due to my slight attitude as I quickly brushed her off.

"Damn, well excuse me, Mike. What's wrong with your black ass this afternoon?"

"Nothing, Nicole," I answered short. It's just that one of the girls didn't make it back yet," I told her.

Once I'd reached the last step, I turned around to listen to whatever she would say next. Her facial expression didn't hide her surprise, as her eyes widened and her mouth hung open as if frozen in place.

"What?" she said. Her bags fell at her feet and each hand landed on a hip. She tilted her head to the side as if doing so would help her better understand what I'd said.

"Yeah, Innocence was left behind, in St. Pete, all by herself.

"Damn, that's fucked up," she blurted out. "You gonna go get her?"

"You damn right I am," I snapped, "I can't just leave her down there caught out like that. Hell she's one of the muthafuckin' Florida Hot Girls," I said, as if she didn't already know.

"You better believe it," Sexy Redd said from the top of the stairs. A towel was wrapped around her body, and one was also around her hair. The most serious muthafuckin' look I'd ever seen was stuck on her beautiful, Puerto Rican face.

Michael Gallon

CHAPTER EIGHT
SAYING GOODBYE TO INNOCENCE

As I continued to converse with Nicole, Sexy Redd stood at the top of the staircase listening to the conversation. She stared at Nicole as she shook her head from side to side, still in disbelief that Innocence had literally been left behind.

"Do you need us to go with you, Mike?"

"Nah, y'all get some rest. We gotta be at the Caribbean Beach Club tonight, and y'all gonna need all the rest you can get. We're expecting a huge crowd to be in the house tonight," I told a confused and nervous looking Nicole.

I walked into the kitchen to get me something to drink. Frantically searching through the fridge, I saw the last carton of orange juice. I quickly poured me a cup. Then, I went back upstairs to take a quick shower before heading to St. Pete.

Back in my bedroom, Redd stood in front of the mirror brushing her wet hair.

"So, are you driving over to St. Pete, or do you want me to drive?" she asked.

"Nah, we taking the limo," I said, "It should be here in about thirty minutes."

"Okay, baby, do you need me to pick you out something to wear?" she offered.

"Yes, please. I'ma go jump in the shower."

"I don't know why your silly ass didn't take one with me," she said, walking her naked body over to the closet.

"Because I know what would have happened if I had." I slapped her on her fat ass butt cheeks.

"Whatever, Michael. Don't act like you don't be wanting this good ass kitty-kat every day and all day," she yelled, from inside our huge walk-in closet.

"Yeah, okay. Just like you be wanting all this good, long ass Jimmy Dean Sausage off in your stomach every day." I laughed.

"Boy, just hurry your sexy, black ass up and take a shower, before I come in there and take what I want," she replied and joined me in laughing.

Forty-five minutes later, we were dressed and walking down the stairs hand in hand. We sat down in the living room, dressed as if we were stars in a motion picture. Redd had on her dark Gucci shades, a pair of black designer jeans, and an orange silk, see-through shirt. On her feet were a nice orange pair of Prada shoes that revealed her well-manicured toes.

Now, your boy was dressed in a pair of white, silk slacks, a black Versace shirt that had a tiger sitting by a river on the back of the shirt, and a nice pair of black Stacey Adams. Of course, I had on a white godfather hat that sat just right on top of my head, which was full of waves that went in a spiral motion.

I had already called the airline to check the scheduled time for the next flight to Jacksonville from St. Pete. The flight attendant informed me it would leave at five thirty and the price was one hundred seventy-five dollars. I immediately booked Innocence a flight. It was the only thing I could do since I had to get her fast ass back home as soon as possible.

Triston picked us up around one fifteen. I had hoped we'd had enough time to pick her up and get her to her flight in time. As I sat there looking out of the passenger window of the plush, black, stretch-limo, I could only imagine what was going on in poor little Innocence's mind.

Triston had one of my slow CDs playing inside the high-dollar car stereo system. "Young Girl" by the group Troop played softly through the speakers. I continued to stare out the window as we hurried down Interstate 4, headed to St. Pete.

Redd slid her nice smelling ass over closer to me. She took my arm and placed it around her neck. "I love this song. Are you okay?" she asked.

"Yeah, I'm alright," I said, still looking out of the window.

Triston passed the Poinciana Exit right outside of Champions Gate. With the music playing in my ear, I dozed off thinking about how I would tell Innocence she had to go back home. She wouldn't be able to dance for us any longer until her situation at home got better.

As I slept, my mind wandered off and into eternal bliss. Again, I saw the face of the young lady whose life I had taken just days prior. This time, it was more apparent what she wanted and what she was trying to say to me. But as soon as she opened her mouth to utter the words, I was awakened by the sound of Triston's voice.

"Sir, we're ten minutes away from our destination."

"Thank You, Triston."

Redd and I tried to stretch out before we arrived at the hotel. We looked at one another, both wondering how we'd fallen asleep so fast.

"The music was sounding so nice, I guess I must have dozed off without realizing it," I said.

She pulled out her pocketbook mirror and checked to make sure her appearance was on point. "Yes, you did, bae. I guess we were both tired and didn't even know it," she said, as she applied red lipstick over her full-size lips.

"I guess so," I said.

Ten minutes later, Redd and I arrived at the hotel. Innocence was sitting in the hotel lobby waiting for us. She was just excited to see us as we were to see her. She ran up to us and gave both of us a tight hug.

"Boy, I'm glad to see you all," was the first thing that came out of her foolish mouth, "thanks for coming. Where is everyone else?" she asked us, as she scanned the lobby for the others.

"They're home," Sexy Redd said. We walked back towards the limo which was parked right out front. "Why didn't you stay with the group?" Sexy Redd asked her, as we climbed inside the limo.

"I was with them until this asshole decided he wanted to get a room in St. Pete. Innocence looked over at me and said, "Mike, I'm so sorry, I promise I won't ever do that again."

I looked over at her with my dark shades covering my dry red eyes. "I'm sorry too, Innocence. . . . for listening to Chyna and then for letting you go. Did she tell you your parents were looking for you?"

"Yes, but I'm good. I spoke with them."

"Nah, baby," Redd said looking at her, "Michael and I have to send you back home. Your father is worried sick about you and we really don't need that type of heat on our heads right now."

She looked at Redd and me with tears running down her pretty face. "Redd, I promise. I'll never do this type of shit ever again!"

"Listen, boo, last night I co-signed for you so you could go make some extra money. Mike knew something like this would happen. For some strange reason, he really didn't want you to go. What if something crazy would have happened to you? We would've all been devastated and in trouble." The whole time Redd was talking to her, she just sat there with her head held down and tears flowing down her lovely face.

I gave her a napkin to blow her nose.

She looked up at me with those pretty brown eyes of hers. "Mike, please... I'm sorry. I'll listen to you the next time, I promise."

I wanted to tell her everything would be okay and that she could stay, but I knew better. She had crossed the line when it came to making the right decisions in this game. I knew it, but she didn't. I was responsible for her safety as well as the safety of all the other females. I had to let her go. I just couldn't take any more chances like that. Plus, her father was looking for her.

"I tell you what, Innocence, make everything good with your family and then call us back when everything is okay. Then I'll come back for you." She put her head down in her lap as I turned away and started looking back out of my window.

Triston weaved in and out of the heavy traffic trying to get us to the airport in time. "Mr. Valentino, we should be at our destination in about five minutes. What airline will she be flying from, sir?"

I was so caught up in my feelings I hadn't heard him talking to me. It wasn't until Redd pulled on my shirt.

"Yeah, I'm sorry, what did he say?"

"Bae, Triston wants to know what airline she's flying from?"

"Aw, I'm sorry. My mind was somewhere else. It's Delta, I believe."

"He said it's Delta, Triston!"

"Thank you, ma'am," he said, as he bent a sharp right headed towards the Delta departure side for flights.

When we arrived at the airport, you could sense that Innocence didn't want to go back home. But it had to be done right, and we had to make our situation safe and comfortable. Not just for her, but for the other females as well.

As we got out of the limo, we hurried through the airport, headed to the boarding gate. Innocence lagged behind as if we were sending her off to a private boarding school for delinquent teens.

When we got to the departure gate, Redd reached inside her Gucci Purse and pulled out some money which she placed in the palm of Innocence's hand. She gave her a nice, big tender hug. Innocence held her head up for the first time since we'd left the hotel.

"Thank you, guys," she said to us, as she walked down the corridor to board her flight back home. She faded away in the distance as she bent the curve to board the plane.

Seconds later, she was out of our sight. And just like that, she was gone. Redd and I were equally frustrated, but we turned to walk back through the airport. I placed my arm around her waist and we held onto one another as if we were leaving also.

"Bae, it was the right thing to do. Once she handles her business back home, we can always go back and get her," Redd said.

"It's not that, Redd."

"Well, what is it, baby?" she probed further.

"Not right now, boo. I'll tell you later. All I want to do now is just get back home so that I can get some rest."

Once back inside the limo, Triston started the car. "Where to, Mr. Valentino?"

I didn't respond and Redd tried to look me in the face. But I was so busy trying to hide the tear from coming down my fuckin' face. Triston turned around and asked me again. By now, Redd knew I was bothered by Innocence's departure.

So, she answered Triston. "Home, Triston. We're going home."

"Michael, that was the best thing for her at this present time. She's still young in the mind and very gullible. You didn't need that added pressure on your head right now. Michael, do you hear me talking to you? I know your ass ain't over there fuckin' crying?"

I was still sitting there looking out of my window thinking to myself. *How in just the short amount of time she'd been with us did she have such an impact on the group and me?*

I snapped back from my daydream to reality. I finally answered Redd who was literally screaming at me by now.

"Redd, no, I'm not fuckin' crying. I heard everything you were saying. It's just what I did, and what I'm gonna, *must* do now!" I replied.

"And what's that, Michael?"

"Getting rid of a nice addition to the group, and now having to suspend another one due to her fucked up attitude. And most of all for placing that young girl in harm's way without fuckin' thinking!"

She slid closer to me, placed her head on my shoulders, and whispered into my ear, "Michael, since meeting you, I've never felt this way about a man. The way I feel about you right now, you have taught me so much in so little time. I know there's a helluva lot more for me to learn. Listen, bae, you're my rock, my everything. I'm gonna need you to be strong for the both of us, not just now, but in the future also."

I placed my nose into her hair and inhaled her scent. I mumbled, "Everything will take care of itself. Let's go home. I've had enough melodrama for one day."

LATER THAT NIGHT AT THE CARIBBEAN, the club was packed as usual. I didn't know if they were there for the girls or the club itself. All I knew was that it looked like it was about to be a good night for the Florida Hot Girls and myself.

As soon as we opened the door to the Boom-Boom Room, there were people coming in, nonstop, throwing money everywhere. We had only been opened for forty-five minutes when my new secretary, Felicia, yelled out to me.

"Michael, I'm gonna need more wristbands. We're already at two stacks and it looks like more people are trying to get back there. What, are you giving away? Free rib sandwiches or something?" she said and laughed.

"Whatever, Ieshia, just keep counting my money," I said, as I walked back inside screaming, "Break bread, don't be scared to break muthafuckin' bread!"

Guys were screaming and yelling and shit like they hadn't ever seen no badass females in one place. I was standing off to the side thinking to myself... *I am the luckiest man in the world to be making all this fuckin' money and having fun while doing it. I would have never imagined I would have all these butt naked ass women up in the club.*

Everything was going smoothly and every song the DJ played made the crowd even more excited. Guys were dancing right along with the females and throwing money at the same time.

While walking around throughout the club watching all the ladies make their money, I couldn't help but think about Innocence and wonder if she was alright. I quickly snapped out of it and watched Redd over in the corner dancing on some nigga who looked exactly like Mike Epps.

Lil Kitty was in the middle of the floor demanding the attention of two Spanish guys who looked like they had spent all their money at the bar. Chazz was behind the DJ booth smoking weed as usual. Even though she smoked mad weed, she always made her money. Strawberry and Lil Red were over in the corner talking to some dude, with no signs of money around them at all.

"Alright, y'all two, don't be looking all sad when it's time to pay your tip out fee later this morning," I said to them.

They turned around and yelled back, "We already got our money, Mike!"

J.K. and her crew of ladies were putting in major work on some nigga name Life and the crew of thugs he'd come in the club with. Mignon and Entyce were cuddled up in the back of the club with two short goon-looking niggas.

"Hey, why you two females ain't dancing?" I asked.

"We over here doing what we do, baby boy. Don't worry, at the end of the night we'll have your tip out fee," Entyce said. Mignon just stood there trying to mean mug me with her cute. sexy ass.

"Yeah, we got these two, pimp. Just worry about the rest of your crew," one of the thug guys tipping Entyce yelled back to me. At that very moment, I knew what they meant. They would probably be leaving with those two guys later that night.

Nicole, with her cute ass, was dancing for four niggas who had come all the way from Jacksonville just to see her perform. The rest of the crew was getting money throughout the club, and I was all smiles.

Chyna was over by the wall looking mad as hell because I wouldn't let her dance. I had to suspend her for what had happened with Innocence. So, she kind of understood the reason why. I really didn't care how she felt, she should have thought about that before she opened her fuckin' mouth. Like I said. everything was going smooth until Ieshia yelled into the room for me.

"Mike, it's some guys out front who want to speak with you!"

I walked out front, and it was like one small guy, with three of his homies, standing around him like he was famous or something.

"You Mike, right?" the little guy asked, with a unit on his frowned up face.

"Yeah, what's up?" I said to him, with my chest stuck out, as though I was about to throw down with him. He then stepped away from his boys and said, "I see why they call your girls the Florida Hot Girls."

CHAPTER NINE
I'M PREGNANT

"And what in the fuck is that supposed to mean, short ass nigga?" I said to the guy. He stood there with fire coming from his flamed nostrils. He was a mere five foot two and weighed around one hundred fifty pounds, soaking wet.

"Because one of your girls burned me the other day!" he hollered out.

"Burned you how? What, she threw some hot grease on your short black ass?"

"Nah, you know what I'm talking about, pimp. The bitch is burning, I fucked her and now my shit looks like fuckin' hickory smoked bacon." I looked over at Ieshia and my two security guards who were over in the corner laughing their asses off. Then the lil' nigga attempted to pull out his dick and show us what he was talking about.

"Man, it ain't funny, look!" he said.

"Hey, man, we don't want to see your dick. Who was the chick you were with?" I asked.

"It was the one they call Do-Dirty. That bitch has my dick looking like muthafuckin' bacon."

Ieshia stopped laughing and said, "All you need now is a girl called Grits and one named Eggs, and y'all can be called breakfast."

While everyone was still there laughing their asses off, I was saying to myself, "Damn, no one knew the identity of the victims at the paper mill yet, so I better act like she's still alive before I give myself away."

"Well, that female doesn't work with us anymore. If I see her, I'll be sure to let her know she has your shit looking like fuckin' bacon." The lil' guy and his crew turned around and walked away angry as hell.

"Man, when you see that bitch again, tell her I'm gonna fuck her ass up," he shouted, as he got closer to the entrance of the club.

"Man, didn't nobody tell you to fuck her raw in the first place, stupid ass nigga!" I yelled back to him, as he and his crew of guys were walking out of the club.

"Hey, Mike, where is Jasmine at anyway? Doesn't she usually hang with Do Dirty?" Ieshia asked, as I had turned around to her and my security guards.

"I have no idea. All I know is she left my house one day to go get her hair done, and I haven't seen her since. I don't know, maybe she decided to quit the group and find a job somewhere else. Anyway, let me get back inside. I have to check on my girl, Redd. She's dancing on some nigga who looks just like Mike Epps."

"Mike, you are so silly, that is Mike Epps!"

"What, when did he get here, and why didn't anyone alert me when he arrived?"

"Disco brought him in through the side door, and security didn't want to alert anyone that he was in the club," she said, as I just stood there dumbfounded that Mike Epps was up in the club and no one bothered to tell me a damn thing. *Damn, this nigga up in my spot, tipping my girl, and rubbing all on her nice caramel ass.*

I stumbled back inside, bumping into people like I was drunk or high on whatever Chazz was smoking on. Now while walking through the club trying to find my Puerto Rican Princess, I saw some of my homie's and a few cousins from my old neighborhood up in the club, just having a good ole time.

When they saw me, they all started shouting out my name. First, it was Big John Baker who was over in the corner throwing nothing but twenties at my girl Carmen.

"Yo', Mike, man I got to have you bring all these fine ass females to Medulla, pimp," he said, while holding up his glass of Crown Royal, looking just like the great Biggie Smalls.

"No problem, Big John, just say when, and have your money on deck, and the girls and I will be there," I said back to him, while cutting him my signature grin.

"Say no more, playa." He reached inside of his Gucci shirt pocket and pulled out two rolls of twenties wrapped in a rubber band and threw it at me. "Count that, playa."

I started counting as fast as my little hands could count. He then slid his head around Carmen's fat ass and said, "Is that enough, big homie?"

After counting around two thousand dollars, I was like, "Yep, just tell me when you want them there, and it's your party, my nigga!"

I walked away smiling and saw my boy, Lewis, had Lil Kitty all to himself over by the bar.

"Hey, Mike, if we would have known it was going to be like this, we would have made sure we would have brought more paper," he said, as Lil Kitty started taking off all her clothes. He hadn't even started throwing any money yet. I guess he must have used his charm and just told her anything.

"Big Baker just gave me a couple of racks, so I guess you guys are going to have a show in Medulla some time real soon," I told Lewis, as Lil Kitty stood butt ass naked in front of him.

I leaned over and whispered into Lil Kitty's ear, "Alright, you keep on teasing me with them lil' ass hips and cute ass pussy, and I'm gonna show you why they call him John Boy."

"Whatever, Mike. You can't handle all this lil tight ass coochie," she said, while displaying that pretty ass smile of hers. She did find out about three weeks later why they called him John Boy. I eventually put so much meat up inside her lil' short ass, she couldn't dance for at least three weeks. One thing she was right about though, was that she was tight as a muthafucker, damn near almost broke my shit when I tried to get off inside her short, lil' ass. But she didn't have to worry about that after she met up with ole John Boy.

Then, I saw my big homie, Calvin J. Brown, over by the DJ booth having a conversation with himself. I walked over to him.

"What's up, Brown?"

He turned around and looked at me as though he didn't recognize me at first, and then said, "Hey, man, how do I get my money back from these hoes, I thought once you tip them they would go home with you?

"What, how much did you tip the female, Brown?"

"I tipped that one chick right over there like two dollars." He pointed over at Tiny. I almost cried laughing when his cheap ass told me he'd given Tiny two fuckin' dollars and thought she was going home with him.

"C'mon, Brown, man," I said, as I turned around and walked away still laughing. That nigga still telling jokes.

Then I saw my nigga, Klaus Sand Daddy Williams, who was still being the player he was always meant to be. He was standing over in the corner of the club with two of my baddest females wrapped up with him. Now, he wasn't throwing out any money at all, but the girls were yelling at the top of their lungs for some reason. "The money is over here y'all!"

He saw me and gave me a quick head nod as he continued throwing nothing but game at those silly ass girls. Like I said, there wasn't a single dollar anywhere to be found around those girls, just Klaus standing there with his arm around both of them, telling them how fine they were, and if they were to leave with him, he would make sure they would be taken care of.

While walking away shaking my head, I saw my boy, Big Pat Blake and his younger brother Dinky Blake giving Chazz and her sister Suga Bear some weed that looked like it had some purple buds inside of it.

"Hey, Mike, I hope you don't mind if we give these two beautiful sisters some of this Cali Bud we just got shipped in?" Big Pat said, as Dinky just sat there laughing 'cause their drunk ass cousin Alganod had just come back from outside telling them someone had stolen the engine out of his car while he was inside the club tipping the females.

"Man, didn't nobody steal your damn engine out of your damn car. You didn't even fuckin' drive to the club. And the last time I checked, you don't even own a fuckin' car, nigga. You high and really tripping. Go sit your drunk ass down somewhere," Dinky told him, as he snatched his blunt out of his mouth.

"Damn, Dinky, you right, man. I don't have a car," Alganod said to himself as he sat down laughing at his own silly mistake.

"Nah, I don't mind. Just don't smoke it round me, please. And, oh, by the way, you two young ladies have a thirty dollar fine to pay for purchasing weed in the club," I said to them as I was about to leave so I could find my girl.

Suga Bear then decided to open her mouth. "No problem, Mike, we have our fine right here between these big ass pussy lips, now come get it," she said, as they burst out into laughter.

Then her lil' sidekick, Peekachu added, "Nah, Mike, I'm gonna put their fine between my ass cheeks, come get it if you bad."

"Man, fuck that, y'all can keep it if it's in her crackhead smoking ass," I said, as I walked away, laughing my ass off.

Before I could get two steps away from them, my homie Howie, slid up under Peekachu's lil' red ass and sucked the money clean out of her ass. Damn, Howie, no wonder they gave him the nickname Fruit Loop as a young child. He was a real high roller ever since his ass was introduced to them prescription pills that always made his ass see everything in two's. In other words, Howie a.k.a. Fruit Loop was always fuckin' high.

As I got closer to where I saw Sexy Redd, I saw my cousin Eddie Valentino Jr, the older brother to Edward Lee Valentino—remember, the guy who introduced me to the business? He was coming out of the bathroom with Mignon, and he was zipping up his pants and shit.

I looked over at her and quickly said, "Alright, that nigga don't produce nothing but babies, so if your ass comes up pregnant, that's on you." I don't know why I said that because soon as I said it, Strawberry's ass came from out of nowhere.

"I want one, where he at?" As soon as she said that, my big homie, Vashawn, better known as Hardwhite, scooped her lil' red ass up and took her right outside to his brand-new white 2000 Cadillac Escalade.

"Don't worry, Mike, I'm about to give her fine red ass just what she wants," he said as they walked outside smiling at each other.

Forty-five minutes later, she walked back in with her clothes on backwards talking 'bout, "I won't do that shit again. That long-winded-ass nigga tried to blow my fucking back out!"

Sexy Redd finally caught up with me. "Bae. look who wants to meet you!" I turned around.

"Oh shit, it's muthafuckin' Mike fuckin' Epps," I said. I was excited since I was meeting a damn celebrity and shit.

"Man, this place is off the chain. How in the hell did you get all these badass bitches up in this muthafucker?"

"Man, it wasn't easy." I answered honestly.

"Man, you a fuckin' pimp, ain't you?"

Sexy Redd cleared her throat. "My man is not a pimp. He's a black entrepreneur who's trying to make an honest living."

Mike started laughing as he stood there looking all around the club. He looked back at Redd and said, "Yeah, whatever she just said. Man, you a fuckin' pimp!" He continued laughing.

"So, you like what you see, Mike?"

"Yeah, man I've been here for like two hours or so. I already threw like two stacks at your girl here."

"So, how long you staying, Mike?"

"I'm about to leave right now. I'm on the way down to Miami to meet up with Ice Cube. We about to start filming this new movie called "All About the Benjamins," but I definitely like what I see here. Here is my number. Call me so we can hook up and shit." He smiled as we walked out towards his limo, parked outside.

"Okay, Mike. Here's my number also. Call me whenever you need the Florida Hot Girls, and I'll render some services to you and your friends," I said proudly.

"Will do, young brother. It's nice to have met you, and nigga always keep it muthafuckin' pimping."

I looked over at Sexy Redd. "That nigga is a complete fool," I said.

"Yeah, he alright. I should have got all that lil' ass knot he had in his hand."

We smiled and went back inside. It was still so crowded, you couldn't even walk through the club.

"Bae, I'm about to go get dressed. I'll be right back," Redd said.

"Alright, I'll be at the bar. You want something to drink?"

"Yeah, get me a coke or something. My throat is dry as hell," she said, as she walked away to change into her street clothes.

As I was walking back to the bar, I got that funny feeling again as though someone was watching me. When I finally reached the bar and ordered Redd and I something to drink, I looked in the mirror behind the bar and thought I had seen Do-Dirty standing behind me. I quickly turned around and shook my head in disbelief.

Man, I must be seeing things, I thought to myself, as I wiped my eyes. I tried to focus on what was real and what was my imagination. As I opened my eyes, to my surprise, guess who was standing right there before my eyes?

Yep, Ms. Fine ass Sharon Connolly. "Hello Michael."

"Hey, Sharon, I haven't seen you in a while."

"Yeah, I wonder why, Michael?"

"You look like you've picked up some weight since the last time we saw each other."

"Oh, you noticed I thought I had too. Remember the last time I was at your apartment?" she asked.

"Yeah, why what's up?"

"Well, I wanted to tell your black ass then, but I wasn't sure."

As I stood there listening to her, I discreetly searched the club for Sexy Redd to make sure she didn't catch me talking to Sharon. "Tell me what, young lady."

"The reason why I'm picking up so much weight, silly."

"Okay," I said, still frantically anticipating Sexy Redd to return.

"I'm pregnant with your child, Michael."

I spit out my drink. I looked at her and replied, "Excuse me, *pregnant?*"

"Yes, Michael. I'm having your baby."

As soon as the words rolled off her lips, Sexy Redd walked up to where we were standing.

"Bae, where is my drink, and who is this pretty little lady standing here?" she asked, as she looked from me to Sharon, and back at me again. "Just by looking at her I would say she was pregnant." Then Redd gazed at her as if totally taken by surprise and added, "And she looks so much like me, she could be my sister!" she said.

"Yes, Michael. Why don't you introduce us since we haven't had the chance to meet each other? And by the way, tell her who the father is," Sharon said, as she stood there with hurt and sadness in her eyes.

"Yes, Michael, please do," Redd raised her hands and slapped them down on her hips. She stared at me and waited for me to open my mouth and say something.

CHAPTER TEN
YOU OWE ME!

"Mr. Valentino, are you okay?" is all I could hear in the background as I sat slightly dazed. I tried to pull myself together from the massive ass whipping the cops had put on me for fucking up one of their own. At first, I couldn't remember where I was, then I looked around and realized they had me propped up in one of my dining room chairs, inside of my utility room closet. Blood and sweat flowed down the side of my throbbing head, as I zoned in on the agent who asked me a series of questions about the girls I referred to as the Florida Hot Girls.

"Now, I want to show you a few pictures, Mr. Valentino, and if you recognize the females in the photos, just write down where you might know them from."

"Listen man, like I said earlier, I have a group of girls called the Florida Hot Girls. We travel around to different places performing at clubs, and, sometimes, bachelor parties. But before I answer any more questions, can somebody please give me a fucking towel so I can wipe away all this fucking blood dripping all over my gotdamn floor!"

"Yes, right away. Hey, Paul, have someone grab Mr. Valentino here a washcloth, so he can wipe away the blood and perspiration."

"That's mighty kind of you, officer," I replied, as I caught the towel in mid-air and quickly began wiping away my own blood.

"Now back to our questions. We have reason to believe that you and some of your associates are doing more than just parties," the tall, slim, dark-haired agent said with a stern look on his young looking face, as if he didn't believe a damn thing I'd said.

"I have no idea what you're talking about, sir," I quickly replied, as I tried to make myself comfortable in the chair I was sitting in.

"Mr. Valentino, just help us help you. As long as we can wrap this up today, your problems will be over. But do understand this, sir, my partners are conducting an interview with your friend, or should I say your *counterpart* right now. What do you think he's saying on your behalf?"

"Quite frankly, I don't give a damn what he's saying, because I know damn well I'm not a fucking Pimp! So why are you guys even here?" I replied, while cutting my eyes over at the other agent who looked like he'd just jumped fresh out of the Academy. "Sir, it has been brought to our attention that you *are* a Pimp, and that you've been operating as such for the last ten years," the agent replied.

It was at that very moment that my mind drifted back to the night at the Caribbean Beach Night Club—I was about to get into a heated argument with the beautiful Sharon Connolly.

Thirteen years prior . . .

"I KNOW YOU HEAR ME talking to your black ass!" Sexy Redd said as I just stood there shocked at what Sharon had just told me.

"Oh shit, chick, Mike is over there between a rock and a hard place, looks like he needs some help!" Nicole whispered to an open-mouth Mignon. Mignon stood beside her and the two of them glared at me as if they were watching a movie.

"Hey Redd, I need some help counting up some of the girls' tip out fee," Nicole cut in, and rescued me from my current dilemma.

"Sure, no problem, Nicole. Mike's black ass seems to need a moment with his lil friend anyway!" Sexy Redd replied. She rolled her eyes at me and Sharon and walked away. She made sure I noticed the way her hips swayed from side to side. That's when I quickly snatched Sharon by her arm and attempted to usher her lil red ass out of the club.

"Sharon, can I please speak with you outside and not in front of all my customers like this?"

"Sure, Mr. Playboy. I just want to know what you're going to do about me and your baby?" By now I was literally dragging her out of the club but she continued to run her mouth. "Michael, you don't have to squeeze my arm so fucking hard," she grimaced, as she turned around and looked me in my red, bloodshot eyes, "I can walk on my own, so let my fucking arm go," she yelled.

"Sharon, I'm just trying to get you out of the club before you make a scene," I replied, just as we'd made it to the door.

"Oh, I'm cool, playboy, it's you who's about to make a scene. I knew I would find your black ass in the club tonight, since you don't know how to return my phone calls!"

"Sharon, I keep telling your lil red ass, I've been very busy trying to put things in place," I said, as she stood with her arms folded across her stomach.

"Yeah, I guess so, since you moved and no one besides a few of your nasty ass dancers knows where you live."

"I was gonna let you know about that," I told her. "Yeah, Michael, I know ... just like you were gonna let me know about your new live-in girlfriend too, right?"

"Sharon, please, lower your voice. People are staring at us," I replied, trying to keep my voice at a minimum.

Again, she looked in my eyes and replied, "You should have thought about that before you invited me over for dinner and turned it into something else. Remember, it was you who promised you wouldn't break my heart," Sharon blurted out as she began to cry.

I kindly took her by her arms but she pulled away from my touch.

"Sharon, listen, if you just let me explain you'll realize it's not what it looks like." Her tears began to flow down her face and caused her makeup to run. I attempted to wipe them but she slowly jerked her head away.

"Why couldn't you explain in front of your lil precious girlfriend?" she snapped, "does she even know about us?" she asked. She looked in her purse for something to wipe away her tears.

Then I asked the dumbest question I could've ever asked the apple of my eye. "Sharon, are you even sure it's my child your pregnant with?"

"Michael, you're the only man I've been sleeping with for the past few months. Yes, it yours and I'm keeping it!" she yelled, as she pulled away from me in anger.

"No doubt, I wouldn't have it any other way!" I replied, sounding like the singer Prince. She stopped in her tracks and slowly turned around to look me in my face. "What? You thought I wanted you to have an abortion or something?"

That's when she ran into my arms screaming. "So Michael, you're not upset about me having your child?"

"Upset about what? I'm about to be the proud father of a beautiful little baby," I said. "Do you know what we're having?"

"No, Michael, not yet, but next week I'll find out if it's a boy or a little girl," she said, as she continued to cry tears of joy in my arms, outside of the club.

"Okay, let me know when and I'll take you. Let's find out together."

"What about your girlfriend, Michael?" she asked, looking me in my eyes. As I stared back at her, I couldn't get over how much her and Sexy Redd looked as if they could've been sisters. I quickly shook the thought off.

"Sharon, you and my unborn child are my main concern right now okay?" I hurriedly replied.

"Yes, Michael," she said, still teary eyed.

"Okay, now go home and get some rest. I'll stop by sometime tomorrow to check on you."

"Okay, Michael, you better come by too," she told me seriously, "don't have me waiting all day for you."

"Sharon, trust me I'll be there. I have a few things to take care of tomorrow, but I'll make it my business to come by and see about you and the baby." I gave her my signature smile.

"Okay, baby, and oh by the way, I'm sorry for coming up here bothering you at your job," she replied sincerely.

"No problem, beautiful. It's my fault. I should've called you earlier and explained my new living arrangements before it came to this," I said, as I continued to stare at her and those beautiful eyes inside of her head. *Damn, if Sharon doesn't look a lot like Sexy Redd, but that's impossible ...* I kept thinking.

"Is there anything else you need me to do?" I asked, as we made our way to her car.

"Yes," she answered, just before she got into the driver's seat.

"And what might that be?" I Smiled.

"Just tell me that you still love me," she said, as she wiped away her last heart-felt tear.

"Yes, Sharon."

"*Yes, Sharon* what, Michael?"

"I still love you, Sharon. Now good night and get home safe." She smiled coyly and drove away. As soon as she was out of sight, I quickly ran back inside the club before Sexy Redd could get outside and show her ass.

I bent the corner of the club about to head back into the Boom-Boom Room, my young, smart-mouth ass assistant stopped me. "Hey Mike, you alright?" she asked. Her hands were filled with twenty-dollar bills.

"Yeah, I'm good. Why you ask?" I asked. My right hand gripped the wall of the club as I tried to catch my breath from running so hard to get back inside.

"Because I saw how my girl, Sharon just went off on your cool wannabe ass," she replied in between counting up my money.

"Whatever. You know Sharon?" I asked.

"Yeah, I've known her since elementary school. And one thing about her is when she really likes someone, she goes all out for that special someone."

"Thanks a lot, Ieshia, just count the rest of my money, please."

"What? Don't turn your nose up at me. She told me she was talking to somebody named Michael, but I didn't know she was talking about you, Mr. Michael Valentino. You're a bad man!"

"Yeah, now how about that?" I voiced and smiled before walking back into the room, not knowing what to expect from Sexy Redd.

Right after I'd entered, Nicole came from around the corner of the room. "I saw you needed a lil help so I ran some interference for your black ass. And, oh, by the way, Sexy Redd is inside the ladies' room," she said with a lil sarcasm in her voice.

"Thank you, Nicole," I replied, as I gave her one of my Denzel Washington smiles.

"No problem, Michael, just remember you owe me!" She gave me a quick wink of her eye and kept right on moving.

Redd finally came out of the restroom and I sat calmly in front of the ladies. Some were getting dressed in their club attire (dressing in) while others were frantically trying to find their personal clothes to put back on (dressing out). Over to the right of me were several of the females who were busy counting up their individual stashes of money. Sexy Redd spotted me and realized I was trying to act as if I hadn't seen her walk back into the room. She slowly strolled over to me and muttered into my ear.

"Michael, I don't know why you didn't wanna talk with your lil side chick in front of me. I was just going to tell her that you and I won't have a problem raising her child."

"What?" My mouth dropped and my forehead grew wrinkles of curiosity.

"Michael, listen honey, I know you had a past before I met you, and if you *are* the father of her child, I have no problem helping you raise your child. Everyone needs their father in their life."

"Damn, you serious?" I asked, and at the same I reached out to place my arms around her tight waist.

"Why of course you young, silly man," she quietly replied. We met each other halfway and kissed one another as if we were madly in love.

"Ummmm, excuse me you two! We're in here with you guys," Mignon interrupted us.

"My bad, ladies. Now that we have your attention, there are a few things I have to say before we head out for breakfast. First of all, I hope you all had a nice and prosperous night. Second of all, your bar fee is only thirty-five dollars—Sexy Redd will come by and collect that for me. Third thing is, we will have a meeting tomorrow afternoon in regard to traveling to Jacksonville on Friday. The meeting will be held at the Olive Garden around one. We can eat lunch and discuss where we'll be staying and what club you all will be dancing at this weekend."

"Excuse me, Mike."

"Yes, Nicole."

"Will we be in the limo, or the truck?"

"Good question, Nicole. It really depends on how many girls are going this weekend. Now are there any more questions about this weekend before we leave?"

"No," Lil Kitty screamed out, while fumbling around with a bag filled with her sweaty ass dancing outfits.

"Good, thank you guys again for a wonderful night, now let's go get something to eat. I'm hungrier than a muthafucka," I said, as we made our exit. Sexy Redd continued collecting the bar fees.

As we were walking towards our mode of transportation, hot booty ass Lil Kitty yelled out, "Hey, where's the lil cutie you call Innocence, Mike?"

"I'll explain her absence tomorrow at the meeting, Lil Kitty," I replied, hoping the other girls hadn't heard what she'd just asked me. We approached the limo and the driver opened the door. Redd climbed in first and I followed.

"While we're on the subject of people missing, where's my lil dog Jasmine, 'cause her lil stank pussy ass got like five of my outfits!" Tiny said to the rest of the girls, as they got inside of the limo one by one.

"You might as well forget about those outfits, child. I guess you ain't heard about her and her crackhead ass friends, huh," Chazz spoke. The blunt hung from her crusty lips which looked dry from smoking weed all damn day long. Just as soon as she blurted that out, she had all the girls' attention since half of them didn't know what had happened to Do-Dirty and Jasmine.

"Go on, what happened to them?" Lil Kitty asked, as she eagerly waited for more info.

"Well, word on the streets is the dead, burned bodies found inside the old paper mill were identified as Jasmine, Do-Dirty, and a dude called Goldmouth and his crew," Chazz stated and continued, "the police said whoever did it tried to make it look like a drug deal gone bad but when they found bullet holes in each victims' skull, their deaths became a homicide investigation." With our arms intertwined, me and Sexy Redd sat quietly and listened to what came out of her mouth. I assumed she was done talking and hoped the conversation would change, however, the other girls just *had* to put their two-cents in.

"Man, that's crazy," Lil Kitty said in a baffled tone, "wasn't Jasmine just at your house the other day, Mike?" she asked, with surprise and shock displayed on her face.

"Yeah, she was Lil Kitty, but we haven't seen her hot ass since she left to go get her hair done on Monday," I replied. I looked around to witness the expression on each girl's face.

"My heart really goes out for Lil Do-Dirty, 'cause her lil grimy ass had like five lil kids to take care of," Kizzy chimed in.

"Hell, if you think that shit is fucked up, how about somebody in Jasmine's family said her mother received a fuckin' black dress in the mail yesterday!" Tiny replied while trying to put on her makeup.

"Damn, in my native country, when a family receives a black dress, that surely means someone has died or is about to die," Sexy Redd replied, as she slid in closer to me.

An eerie silence filled the limo until Nicole opened her mouth. "I really didn't have a problem with Do-Dirty until the lil heifer tried to steal my damn money bag one night after a show," she told the girls as she shook her head from side to side, "you know God don't like ugly, and He ain't too fond of cute either," she added in a matter-of-fact tone. The last words that left Nicole's mouth caused a few of the girls to put their heads down as they sat in silence, seemingly with thoughts of Jasmine and Do-Dirty on their minds.

The limo continued to cruise through the streets as the driver tried to get us to the Waffle House before the crowd got there.

When we arrived at the Waffle House off of Hwy 50, there were seven girls with me including Sexy Redd. Since there were only a few customers inside, we decided to eat there instead of taking our breakfast home. Everyone grabbed themselves a booth and sat down, anticipating what they were going to order.

We had been there for about ten minutes when Lil Kitty made an awful discovery. "Mike."

"Yes, Lil Kitty," I replied, while waiting on the girls to decide what they were having for breakfast.

"Ain't that Charlie B?" she asked and pointed her finger, "right over there pouring them folks some coffee."

I slowly looked up at one of the ex-members of the group. "I'm not sure, but it does kind of look like her. Damn, didn't know she was working," I replied, with a good ole pork chop breakfast on my mind.

"She's cute, Michael, why did she quit the group anyway?" Sexy Redd asked, as she placed her menu back in the slot on the table.

"Girl, they say she had some beef with you know who—Mike's ole girl, Ms. Stank-attitude-having Ms. Kitty, so Ms. Kitty fired her," Lil Kitty replied.

"That's so fucked up, Mike, why don't you bring her back?" Sexy Redd suggested. She motioned the waitress to come take our order.

"That's up to her," I replied. Mignon looked over at me and shook her head from side to side.

"See, that's why I had to get rid of Ms. Kitty, she was just too fucking mean," Sexy Redd voiced as she placed her order.

"Calm down, guys. If y'all want her back on the team, why don't y'all just ask her to come back," I told the girls, as I placed my order.

"Excuse me, Charlie B, can we talk to you for a quick minute?" Entyce yelled out to her from our table. When Charlie B realized it was the old crew, she gingerly walked over to the table with a genuine smile covering her beautiful face.

"What's up, ladies? I still see you hot girls still out here making that paper," she said, as she looked around the table at the stable of gorgeous women with me.

"Yes, that, we are," Lil Kitty replied. She pulled out her lil wad of cash to show Charlie B. "I made eight hundred dollars tonight. The girls and I just wanted to know if you wanted to come back to the group?"

"I don't know about that. What does Mike have to say about that?" she asked. She cut her eyes over at me. By now, I had picked up my knife, ready to cut into my mean looking pork chop breakfast.

"Why are y'all looking at me? Hell, I wasn't the one who fired her," I told them, with hot sauce and eggs hanging from the corner of my mouth.

"We know that Mr. Smart Ass, but the poor girl is asking you if it's okay with you if she comes back to the group," Sexy Redd interjected, as she sipped from her glass of Orange Juice.

"Redd, it's up to you all. You ladies are the ones who control who's in or who's out."

"Mike, you need to stop trying to be so hard on the girl. Damn, look where she's working since leaving the group," Nicole voiced, with a mouth full of waffles and syrup.

"You know, you're right. I usually say you girls are gonna end up working at McDonalds when y'all leave the group."

Sexy Redd stood up and walked Charlie B off to the side, away from me and the rest of the girls.

"Listen, Charlie B, I'm the new bitch in charge now. I got rid of Ms. Kitty, and I'm the one who's fucking Mike now and forever, so you're welcome to come back into the group if you like. Here's a thousand dollars—put this in your bra, and just pay me back when you come back to the group, or should I say back to the *family*. We leave for Jacksonville Friday, and it would be nice if you could make the trip." Sexy Redd winked her eye at her and walked away with a smile on her face.

Minutes later, we paid our tabs and tipped our waitress two hundred dollars and left. The waitress we tipped stepped to Charlie B as we climbed back into our limo.

"Hey, do you know who those people were?" she asked, as she stood in amazement at the large tip we'd given her.

"Hell yeah! You don't know who they are?" she asked the lil slim, white female who had been our waitress.

"No, but they sure as hell left me with a big ass tip," she replied, as she smiled at Charlie B.

Her and the waitress stood at the glass window admiring the limo as it pulled out of the driveway. Charlie B looked back at her lil petite white friend and replied, "Girl, those bad ass females you just served were none other than the world famous Florida Hot Girls!"

"You know them bad ass bitches?"

Charlie B pulled out the original Florida Hot Girl chain that she'd worn around her neck faithfully.

The lil slim white girl's eyes grew larger. "So were you a Florida Hot Girl too?" she sputtered out in disbelief.

Charlie B cut a nice seductive smile back at her and then replied, "Yes, once a Florida Hot Girl, *always* a Florida Hot Girl. And don't you forget that!"

That night was the last night that the Waffle House located on Hwy 50 ever saw Charlie B or the waitress we tipped the money too. Both of them were inside of our limo headed to Jacksonville, ready to embark on their new careers with the Florida Hot Girls that weekend!

Michael Gallon

CHAPTER ELEVEN
HER DEPARTURE

Thursday 12:15 p.m. ...

Thursday afternoon, I woke up knowing that some of the girls didn't have a ride to the meeting, so I picked a few of them up, and had our limo service pick up the rest. We sat at our usual table in the back of Olive Garden, to eat and discuss the agenda for the weekend. Chyna, who I was still partly mad at for fucking up my plans with Innocence, had to open her mouth first.

"Damn, Mike, can we at least eat first before you start your meeting?"

Before I could answer, Nicole leaned over my left shoulder and mumbled into my ear, "When are you going to get rid of her disrespectful ass, 'cause I'm 'bout tired of her lil red ass."

In time, lil one, just give it some time," I whispered discreetly. I smiled at Chyna because I knew she was about to make a spectacle of herself as usual.

"Alright ladies, please listen up while you eat your lunch. When we get to Jacksonville this weekend, all of you will be dancing at Black Magic, and you'll be staying at the Laquinta Inn right next to Denny's. Please make sure you have enough money for your room and enough to eat with. At the present moment, it looks like there will be around eleven girls going with us this weekend, so we'll be taking the limo." As soon as I finished with my little speech, Sexy Redd stood up with a speech of her own that I hadn't been aware she'd be giving.

"Excuse me, ladies, we've been making a lot of money in the past few months, and with that said, all of need to start saving your money for a rainy day. Michael and I have been on the road with you ladies every step of the way—the stress and toll that all of you have put on him, leaves me with no choice but to take him on a small vacation very soon. So save your money, that day may be here sooner than you think!"

What in the hell is she talking about? I thought, as I sat there listening with an alarmed look on my face. *I can't leave my stable of beautiful women right now even if I wanted too!* These girls needed me more than life itself. And who would I leave in charge ... *it sure as hell won't be mild-mannered Andre.* His head was so far stuck inside Lil Kitty's ass, he wouldn't know what to do with all the gorgeous women I had acquired after a few months of starting the group. I was still sitting there stunned half to death when Sexy Redd sat back down and leaned over and whispered to me.

"Michael, I know you weren't prepared for what I just said to the group of ladies, but I'll explain everything to you when we get back home."

The ladies who were all just as stunned as I was, sat there cautiously whispering to one another.

"If Mike takes a vacation, how are we going to make our money? This is my life, and this is what I do for a living, and besides that, I don't plan on stopping any time soon," Nicole whispered to Mignon. Mignon just sat there shaking her head in agreement to what Nicole had said.

While those two went on in detail, as to what to expect next on the agenda, the rest of the ladies continued eating and talking amongst one another. Before we knew it, the waitress was bringing out our individual tabs so we could pay our bills.

"Excuse me, Michael, you never told us what time to be ready tomorrow."

"My bad, Chazz, be ready around this time tomorrow. The limo will pick you guys up on the way out of Orlando."

As we were all leaving, you could tell the message Sexy Redd had delivered had some of the girls confused as to what to do next.

None of them had even seen it coming, but neither had I. But after I got inside the car with Sexy Redd, she explained her motive. It was her way of trying to let a few of the females know that if for some reason I didn't call them or pick them up, their time in the group was over—specifically, the girls who were about to get fired. I could've come right out and told them face to face, but I had tried that in the past and they would plead with me not to let them go.

Firing someone was tactic that would always lead a person to retaliate in some type of way, and I would find that out sooner than later.

"Girl, you had me going and shit, hell, I can't take a vacation when it comes to the girls and this group," I told her, as soon as she finished telling me her plan, "this is my family and if you take away the Florida Hot Girls, you might as well kill me. Like I always say, "Without me there is no you, and there is no you without me." Redd smiled at me as she backed out of the parking lot and headed back home.

Once she'd made a right onto Colonial, I laid my head back on the headrest and closed my weary eyes. I knew the drive home would take at least twenty minutes, so I figured I would catch me a quick nap. But to my surprise, Redd had us back home before I could even close my eyes good.

Maria, the part-time maid, met us at the front door. "Hola, señor and señorita," she voiced, with a somber look on her face. We greeted her as usual, but something seemed out of place when she lowered her head and motioned for Sexy Redd to follow her up the stairs. Swiftly, Sexy Redd walked behind Maria and up the stairs. I stayed down stairs with the females who were living with me and chopped it up with them for a few minutes.

While sitting at the bar, I saw the few Puerto Rican gentlemen who worked on the lawn, gathering around one another outside, as if something serious was about to kick off.

Moments later is when I heard a loud scream resonating from upstairs in my bedroom. I quickly jumped up from the bar stool and ran towards my bedroom door. The closer I got to my bedroom, the more I could hear Sexy Redd screaming and crying through the door as if something awful had happened to her. I quickly snatched the door open, just as she ran towards me and fell onto my chest.

"Redd, what's wrong, what happened?" I asked her as she could barely stand up. She couldn't move her mouth and Maria came and removed her from my arms. "Maria, what is it, what's wrong?" I asked a frightened looking Maria.

Sexy Redd pulled herself together and looked up at me as I stood there not knowing what had just transpired.

"Michael, I have to leave the country right away. I don't know when I'll return, but please understand you mean the world to me. I will never stop loving you and I hope you never stop loving me. Something terrible has happened to my family back home and my safety here in your country has been compromised. I must leave immediately. My father has already sent his private jet to pick me up at the airport."

"What? Your family has their own private jet plane?" I asked, as I stood frozen, stumped, and confused.

"Yes, and a whole lot more than that. The bad news is that my younger brother has been found dead!"

"Ah, na ... I'm so sorry to hear that. Do they know what happened or who did it?" I sat down next to her and tried to comfort her.

"No, and I think I need to explain a few things to you. Maria is not really some part-time maid. She is my father's sister, in other words, she is my aunt, and she was sent here to watch over me. Raoul and Sergio, the two gardeners down stairs, are my cousins, also here to protect me."

"Damn, so damn near every Spanish looking person around this house is your relative?" I replied, as I continued looking down at her.

"Yes, Michael. You see, my father is a very well-known man in the drug game, and it looks like some of his competition is trying to erase my entire family off the face of this earth."

"Damn, he's that powerful, huh?"

"Yes, Michael. Have you ever heard of Pierre Santiago?" she asked, as she wiped away her tears.

"Oh shit, that's your father?" I quickly fell back in shock.

"Yes, Michael. And it looks like his daughter, Rhynyia Santiago, is now the next one in charge if something bad was to happen to him," she replied, as she slowly walked over to the dresser to begin packing her bags.

"No, don't worry about that, Rhynyia, I shall pack your things for you. Do whatever it is you have to do. We have to be leaving as soon as possible," Maria voiced as Rhynyia sluggishly moved about the room.

"Damn, but you told me your name was *Nyia.*"

"I know, Michael, there are a few more things that you don't know about me, and it's best that you *never* know. One day I'll explain it to you, but as for now, it's best you don't know. You always told me the less you know, the less you would have to ever tell someone," she said, as I stood back staring at the female I thought I knew.

"Why all the secrecy? When were you going to tell me?" I asked. I couldn't help but wonder what else she'd been keeping from me.

"It's for your own protection and safety, Michael. When the time presents itself, I will explain everything else, but surely not now like this. Please, don't be angry with me," she said, as she searched the room for her belongings.

"How can I be mad with you at a time like this, Rhynyia? Hell, you just lost your brother, and besides, I love you too much to be angry with you."

"No problem, baby, I knew you would understand," she replied, as Maria quickly darted out of the room with a few of her overnight bags in tow.

"But Redd, why did you do all those things if you didn't have to?" I asked, as I tried to get next to her.

"The world will never know why one does the awful things that we do. Just know that you are my everything, and one day I shall return to claim what's mine." Her answer shocked me as she stood by the window of our bedroom looking out over the front yard. Then she moved in closer to me and ran her right hand down the side of my puzzled looking face.

"I have to leave now, Michael, and I can't let you accompany me to the airport, for it is far too dangerous. For all we know the people responsible for my brother's death might already be somewhere here in Orlando."

I turned to her with a tear running down my face. "But Redd, it might be months before we see each other again."

"Michael, we both have to have faith that we will be back in each other's arm again real soon. Just trust me when I tell you, it's for the best that you stay here."

I looked at her as if she had just shitted on my frail heart. Then came a knock right before Maria whispered through the slightly ajar door, "Princess, it is time."

CHAPTER TWELVE
PRINCESS

At first I thought I was hearing things, so I looked at Rhynyia, and asked, "What did she just call you?"

"She called me *Princess*, Michael."

"I thought your name was Rhynyia or Nyia?" I replied.

"It is, Michael. My name is Rhynyia when I'm here amongst you and everyone else. However, in my part of the country, I'm a Princess, heir to all of my family's wealth and popularity. You see, I'm from a small island outside of Puerto Rico known as Vieques, in which my family is royalty. You see, my father and his father before him, obtained all of our families' wealth and fame through the illegal drug trade in the early nineties. My brother was to take over the family empire once my father decided to turn over his power and reign. But it seems like someone has decided to kill my poor, innocent, younger brother before all that was to take place."

"Wow, a fucking Princess, huh?" I replied, as I scratched the top of my aching head.

"Yes, Michael, now please let me leave before things get really out of hand."

I wondered if her words really meant I could get hurt by one of her bodyguards. She moved closer to the door and turned around to look at me one more time.

"Thank you." She rubbed her petite stomach and smiled back at me.

"Thank you for what Rhynyia," I asked as I stood there still in shock from all I had heard.

"I should have told you this the other night, but things were moving so fast it just slipped my mind."

"Told me what, Rhynyia?" I asked her in frustration.

She paused and hesitated for a brief moment then she slowly held her head up. She looked me directly in my eyes and softly whispered, "Michael, I'm also having your child." With tears in her eyes, she walked out of the door, and out of my life. I was shocked and confused at the same damn time.

"Rhynyia, wait, wait! Please, wait!" I yelled. With her aunt and bodyguards by her side, whisking her away, she continued to walk away from me.

I tried to run behind her, but one of her father's six-foot-four henchmen turned to me with a stern look on his face.

"Sir, it is best that you let her leave without you making a spectacle out of yourself and others. Her safety is in our hands right now! Please, return back to your room and wait until we have left before you attempt to follow us!"

Just as soon as he closed the door to my room, I heard more heavy footsteps walking throughout the house. They were too loud to be the footsteps of the girls, so I knew it had to be more men walking throughout the massive structure that we called home. I stayed in my room and watched from my bedroom window as the heavy-guarded convoy of black automobiles headed to the airport. I wondered when, or if, I would ever see my precious Princess Rhynyia again.

Minutes later, is when Nicole ran into my room sounding all hysterical, yelling and asking all kind of mad questions.

"Michael, who were all those people dressed in black, and where are they taking your girl Sexy Redd?" I just stood there, looking down the street at the convoy of cars driving away from the house.

My mind tried to comprehend the fact that Rhynyia had just told me she was having my child. *Damn, why didn't she tell me earlier that she was pregnant with my child, and what other dark secrets was she keeping from me?* "All this time I had been living with someone who was fuckin' royalty in another country, and didn't even fuckin' know it," I said to myself.

I could hear Nicole's big mouth in the background. "Mike, do you hear me? What's really going on?" she yelled, as she stood in front of me and questioned my black ass, while wearing nothing except a pair of tight ass boy shorts.

"Nothing, Nicole, everything is fine. Just go back to what you were doing and I'll talk with you in a few minutes," I replied. I slowly turned back to watch the last car of the convoy bend a right, headed out of the subdivision.

"What about Sexy Redd?" Nicole screamed.

"Nicole, she had to go back home for a while, but she'll return when everything calms down."

"When everything *like what* calms dow*n*, Michael? she emphasized with curiosity. What are you talking about?" she probed with an uncertain look cast over her face.

"Nothing, Nicole!" I replied. I walked over to my bedroom door so I could usher her out of my room. When she looked back at me with her nose twisted up in the air, I gave her one of my nonchalant smiles.

"Umph, I know what that means ... now that she's gone, your ass is about to be off the chain all up in here and shit."

"Whatever, Nicole, I'll speak with you in a few minutes. Now please let me get myself together," I responded, as I eased her out of my bedroom door. Just as Nicole was pushed into the hallway, she placed her back up against my door, to witness Mignon coming out of her room with a quizzical look on her face.

While the two of them were standing outside of my room, looking at one another, wondering what had just transpired. I walked over to my stereo sound system and placed one of my slow CDs inside of the turntable. "Yearning For Your Love" by the Gap Band blasted through the speakers.

I heard Mignon scream to Nicole, "Oh shit, girl, that's my muthafuckin' jam!" Nicole cut a sinister grin over at her friend, and the two began singing along with the nice, slow ballad.

I sat on the edge of my king size bed and listened to the melodic voices croon the classic love song. For the first time in a long time, I shed a tear for my Princess, who had just waltzed out of my life. Knowing she was gone, I knew my heart would be yearning for her love until she returned back to me.

"Now please tell me what the hell is going on. What was all that noise?" Mignon asked Nicole just as the song ended.

"Chick, Sexy Redd's people just came up in here and snatched her lil ass up! It's like them bitches kidnapped her ass and shit," Nicole voiced, in an excited tone.

"Is Mike okay?"

"Yeah, girl, I guess so. Don't you hear his ass in his room with the music turned up all loud and shit?" Nicole replied.

"I hope ole boy ain't in there crying."

"Whatever, Mignon, you know that nigga stronger than that," Nicole told her. Their voices became distant and muffled as I heard their footsteps heading toward the down stairs part of the house.

I had just wiped away the last tear when I decided to walk downstairs for something to drink. I got down stairs and spotted the two of them about to walk outside to the pool area, when Nicole saw me at the fridge.

"Hey, are you okay?"

"Yes, Nicole."

"We heard you playing some real nice slow music inside your room. Do you need some company?" Nicole asked.

Mignon stood at the door of the kitchen while giving Nicole the side-eye. *No this hot ass female didn't just ask the man if he needed some damn company!* She thought to herself.

"Nah, not right now, Nicole, I'll be okay. I have a few things to sort out right now." I turned to walk back upstairs.

"Damn, hot ass chick, the bitch hasn't been gone a hot minute and you already trying to get in her fucking spot!" I heard Mignon say to Nicole.

"Girl, mind your damn business. It ain't even like that. If that nigga can't get his head in the game, we all gonna suffer a loss!" Nicole replied, as she turned to stare at Mignon.

"She's right, Mignon … if Mike stops working because he's lost the love of his life, we're as good as done!" Strawberry concurred. She walked out of the pool house and started drying herself off.

"Damn, bitch, where did you come from?"

"Out of the pool house, 'cause when I heard all the commotion going on inside the house, I thought something was about to go down, Mignon. Shiit, I came out here to the pool house to get that muthafuckin' Choppa, bitch."

"I see, so what, you saw her leave too?"

"Yeah, Mignon, and just like Nicole just told you, let's hope Mike's okay"—Strawberry shook her head from side to side despondently—"Lord knows we can't stay afloat if he sinks into a sea of depression."

"Listen, ladies, I've been here just as long as you all have. and one thing I know about Michael Valentino, is he always bounces back, no matter what the circumstances might be. One thing for sure and two things for certain: he is not gonna let this stop him from taking us to our shows, 'cause he loves the group just as much as we do, and he for damn sure ain't gonna let it stop him from gettin' to that bag," Mignon said to the two girls.

It seemed as if the girls were maturing, and not only as a group of female strippers, but it was more so the closeness of the bond they'd formed. They were closer than anyone could ever imagine.

Meanwhile ...

WHILE THAT WAS GOING ON between the girls, I was upstairs sitting on my bed. It had to be one of the saddest days of my life. I sat in deep thought staring out of my bedroom window, as the music played in the background. The song playing was "I Want My Girl," by Jesse Johnson, former bass guitar player from the group *The Time*. I didn't want to do anything or be bothered by anything or anyone. All I wanted was to have Rhynyia back in my arms where she belonged. I continued to sit there, deeply lost in some type of trance.

My phone rang in the distance. Not knowing who it was on the other line didn't faze me at all. My whole world seemed as if it was crumbling right in front of me. At that very moment, nothing really mattered to me except Rhynyia and my unborn child she was carrying. Seconds turned into minutes, and minutes turned into hours. I must have dozed off for a few hours. I rolled over to see the message light on my phone blinking. When I stumbled out of bed to retrieve my phone from off of the dresser, I noticed one of the dresser drawers slightly ajar. I slowly pulled it open to find a letter Rhynyia had left for me:

Michael, I never thought this day would come nor did I ever wish for something like this to come between us. By now, you know who I am, and what I stand for. My life has always been one of secrets and lies. But believe me when I tell you, my life with you is no secret or lie. In just the short time that I have been with you, I have grown to love you more than life itself. Please be patient and I promise to come back for you one day, as soon as things in my country are taken care of. My family has always tried to keep me hidden from society due to their worldwide wealth and fame. When I turned twenty one, I told my father I wanted to come to America so I could start my own life. He sent me here, to Orlando, to get away from my country, and to find the mother I never knew.

I never imagined that a man like you would be placed in my life. When I met you that day at the grocery store, I was a little reluctant to talk with you. Then I saw you again one day with your group of women in the mall. That's when I was like, he must be all of that and a bag of chips. So, I took a chance and I'm glad I did.

Since we've been together there has never been a dull moment. You have shown me so much in just the short time we've been by each other's side, and I'm very grateful to you for that. I just wish we could've had more time together. I know I'm not there with you, but always know I won't be far away from you.
Love Always,
Princess Rhynyia Santiago . . .

CHAPTER THIRTEEN
BLACK DRESS

Just as soon as I'd read the last word of the letter, my phone started ringing. I quickly answered it on the first ring.

"Hello."

"Michael, what's up? Are you still coming over?" the woman on the other end of the phone asked. I could hear the excitement in her tone.

"Yes, I'm on my way right now."

"Is there something wrong, Michael?" she asked. "You sound like you've been crying."

"Nah, everything is fine, Sharon. Just let me put on some shorts and a shirt, and I'll be there in a few," I replied, trying to get off the phone before she found me out.

"Hurry up, because me and your child are starving," she replied.

"I hear you, Sharon. Just as soon as you let me hang up the phone, I'll be on my way."

"Bye, baby, I love you."

"Love you too, boo." I slowly hung up the phone and wiped the stained tears away from my face. I headed to my walk-in closet to find something appropriate to wear. For a brief moment, I just stood there, debating what to wear.

"Who do I think I'm fooling? I don't love nobody but my damn Florida Hot Girls," I uttered to myself.

Thirty minutes later, I had finally decided what to wear over to Sharon's house, so I was on my way. I knew she wanted to go out and grab something to eat so I'd worn something casual—a pair of black tailored slacks, a nice white, silk dress shirt to match, and on my feet, a pair of my black signature Stacey Adams. Knowing her, she would want to have dinner at her favorite place, Red Lobster, so I choose the black, big body Benz to drive her there in style. Hell, she deserved it.

"And besides, she's about to become the mother of my child," I said to myself, as I pulled out of my driveway headed for Kirkman Road.

On the way over to her house, it had dawned on me that it had been a while since I'd been able to drive somewhere all alone. Usually, I'd have Rhynyia or one of the females from the group as my passenger. I must admit, it felt good to be driving over to her place by myself. It gave me some time to actually clear my thoughts and get my hazy mind together. Besides, since I was riding by myself, I was able to finally enjoy some of the slow music I'd downloaded earlier in the week.

I casually leaned over to my console and picked out volume two of my midnight slow-jam collection and slid it into the disc. A casual smile emerged on my face when the song, "Red Light," by André Cymone serenaded through the Bose stereo system. For those who don't know who André Cymone is, he was the first bass player Prince allowed to play in his very first band.

The song was sounding so nice and pristine that without even knowing it, a few tears had snaked down the side of my face. As I listened, I thought about Rhynyia and realized how much I was going to miss her being by my side. Before I even knew it, I had snot *and* tears darting down my face. I dully looked over in my rearview mirror. *Hell, I can't show up at Sharon's house looking like this ...* I was too far away from my house to turn around and I was too close to her place to let her see me in the shape I was in.

I pulled over to the park that was just around the corner from her house, so I could pull myself together before she could lay her eyes on me. I opened the door of the Benz and damn near stumbled out of the car, trying to balance myself from falling. I propped myself up against the inner portion of the car door and that's when everything went south for a brother. I began to cry even harder. I mean, for about twenty minutes, I was actually cried like a grown fuckin' baby.

It was the first time I'd cried like that since ... hell, I can't even remember. All I know is it hurt me so bad to lose the woman who would've been any man's dreams. And to make matters even worse, the song playing inside of the car was "Back in My Arms" by the group Silk.

Rhynyia and I had just been together planning our future, making sure things were bright for whatever we decided to do, and then she got that damn phone call, and just like that, she was gone. As I cried and reminisced, bent over my car, my phone started ringing once again. The ring tone was the clue that let me know it was Sharon calling. I wiped the last few tears, then wiped my nose with one of the Kleenex tissues.

"Hello," I struggled to say.

"Michael, where are you?" she yelled, sounding as if she had been crying with me.

"I'm right around the corner from your house, Sharon," I replied, while wiping away tears and snot.

"Okay," she said, between sniffles.

"Hey, Sharon, I may not be the smartest man in the world, but why does it sound like you're crying?"

"It sounds like you're crying too, Michael. What's wrong?"

"It's nothing. I'll explain everything to you when I see you," I told her, "now what about you?"

"My mother just called me, Michael, and it appears that one of my cousins was found dead," she replied, sounding as if she was trying to hold back more tears.

Damn, I thought that I had problems, now Sharon gets bad news that someone in her family was found dead, I thought to myself. I knew she was really going to need my support so I had to pull myself together—not only for myself, but for her as well. Besides, I was the man in the relationship and men weren't supposed to cry.

Moments later, I was pulling into Sharon's driveway. Before I got out of the car, I looked myself over to make sure my appearance was on point. After that, I was out of the car and headed for her front door.

She must have been waiting on me because she opened the door just before I knocked. She looked as if she had been crying all afternoon. Her eyes were swollen and red with tears that rolled rapidly down her small but cute face.

"Hey, Michael," she said, as she ushered me inside while trying to hide her face.

"Hello, boo, are you alright?" I asked, as I placed my arms around her fine, petite body.

"I'm fine now that you're here. Thanks once again for coming," she replied. We walked over to her living room sectional and held on to one another as if there was no tomorrow.

"I told you last night I was coming over today to speak with you about the baby. But since there's been a death in your family, I guess we'll talk about that later."

"Yes, baby. I can't believe she's dead," she replied.

"*She*? Damn, it was your cousin, a female?" I replied, as I slowly pulled down my Versace shades.

"Yes, my mother's sister's baby girl."

"Damn, not her baby girl, that's terrible. Do they know what happened or who did the dirty deed?"

"No, all they know is she was shot two times—once in the middle of her head, and the other one in her stomach. But the fucked up part about it all is that whoever did it set her and her friends on fire. So now, the families of each victim have to bury them in closed-casket ceremonies," she sputtered. She fell into my arms and sobbed for her cousin as if she had been her very own child. At first, it didn't dawn on me as to who her cousin was. Then I looked up and saw a picture of her cousin on the fireplace mantle.

"Is that her right there?"

"Where?" she said, as she picked herself up off of my chest.

"In the picture with you and the bright faced young lady," I uttered, as I pointed at the picture on the fireplace.

"Oh, right there. Yes, that's her behind my mother and me," she replied, as she wiped away her tears.

"Damn, that's some sad ass shit. I hope they find the person or persons responsible for what happened to her and her friends."

"Yeah, we all do. Now let me go finish getting dressed so you can take me to my aunt's house, if you don't mind?" she asked, as she stood in the hallway of her home.

"Listen, Sharon, I'm here for you, ma, so whatever you need me to do, I'll do," I replied, as I walked up to her and placed a kiss on her salt-tasting right cheek.

"Thank you, Michael. It'll only take me a few minutes, so please make yourself at home," she replied, then turned to walk away. Her nice ass swayed from side to side causing me to pull on my man hood. I thought about how we had become close with one another since the day she'd come into my office without panties on.

"She must have really wanted my attention that day," I said to myself, as I gazed at her until she'd vanished behind her closed bedroom door.

I turned to walk back towards the picture that had caught my eye earlier. For some odd reason, I feared I might know the female in the picture. The closer I got to the picture, the closer it felt as if my heart was about to drop out of my chest. To stall myself from getting closer to the picture, I found myself admiring how nice her place was.

I had only been there a few times, and I swear each time I'd been there, her place was always clean and smelling good. I really loved the way she had the entire home decorated. She had even started decorating the third room for the baby. Sharon was really the wifey type. Everything about her exuded what any smart man would want in a future wife.

Her place was a nice, modest three-bedroom, two-bath home that the average woman wouldn't be able to afford on her own. But somehow, some way, Ms. Sharon had her shit all together. She was a beautiful woman with a lot of potential. Hell, she even knew how to cook. There was never a dirty home to go to whenever I went by her place. In a sense, Sharon was more than perfect—the chick was flawless.

While still walking around her home, I found myself observing the picture on the mantle that had caught my eye earlier. A short looking girl stood in back of Sharon and her mother smiling as though it was the happiest day of her short-lived life. I took the picture down to examine it closer.

"I'm fuckin' trippin'," I whispered out loud, "that can't be her … I must be seeing things." *Sharon's mother looks just like Sexy Redd, only an older version.* Just as the thought had crossed my mind, I quickly turned around and realized Sharon had been behind me looking just like Do-Dirty.

"Michael, are you okay?" Her voice resonated throughout the air in her home. All I could do was stand there stuck in another trance, or better yet, spaced out. "Michael, Michael!"

I shook my head back and forth a few times and answered. "Yeah, I'm sorry, Sharon .., you just remind me of someone who used to dance for me at one point and time," I replied. I continued to look at her as if I had just seen the ghost of Do-Dirty.

"Boy, please," she said, "come on, let's go. My mother and everyone else is over at my aunt's house waiting on us," she said, as she took me by the hand and led me out the door.

"*Us?*"

"Yes, *us.* I told them my new man would bring me over to the house, so I hope you're ready to meet my family."

"What about you and the baby being hungry?" I quickly asked.

"We are, but we can all grab something to eat at my aunt's house. The whole family is over there anyway due to her daughter being murdered the other day."

"Damn," I uttered under my breath. I knew I'd told her I would take her over to her aunt's house but I didn't think I would have to meet the entire family. I had to come up with some type of excuse not to get out of the car once we got there.

As I opened the car door for her to sit her lil fine ass down, she turned around and hit me with something I'd just heard after leaving the club a few nights earlier.

"How about my aunt told my mother she received a black dress in the mail yesterday."

CHAPTER FOURTEEN
HER GHOST

As I closed the door of my car, I had to take a step back for a minute. I was really confused now. Not only was the girl in the picture with Sharon and her mother the striking resemblance to the female I'd just killed a few days earlier, but Sharon's damn mother looked as if she could've been Rhynyia's twin sister.

Damn, what was really going on, and why was it going on around me and my spiraling out of control? As soon as I got inside of the car, Sharon began badgering me with question after question.

"So, Michael, what do you think it means?"

"What's that, Sharon?" I replied, trying to act as if I didn't know what she was talking about.

"The black dress."

"Oh that … I really don't know, Ms. Lady," I replied, as I put the car in drive. I couldn't help but think of what I'd seen in the picture back at her house.

"Whatever it means, it doesn't sound right," she continued, "somebody's playing games with our family, Michael." I listened intently as I jumped onto Interstate 4. She paused, then added, "And when I find out who it is, they're gonna have to pay the ultimate price," she said, in a tone more serious than I'd ever heard from her.

"Damn, lil mama, and what is that?" I asked. I tried to keep my eyes on the road up ahead.

"Don't play with me, Michael, your black ass know exactly what it means!"

"Damn, you serious as a muthafuckin' heart attack, I see!"

"You damn right! Now get me to my aunt's house, please."

"No problem, 'Miss Daisy'. What's the address to your aunt's house?"

"Whatever, smart ass! She lives over off of Pine Hills and Silver Star, right behind the Winn Dixie shopping center. You should know where that is, it's right by your old job, remember?" she muttered, as she cut a lil smile over at me.

"Yes silly, how could I forget. That's where I met your lil no-panties-wearing-ass at."

"Shut up, boy," she chuckled out softly, "you liked what you saw that day. You should've seen the way your mouth fell open when you saw my lil cootie cat."

"Yeah, you right. "At the moment I didn't know if I should've ate you out, or kissed them sexy ass lips of yours."

"Whatever, Michael. "When you found out your wife, Mrs. Camisha Valentino, was in the building, you should've seen the expression on your face!" She laughed as she tried to demonstrate how I was looking.

"So I was looking fucked up, huh?" I asked, as I cut a smile back over at her.

"Hell yeah, you should've seen how scared you looked when you told me to get myself together because she was just around the corner of your office door."

"Whatever."

"You know, while we're on the subject, I've been meaning to explain that day to you because I know you probably thought differently about me since I presented myself like that.

"Nah, not really, Sharon, it really never crossed my mind."

"Whatever, boy."

"For real," I replied.

She started telling me how she had first saw me at one of my seminars and thought I was a very handsome man and how she had planned to try to seduce me. So with my left hand on my steering wheel and my right hand on the console of my car, she placed her left hand on top of my right hand and placed it inside of her inner thigh.

"And guess what Mr. Shy Ass? I'm not wearing any panties right now either. But that doesn't mean I'm fast in the ass. It's just that when I see something I want, I'm going to get it one way or another."

"Damn, one of your elementary classmates said the same thing about you the other night."

"They said *what* about me, Michael?" she asked, as she turned to face me in the car.

"Nothing really. It was your girl Felicia, my assistant. She told me you and her were classmates, and when you really like someone, you really like them."

"Okay ... what else did she tell you about me, Michael, since she claims to know so much about me?"

"Nothing Sharon, that was it."

"Oh, okay, I'm just checking. And like I said, just because I came into your office that day without any panties on, doesn't mean I'm a nasty, fast ass chick like some of your hot ass dancers."

"Okay, whatever, *Ms. Fast Ass!*" I laughed jokingly.

"Michael, I'm serious, I was just trying to get what I wanted, and what I wanted was your black ass," she said, looking so serious, I actually started forgetting all about my precious Sexy Redd.

I took my eye off the road and looked at her for a brief minute. It wasn't until I looked back up into my rearview mirror and saw the face of Do-Dirty sitting in my back seat, with the one bullet hole in her bleeding head that I momentarily lost control of my car.

"Oh shit!" I shouted.

Sharon, thinking fast on her feet, grabbed the steering wheel and kept us from crashing into the other lane, just missing a Publix semi-tractor trailer carrying frozen produce to another one of its grocery stores.

"Michael, what's wrong, are you okay?" she screamed in fear.

"I'm good. I thought I saw something in the middle of the road," I lied, while double checking to make sure Do-Dirty wasn't really sitting in the back seat.

"Bae, you should really get that checked out. You've been acting really strange the last couple of hours. Are you sure everything is alright?"

"Yeah, Sharon," I quietly replied.

"It's like you've been blacking out and then coming back as if you don't even realize you're blacking out," she stated. I continued driving, thinking to myself about how right she was about my current situation.

Ever since I had taken Do-Dirty's life, it seemed as if her ghostly spirit had come back and attempted to take my life. Whatever it was, something was definitely happening to me. Since that awful day at the paper mill, there had been nights I couldn't sleep. Could it be she was haunting me, and her soul couldn't rest until her murder was solved? I didn't have a clue. All I knew was I was a hot mess, and it seemed as if it was about to get even worse.

Sharon, who was on the passenger's side of the car, was still running off at the mouth.

"Okay, Michael, it's apartment 216 in the back," she said, which brought me back to reality.

I had just turned into the large, but dense, apartment complex, and I felt a sense of urgency because I couldn't shake feeling like I had actually been there before. *But for what and for who?* I questioned myself silently. Due to all the kids running around, playing amongst one another, I drove through the complex slowly. The place looked familiar and the surroundings were the same, but something just didn't sit right with my conscience. I was somewhere I had been before, but I just couldn't remember who it was I had previously been out there to see.

Once I pulled the big black body Benz into the parking space of those apartments, my memory tediously started to kick back in. Yes I had been there a few times before to pick someone up, the question I had now, was that female still dancing with me or had she quit the group. I I had just placed my car in park, when Sharon looked over at me and asked me the million dollar question.

"Okay, Mr. Michael, are you ready to meet some of my family?"

"Sharon, if it's okay with you, can I just sit out here and try to figure out why I keep having these moments when I black out, and then zone back in?"

She looked up at me with those cute ass eyes of hers and replied, "Seriously, Michael?"

"Yes, bae, I have to figure this shit out before it kills me, or even worse, us *and* the baby. You see what almost happened back there in the middle of traffic," I replied, as she sat there looking as if I had just rained on her parade.

"Michael, this is my family and I really wanted to introduce you as the man in my life. Now how does it look for me to go inside my aunt's apartment and you stay your ass out here in your damn car?" she replied, with anger resonating throughout her voice. I remained fastened to my seat, as her words rolled off of her sensuous lips. I wasn't trying to hear a damn thing she'd said because I was too entrenched on what was transpiring in my head.

"Alright, I'm coming. Let me get your door," I said. I opened my door, still pondering why the place seemed so familiar.

I had just gotten around to her side of the car and opened the door, when out of nowhere, three little kids came running up to the door of my car. As Sharon slowly emerged from the passenger's side of the car, she stood up and brushed her hair out of her face. Then it was as if the moment had slowed down in time.

One of the kids yelled, "Hey, Cousin Sharon and Mr. Michael!" I was completely caught off guard as I turned to see the face of the child who had just called out my name.

At first, I thought my past was about to catch up to me. *Could it be a child of an old female I had dated, or a child of one of my dancers who I couldn't seem to remember?*

"Hey, Rachel, how are you?" Sharon asked the young girl. She couldn't have been more than seven or eight years of age.

"Fine. Are you here to see my mother?" the young child asked. I looked down at her as she stared back in the eyes of her cousin. Sharon kneeled down to hug her.

"No, Rachel, I'm here for the family."

"Oh, because my mother is dead. Somebody killed her and her friends the other day," the small child said, as sadness filled her tone. Sharon pulled the young girl closer into her chest.

"I know, honey, and that's why we're here. Are you okay?" Sharon asked the young girl with her arms around her small back. She continued to embrace and comfort her at the same time.

The young girl looked up at me, and she looked as if she and her mother had been twins. I blinked my eyes once or twice and tried to erase the sight of the young girl's face. But just as I opened my eyes, instead of seeing the young child's face, I saw Do-Dirty's face. The hole was right there in the middle of her head, and it was bleeding while flies and gnats feasted on the open wound. Blood streamed down her head and onto her face and lips.

"Oh shit!" I yelled, as I began to stumble backwards. I reached out and tried to catch my balance. Sharon hastily stood in my path to help prevent my fall.

"Michael, Michael! Oh my God, not again," she screamed as I fell back onto my car. My body shook violently as if I was having a seizure or something.

Everything went black and all I heard was a bunch of screaming and yelling, then I began to lose consciousness.

CHAPTER FIFTEEN
SHORT-NECK HAVIN' ASS!

Back at the house, the girls who resided with Rhynyia and I were just about to settle in to eat their leftovers. However, someone had already beaten them to the punch.

"Hey, does anyone know what time Mike is coming back home?"

"He didn't say, Nicole. He just walked out of here headed to heaven only knows," Strawberry replied, as she sat at the bar area eating a huge bowl of Frosted Flakes cereal.

"Well, where ever his ass is at, I'm fuckin' starving," Nicole replied. She stared as Strawberry smacked her mouth while eating the cereal.

"I'm starving too, ladies," Entyce yelled, "let's order some pizza," she suggested, while walking out from the living room area of the house.

"Sounds good to me!" Mignon screamed, as she ran down stairs to mingle with the girls.

"All y'all yelling about pizza, what about our doggy bags from earlier today?" Nicole replied, as she bent over and searched through the fridge for the leftover food.

"Sorry, mates, I ate all that shit up earlier," Entyce replied, in her English accent. She leaned over the bar and looked at Nicole bent over searching through the fridge.

"No you didn't eat everybody's food, Entyce!" Nicole screamed. She slammed the door to the fridge and turned around to give Entyce a unit.

"Sorry, Nicole. I didn't think you guys were gonna eat it, so I did what I do best and fucked that shit right on up. Hell, I thought y'all was still shaken up over Sexy Redd leaving."

"Fuck that shit, Entyce. I could care less about the hoe leaving! All I care about is my damn food from Olive Garden that your big headed ass ate," Nicole voiced in anger. Strawberry and Mignon just stood there motionless as Nicole kept ranting about her food being gone.

"Sorry," Entyce replied. She held her head down pretending like she really gave a fuck.

"Well, Entyce, since you ate all our fuckin' food, it's only right that you pay for the pizza."

"No problem, Nicole. What kind of Pizza y'all want?"

"It doesn't matter as long as it has meat on it!"

"There your ass goes, Strawberry, always wanting some meat in your big ass mouth!"

"Whatever, Nicole! You like meat in your small ass mouth too."

"I never said I didn't but I would rather have *my* man's meat somewhere else instead of in my mouth, if you get my drift, chick!" The ladies burst out into laughter.

Minutes later, they calmed down when Mignon struck up a very sensitive conversation.

"Hey, let me ask you ladies something while we're all here in attendance."

"Go ahead. What is it now, professor?"

"Whatever, Nicole. Has it crossed you ladies' mind as to who took out the niggas who tried to rob us at gun point the other night?" she asked, with a look of concern written over her face.

"You know, I've been thinking about that for the last few days myself. I just can't believe Jasmine and Do-Dirty had something to do with them trying to rob us," Nicole replied. Mignon leaned up against the counter and sipped on a cold refreshing bottle of sparkling water.

"Girl, I knew the same night that shit popped off Jasmine's pretty ass had something to do with it," Entyce voiced, as she walked back into the kitchen with the house phone in her hand.

"How do you know that, Entyce?" Strawberry asked, as she put another spoonful of Frosted Flakes in her wide mouth—milk dripped down the side of her face.

"Because, Strawberry, not one of those guys even touched her ass that night they were up in here tryna rob us!" Entyce told her, as she slammed the cordless house phone down.

"Ump, you do have a point there, Entyce," Mignon replied, while chewing on a handful of green, seedless grapes. "Now that you mentioned it, not one of those damn guys said a damn thing to her that night and now look at where she's at—somewhere pushin' up daisies right along with the rest of them fools," Nicole added, as she rolled her neck and eyes simultaneously.

"So here's the question I need answered: do y'all think Mike and Sexy Redd had anything to do with murders?"

"I really can't say, Mignon. Mike was here with the security guy all day while Sexy Redd was at the mall with us," Nicole voiced, as she peeped out of the window and hoped the pizza guy was somewhere near the house with the food.

"Well, all I can say is whoever it was made sure it would be a while before they found out who *really* did it."

"You do have a point there, Entyce," Mignon stated, as she scooped up another handful of seedless grapes.

"Yo, Entyce, what time is the pizza guy gonna get here?"

"They said thirty minutes, Nicole."

"Damn, it seems like it's been an hour already," Nicole sputtered. She rubbed her stomach with a grimacing look on her face to let the girls know she was starving.

Ding-Dong! Ding-Dong!

"Finally! Speak of the devil and he shows up," Nicole said loudly. A smile covered her face.

"Strawberry get the door," Mignon yelled. She hurried to the kitchen to grab a few paper plates from the pantry.

Strawberry looked out of the window. "Wow, the pizza guys around here sure as hell look better than the ones where I come from, and they don't even bring the pizzas to the door with them."

Nicole went to the window, to see what the hell Strawberry was talking about. "Girl, move your apple headed ass out of the fuckin' way," she nudged Strawberry playfully.

"Damn, Strawberry, that's not the damn pizza guy. Shit, he ain't even got nothing in his hands," Nicole grumbled. She turned back to look at the expressions on her friends' faces. "Who is it?" she yelled through the door.

"It's Richard, Mike's cousin from Orlando," the guy on the other side of the door replied.

"Oh, that's the cousin Mike's gonna hire to help with the girls," Mignon informed her while finishing off the handful of grapes.

"Well is someone going to let his ass in, or y'all gonna just let him stand outside?" Entyce asked. She sat back down at the bar.

"Hello?" Richard shouted from behind the door.

"Hold up, Richard, while we put on something presentable." Nicole yelled, as she backed away from the door and ran up the stairs to change.

Entyce went to the door to open it and let him in. "Move, Strawberry, while I let his ass in."

"I hope he don't try to rob us," Strawberry told Mignon, who was already halfway up the stairs.

"Shut up, Scary Sherry," Mignon uttered.

"Well, hello, ladies," Richard said, with a giant smile covering his face. He entered the house and immediately noticed how beautiful the women were.

"Hello to you as well, Mr. Richard," Entyce replied. Her and Strawberry were still downstairs waiting on the pizza.

Richard stood in the kitchen area gazing at Strawberry and Entyce. "Is Mike here?"

"Not right now"— Strawberry turned around and placed her empty bowl in the sink— "he stepped out earlier and hasn't been back since. Was he expecting you Richard?"

"Yeah, he had mentioned something to me about a job."

"Well, who knows where his ass might be." She turned her focus back to Richard and took her seat back at the bar. "Have a seat, he might be back soon."

"Yeah, that's Mike for you." He snickered. "He probably forgot I was even coming."

"I tell you what .. let me call him and find out what time he's coming back," Entyce said, and picked up the cordless phone.

"That's cool. You got anything to drink?" Richard asked, while rubbing his hands together.

Nicole answered his question as she waltzed back down the stairs. "Sure. Grab the man something to drink, Strawberry, and stop staring at the poor boy as if you about to eat the man."

"Shut up, Nicole! He ain't worried about me 'cause he too busy observing the way your lil plump ass is stickin' out of them shorts pulled up, all in the crack of yo' funky ass."

"Whatever, chick, ain't nothing funky about all this lil chunk of fine, natural, red ass," Nicole replied. A smile spread across her face. "I must admit, Mike does have a house full of beautiful women around him," Richard voiced, as he gulped down a cold glass of Pepsi.

Strawberry gawked at Richard. "Well, thank you Richard. Mike didn't tell us his cousin was just as fine and handsome as he is."

Richard smiled at the women. "You got my cousin fucked up if you thought he was gonna tell you how fine *another* nigga looked."

"Oh well ... I called his phone and it went straight to voicemail," Entyce let him know, as she stepped back into the room.

"He might just be in a bad area for cell reception, Entyce—try back in a few minutes," Nicole suggested. Again, she got up to look out the window for the pizza guy.

"You might be right, Nicole." Entyce agreed.

Nicole stood in the window with a puzzled look on her face. "Entyce, you sure you called the right pizza place?"

"Yes, ole greedy ass girl."

"Well, I wouldn't be like this if your bald-faced ass hadn't ate everybody else's leftovers."

"My bad, sis."

"That damn man already thirty minutes late. We should get those damn pizzas for the free," Mignon stated, as she walked back down the stairs rubbing her stomach.

"You know when I pulled up I saw a pizza guy looking around the neighborhood as if he was lost," Richard said, as he grabbed himself another cold Pepsi.

"That was probably his ass. When he does finally get here, I'ma cuss him the fuck out. He must don't know who he got fucked up!" Nicole screamed. She, too, paced back and forth while rubbing her stomach.

"Damn, lil mamma, who are y'all badass group of females?" Richard asked with a quizzical look on his face.

"Hell, you don't know? We the muthafuckin' Florida Hot Girls!" Nicole replied, as Mignon laughed out loud. Then with their hands held high, and palms wide open, she and Mignon high-fived one another knowingly.

"If you ask me it looks like y'all the muthafuckin' *Hungry Ass Florida Hot Girls* right now," Richard replied. Everyone burst out laughing just as the pizza guy rang the doorbell.

"Shut that ass up, Richard. I can tell you and Mike are cousins," Nicole sputtered, as she got up to answer the door.

"And why do you say that shorty?"

"Cause you and him both got jokes—oh silly ass, short-neck having ass nigga!" Nicole replied. All the girls burst into laughter at her remark.

CHAPTER SIXTEEN

BLAM! BLAM! BLAM!

"Sorry it took so long," the freckled faced, young white delivery guy, uttered. "I got confused by the different house numbers displayed on the garage doors throughout the subdivision," he said nervously.

"No problem, how much do we owe you?" Entyce asked the young man.

"No charge, ma'am. Since I was late I'm going to have to pay for them out of my own pockets," the young man replied. Entyce stood in the doorway with a devilish grin covering her face.

"Okay thanks, have a nice evening, see ya!" she yelled, as she closed the door. Nicole gazed at her with her mouth wide open. She was in disbelief of what had just transpired.

Entyce walked by her laughing, causing Nicole to question her. "Entyce, what was all that about?" Nicole asked, while reaching for two slices of the extra meat pizza.

"Sorry, mates, I gave them the numbers to the house backwards so we could get the pizzas for the free."

"Girl, and you had me up in here hungry and shit! If you didn't wanna pay for the food, I would have paid for it myself, with your cheap ass!"

"Whatever, Nicole, yo' ass eating, right?" Entyce asked, as she brashly chewed on her slice of pizza.

"So y'all always act like that amongst one another?" Richard asked, as he tried to sneak himself a slice of the nice smelling pizza pie.

"Yep," Strawberry answered, with hot cheese hanging from her opened mouth.

Over at Sharon's aunt's house ...

WHILE THE GIRLS AND MY COUSIN Richard were back at the house eating pizza, all hell was breaking loose over at Sharon's aunt's house. I grabbed for my chest and fell backwards onto the passenger's seat, and Sharon had gotten hysterical trying to get me to respond to her. I had gone into total shock.

"Michael, what's wrong with you?" I vaguely heard her asking me loudly. However, my mouth wouldn't move and my body shook violently. Beads of sweat rained down my face as if I'd been caught in a storm without an umbrella.

"Baby, I'm right here, talk to me, Michael … what's wrong? Please, say something!" I couldn't talk and I continued to shiver and perspire as if I'd been shot and pierced by multiple bullets.

I remember hearing Sharon scream to her mother. Within minutes, her mother noticed all the commotion going on outside of her sister's living room window, and she quickly ran outside.

"Mom!" Sharon yelled. She pushed my legs inside the car and slammed the car door closed.

"I ain't no doctor, baby, but it looks like the poor man is having a stroke or something," she said, as she peered at me through the window, "Oh my God, someone call 9-1-1!" her mother yelled in a panic.

"Mom, it'll take too long for them damn people to get here! I'ma have to take him myself!" Sharon jumped into the driver's seat of my car. Before I knew it, she was whipping that big, black-body Benz out of that apartment complex, doing at least thirty-five miles per hour.

Once at the entrance, she quickly made a right turn onto Pine Hills Road and headed towards the light on Silver Star. The light was red as she merged into the turning lane without even checking for oncoming traffic. She ran the stoplight as if she was the driver of an EMS vehicle headed to the hospital. She must have had a clear path up ahead because she had picked up speed, now doing sixty-five miles per hour around the turns and bends located throughout Silver Star Road.

Sharon drove the big black-body Benz as if she was a NASCAR driver. She was going so fast, before I knew it, I had passed out in fear for my life. *Was my life about to come to an abrupt halt just like that? Had I taken my last breath?* And to think, the last person's face I'd seen was that of the female I'd just taken out a few days prior.

As I drifted off into a comatose state of mind, I asked the Heavenly Father not to let me die this way. I was going in and out, just as Sharon was going in and out of traffic, trying to get me to the hospital. I felt her reach over then into my pocket before she pulled out my cell phone.

"Okay, where is her number?" she said to herself, as she scrolled through my phone.

"Okay, got it!" she yelled out. "Hold on bae, hold on," she shouted as she looked over at me, "I'm gonna get you there ... just don't die on me and your child!"

A Few seconds later, I could hear her yelling through my phone at the person she had called. "Hey, Felicia!"

"Yeah, who is this?"

"It's Sharon, girl. Hey, listen, something is wrong with Michael and I'm taking him to the hospital right now!"

"Is he okay?"

"I don't know right now. All I know is that something is definitely wrong with him," she replied on the brink of tears.

"What hospital are you taking him too?"

"The one off of Turkey Lake Road—call the girls who stay with him and let them know," she told Felicia.

"Alright, Sharon, will do."

"Bye," she ended the call.

She was still flying when I heard sirens blaring behind the car. Scared shitless, part of me was relieved when I'd heard the sirens, because based on the way she was driving, I didn't think I'd make it to the hospital anyway. The funny thing about it was, she wasn't slowing down, not at all. She kept right on flying as if she didn't care. All she wanted to do was get me to that damn hospital, dead or alive.

With my eyes still closed and frightened half to death, I could still see the face of young Do-Dirty, lethargically walking up to me with the gunshot wounds ever so apparent. She had tears and blood streaming down her face. I tried to back away from her but it seemed the closer she got to me, the more it felt as though my feet were stuck in cement. She stood in front of me and slowly opened her mouth to speak.

"I just wanted to feed my kids and give them a better life, but no, Michael, you had to go and shoot me in my head and stomach," she recalled, as I just stood there cemented to whatever was keeping me from moving.

"It wouldn't have been like that, but you and your counterparts tried to rob me. I had to make sure I didn't allow you guys a second chance at my life or the Dynasty I'm trying to create," I replied, as I stood face to face with the woman who I'd shot and killed.

***

"OKAY, WE'RE ON THE WAY right now, thanks again, Felicia." Nicole had just hung up with felicia and everyone had been listening to her end of the phone call.

"Hey, guys, that was Felicia, Mike's assistant," she announced as she dully turned around to reiterate Sharon's information.

"Okay, what's up?" Mignon asked, as she sipped on her beverage of choice.

"Something is wrong with Michael," she uttered, as she began crying. Her emotions got the best of her and she fell into Entyce's arms.

"What?" Mignon yelled. She jumped up which caused her to knock over her drink.

"Something is wrong with Mike, and Sharon is rushing him to the hospital right now," Nicole voiced again, as Entyce helped her to her seat.

"Oh shit! Well what are we waiting for? Aren't we going to the hospital too?" Strawberry yelled. The slice of sausage pizza she'd been eating fell from her hands.

"Yes," Richard voiced. Shocked by the news, he, too, dropped his slice of pizza.

Everyone was in a panic as they scattered to their individual rooms to grab their personal items and identification. Deep in thought, Richard stood in the doorway of the living room while the girls went to their rooms.

"Damn, I sure hope cuz is alright," he muttered to himself. He looked around at all the nice pictures and different cultural artifacts I'd placed nicely throughout the spacious living room. The room was decorated with items from Rhynyia's culture as well as mine. We always said it gave our living room the ancestry history that we as a people had grown accustomed to leaving behind.

In the meantime ...

ACROSS TOWN, SHARON HAD finally pulled over for the two police officers who had been chasing her. Just as she pulled over, she nervously began fumbling through my car for her driver's license. When she found them, she jumped out of the car screaming, "I have a medical emergency!"

The two officers jumped back in fear for their lives and quickly drew their police-issued revolvers.

"Freeze, ma'am! Put your hands up," the lead officer yelled.

Sharon didn't freeze; instead, she continued running and screaming in the officers' direction.

"Ma'am, I'm warning you ... freeze and drop whatever is in your hands, right now!"

"I have a medical emergency dammit! My gotdamn boyfriend is having a stroke or heart attack!" she screamed desperately.

"Ma'am, please refrain from the abusive language and place your hands behind your back," the officer recited.

"Fuck that, I need to get him to the hospital right now or he might die!" she screamed, as she got within inches of the officer.

"Ma'am, I warned you!"

Blam! Blam! Blam!

Michael Gallon

CHAPTER SEVENTEEN
BACK FROM AMONGST THE DEAD

The officer shot three piercing rounds into the midafternoon sky yet my girl Sharon didn't even flinch. She stood firm and direct, as she stared the officers down.

"Okay, now that we have your attention, ma'am, please do as we ask, or the next time I fire my weapon I won't miss!" the officer barked.

"Sir, like I stated before you wanted to play muthafuckin' John Wayne, my boyfriend needs immediate medical attention! Would it hurt you two fine officers of the law to check for yourselves, please?

"Let's go check this out, John Wayne," one of the officers said to his partner. They placed their weapons back into their holsters.

"Stay behind the car while we go check this out, ma'am." The two officers then lazily walked to the passenger's side of my car.

"No problem, sir, just do your fuckin' jobs," Sharon snarled at the young officer. Both officers kindly took their times approaching my vehicle.

The officer who seemed as if he was in charge tapped on the window rapidly. After he realized I wasn't moving, he began frantically knocking on the window with a slight bit of urgency.

"Hey, Tom, this guy isn't fuckin' moving for real!"

"What? You thought I was fuckin' playing!" Sharon yelled from behind the car.

"Move, John, let me see something." Officer Tom Stevens pulled open the door on the passenger's side and observed me lying unmoving as if I were already dead, or in some type of diabetic, comatosed stage.

"Ma'am, what did you say was wrong with him?" the officer yelled.

"Like I tried to explain before, he's having a stroke or some type of seizure! I'm not a doctor and neither are either of you! Now can we get him to the hospital, please?" Sharon pleaded.

"Let us call for an ambulance, ma'am. Just remain calm, please," the officer suggested in a reassuring tone.

"The ambulance will take to fuckin' long," Sharon rebutted. "Why can't you two officers just give me a police escort? It would be much faster," she concluded. More afraid than angry, she eyed the two officers with desperation in her eyes.

"She's right, John—the ambulance will take entirely too long, and the department can't stand another death on their hands as a result of a couple of their own officers not thinking fast on their feet."

"You're right, Ma'am. Please follow close behind us as we try to get you and your boyfriend to the nearest hospital."

"Thank you," Sharon replied, as she jumped back in the car, behind the steering wheel. She cut her eyes over at me. "Hang on, nigga … you're not about to die on me … not right now, and for damn sure not like this!" I could hear her, but I couldn't respond. She slammed the car in drive and sped down the busy intersection, behind the police escort as if she was an actual cop herself.

They got me to the hospital where the doctors and nurses were waiting on our arrival.

"Okay, ma'am, we can take it from here," the tall, white, slim doctor said, as they wheeled my cold, stiff body down the hallway of the hospital.

"I hope he's okay, Ma'am. And we do apologize for our actions earlier," the officer she referred to as John Wayne acknowledged.

"No problem, officer. I know you guys were just trying to do your jobs," Sharon replied, as she finally allowed the tears to flow down her face.

"Excuse me, Miss. You're with the gentleman, right?" the nurse asked Sharon.

"Yes, I am."

"Could you tell us his name and what happened to him?"

"His name is Michael Valentino. He just passed out and it was like he had suddenly blacked out."

"And how long has this been happening?"

"I really can't give you an actual time frame. All I know is that it seemed to start the day after my cousin and her friends were murdered at the old paper mill. So it's been at least a few days or so,"

Sharon replied, as she hastily walked behind the doctors. By now, she was trying to gain her composure because she was still shedding crocodile-like tears.

"Okay, please calm down, Ma'am. I know it's hard but we need you to stop crying so we can understand what you're trying to tell us," the doctor advised.

Sharon took a deep breath and relaxed for a minute before she continued with what she was trying to say.

"It's like he saw something and went into some type of shock, and afterwards he just passed out."

I could hear her as she explained her recollection to the doctor, but that wasn't why I'd passed out. I passed out because she was driving my damn car so fucking fast, it caused me to blank out. Nonetheless, after telling them what happened the doctors immediately placed me into one of the available rooms. I had a pulse and my heart was beating normal, which meant I was still alive. I was breathing normal on my own, so I didn't need any oxygen.

"Nurse, get me his vitals, and once you have them, get me someone down here who might know what's wrong with him!"

"Yes, sir, right away, doctor." I could hear the doctor and the nurses but they couldn't hear me.

I frantically tried to wake up. I needed to get their attention so they wouldn't start cutting on me in an effort to find out what was wrong with me. My eyes wouldn't open. I tried to move anything that would move one of my limbs so they wouldn't think I was in some type of coma.

After a half of an hour of laying with my ass cheeks hanging out on the cold slab they used for a table, I came to the realization that my black ass was between a rock and a very hard place. What was wrong with me? This time when she appeared it was as if I was in some type of dark hole or tunnel. Only this time she looked different. There were no wounds or oozing to indicate I'd shot her. Her face was wiped clean.

"Do—Dirty, is that you?" I asked, as she became more vivid in my realm of eye sight.

"Yes, yes, it's me Michael." The way her voice echoed in the dark place we were in, made it sound as if she was in another world, "I never meant for what happened to happen to you. I'm so sorry," I said. I just stood there in total amazement of what I was seeing and hearing.

"My soul is at peace now, Michael. It wasn't your fault you did what you did. If you hadn't, we would've possibly tried to rob you again, and who knows who we might've killed the second time around. I made some very bad decisions in my short-lived life and now my soul has to deal with the consequences. You, on the other hand, still have a chance to correct your mistakes. Now go ahead and make the right choices in your, somewhat, very complicated life."

As soon as the last sentence rolled off her lips, a tall, very dark man emerged from behind her with what looked like a garden shear in his hand. He had on a long black gown that covered his entire body. His hands were skeletal-like with a hook on the end as they grasped the garden tool. I couldn't see his face due to the black hood he had over his head. I looked down at his feet and noticed they weren't touching the ground.

"Oh shit, the Grim Reaper!" I must have said it out loud because the shadowy figure turned to me with nothing but an empty skull inside of the hood.

"You muthafuckin' right," the figure said. "The time has come for you to leave. Say your last goodbyes and prepare yourself for the afterlife that your previous life has caused you to enter into," the voice of the dark, ghostly figure slowly voiced.

"Goodbye, Michael, please help take care of my kids and let my kids' father know I tried to be the best mother I could possibly be. Don't let them grow up to be like me!"

"Do-Dirty, wait, wait! I have something to tell you," I screamed but it was like she couldn't hear me. Who in the hell is her baby's father?" I asked myself as I stood there deep in thought. And just like they had appeared, her and the ghostly figured man had vanished right into thin air. I stood there still and stiff, wondering what was next for me.

Minutes later, I slowly turned around to see a very bright light up ahead of me. At first, I was frightened by the enormous beam of white light. It wasn't until I heard her voice calling me.

"Michael, Michael, please come back to me! Don't leave me like this, not now, not when I'm going to need you the most!"

My eyes numbly opened to witness Sharon laying there on my chest sobbing.

At first, I lay there looking around the room, searching for an explanation as to why I was there in the first place, stretched out on that table they called a bed. To see her crying in such a desperate manner caused me to feel a certain way about the beautiful, young lady. I couldn't just lay there and witness all the pain and sorrow she was going through. So, I slowly moved my head from left to right and then lifted my hand up and placed it on the back of her head ever so gently.

"Hey, you," I whispered in her ear. "What's up with all the tears?" Her head suddenly snapped back as she looked directly into my eyes.

"Michael, your back! Oh thank, Yahweh," she screamed in joy and sheer excitement. She began kissing me all over my face.

"Sharon, where am I?" I asked while trying to keep her under control and look at my surroundings all at the same time.

"Boy, your crazy ass is at the damn hospital!"

"*Hospital*? For what?" I asked with a shocked expression on my face.

"Michael, you can't be serious. You were at my aunt's house when you blacked out again."

I slowly came around and mumbled, "I remember now. Then you pushed me inside of my car and sped off driving my car like you had lost your rabbit ass mind."

"Boy, shut up. I was trying to save your life," she replied, as she sat there crying and smiling. "Nurse, nurse, he's awake," she yelled, as she stuck her head out of the door of the room. She wanted to alert anyone in ear distance to let them know I had come back from amongst the dead and was back with the living again.

Michael Gallon

CHAPTER EIGHTEEN
SHE'S DEAD

The doctor and a few of the nurses immediately ran into my room and began checking my vital signs once again. No one bothered to ask me how I was feeling.

After several minutes, one of the doctors who had been asked to assist looked down at me. "Mr. Valentino, I'm doctor Ruiz, how are you feeling?"

"I guess I'm feeling fine, doc. Why? What happened to me?"

Sharon was standing over near the nurse and didn't give the doctor a chance to answer before she took it upon herself to speak. "Yes, doctor, he's been acting like this for the last few days," she told him, as if she'd been asked.

"Well, the tests we ran all came back negative. Have you bumped your head in the last few days, or has anyone hit you in the head?"

I started to answer *yes* and inform him of the intruders we'd had at the house the other night. However, just as I started to answer, I realized who was around me and quickly decided it best to rethink my response.

"No, sir, not that I can recall." *Now, if you've been paying attention to the story, you all know that was a lie—if you recall, a few nights ago, Goldmouth had hit me across my head when him and his dumbfounded crew of thieves tried to rob the girls and me.*

By the time I had finished lying to the good doctor and whomever else was standing around, in came the girls and my dear cousin, Richard Valentino.

"How is he? Is he alright?" Nicole asked the doctor in a panicked tone. She had wiggled herself through the crowd of people standing in my room, to get closer to where the doctor stood by my bedside.

"Yes, ladies, he's fine, he just became alert," one of the doctors replied. Everyone in the room stood around me, happy to see I was okay.

"Wow, Mr. Valentino, you seem to be a real celebrity around here. Are all of these ladies family members?" the short, white, stubby doctor asked, with a devious grin plastered on his face.

"Something like that," Strawberry answered modestly, "we're part of a family of young ladies known to the world as the Florida Hot Girls"—she looked at me proudly—"and the young man lying there in that makeshift bed is supposed to be our fearless leader, Mr. Michael Valentino," she blurted out, with a giant smile covering her reddish face.

"The Florida *what*?" a second doctor asked. His face displayed a shy grin.

"Nothing, Doc. When can I leave?" I arched my back and sat up slowly before trying to get to my clothes.

"Well, there's one more test I have to run. If that one comes back negative, I can arrange for you to leave tonight, Mr. Valentino," the doctor said. Then he turned to head to the door.

I could still see his head shake from side to side as he walked away. "The Florida Hot Girls," he mumbled his astonishment as if somewhat confused. When he reached the exit, he quickly turned to me and the girls. "Oh, *strippers*, right?" He took another glance and admired the sheer beauty of the women who had come to check on my health and wellbeing.

"What's up, cuz, are you okay?" Richard asked, as he extended his hand for me to shake.

"I'm fine, cuz. What's up with you?" I replied, as I shook his hand.

"Man, for a minute, me and the girls thought we'd lost you."

"Nah, cousin, looks like I'm gonna be here a little while longer," I replied. while changing my position in that narrow ass bed.

"I came by your house like you asked, but the girls said you weren't there so I hung around anyway. I'm Glad I did, due to what happened to you."

"I'm mighty glad you did, cousin. I see the girls really needed you."

"Yeah, they did," he agreed.

Sharon maneuvered her way through the girls as they stood crowded around my bed. She gawked at Richard as if she was trying to remember where she knew him from. She looked down at me and then back up at him.

"Wait a minute ... no wonder you two look so much alike," she muttered out loud.

I looked back at her and smiled. "Yeah, Sharon, he's my cousin," I told her.

"Mike, you're not going to believe this."

"Believe what, Sharon?"

"Richard is the father of the young girl you saw at my aunt's house," she replied, with a somber look on her face.

"What?" I asked.

"Your cousin Richard here is the father of two beautiful daughters that he and Do-Dirty had together."

I slowly looked back at Richard. He smiled at me, and then Sharon. Richard looked around the shocked-filled room and the expressions on the girls' faces said it all.

"Yes, sir, I sure am," he concurred. "By the way, how's her little fast ass doing anyway?" he asked. Sharon's eyes widened and her mouth drooped. Stunned and perplexed, she didn't know what to say. She studied Richard's face and realized he was clueless. Why else would he have been standing there, showing off all thirty-two of his pearly-white teeth.

"How's who, Richard?" Sharon asked to be sure. "Your kids or Do-Dirty?"

"Do-Dirty of course. I've been trying to get in touch with her for the past few days."

Sharon quickly looked over at me. The feeling of guilt plagued my body from my head to my toes, as I lay there shocked to learn the female I'd killed was the mother of my cousin's two children. I closed my eyes and replayed Do-Dirty's last words as the grim reaper ushered her thieving ass away. Then, like a bolt of lightning, it hit me. She must have known Richard and I were cousins, and that our paths would cross in more ways than one. My body felt numb and I was paralyzed by what I'd just heard. Not only did Richard and Do-Dirty have kids together, but she was Sharon's cousin as well.

No longer wanting to prolong the inevitable, Sharon's eyes filled with water. She inhaled, then exhaled deeply before she informed Richard with the awful news no one in life ever wanted to hear. "I'm sorry, Richard"—she paused and cleared her throat, trying to remove the lump that had formed in it—"you must not have heard yet."

Richard's boyish smile quickly vanished. He appeared to become frozen in place as he focused on Sharon. He held his gaze without blinking. "Heard what?" he asked reluctantly.

"She's dead ..."

CHAPTER NINETEEN
BEHIND ME

"Who's dead, Sharon?" Richard's entire demeanor changed. I watched him choke up, though he tried to maintain his tough exterior.

"Do-Dirty, Richard, Do-Dirty! I'm so sorry!" Richard's eyes immediately watered up as he abruptly turned and ran for the door. When Nicole heard Do-Dirty's name, the pizza she'd eaten earlier erupted from her mouth like a volcano, and landed all over Strawberry's back.

Strawberry, who just happened to be blocking the garbage can, went off instantly. "What the fuck, Nicole! You couldn't hold that shit before you threw up all over my fuckin' back?" She took off the soiled shirt which she now considered destroyed.

Nicole hurried over to the sink and quickly rinsed her mouth out. After she'd gathered herself, she turned her attention to Strawberry. "I tried to go around your wide, flat-ass booty but you didn't move out of the way fast enough! I'm sorry," Nicole echoed.

My thoughts were on my cousin, so I didn't bother trying to intervene with the girls' BS. "Go get him, Sharon, and please don't let nothing happen to him," I uttered, as she darted out after Richard. I turned to the room of ladies who stayed at the house with me. "Listen, no one is to know a damn thing about the shit that went down at the house the other night, and I mean no one," I said in a hushed tone of voice, "we take what we know to our graves ... Do you ladies understand?"

"Yes, Mike, not one word. You can trust us," Entyce mumbled. From a distance we could see Sharon consoling Richard as he cried on her shoulder.

"Who do you think took them out anyway, Mike?"

"I have no idea, Mignon. All I know is whoever the culprits were, they did us a big favor. The only problem we have now is I just hope they don't come to us asking for what the thieves wanted."

Nicole stood at the sink wiping the sausage-pizza puke from her mouth, in an effort to clean off any residue. She walked closer to the side of my hospital bed. "You got a point there, Mike," she agreed in a serious tone.

"Do me a favor, ladies. Start getting my things together so I'll be ready to go when the doctor gets back in with my test results."

"Sure thing, Mike," Mignon stated.

Sharon walked back in with tears in her eyes. She'd been crying with Richard when she noticed the ladies helping me get my things together. "Michael, I never knew Richard was your cousin."

"Yeah, his grandfather and my grandfather were brothers, so that makes us first cousins. By the way, you never told me the name of your cousin they found dead."

"I was about to tell you before you passed out. Her mom said she used to work for you before you fired her. Her name was Do-Dirty."

"Damn, lil Do-Dirty was the one who got killed at that old paper mill?" I was acting as if I didn't know that she was dead.

"Yes, her and a few others that the authorities are still trying to identify."

"Damn shame," I replied, trying to look as innocent as possible. I was mortified as Sharon continued telling me the story of how Richard and Do-Dirty had met one another. She also let me know she was the God-parents to both of his daughters.

"I didn't even know they were dating," I said. It happened to be the only truth I'd told thus far.

"Yeah, that's how she was—very quiet about who she was dating." We were still talking when the nurse walked back in with a smile over her face.

"The doctor says you can leave whenever you're ready, Mr. Valentino."

That was all I needed to hear. I quickly jumped out of bed and rushed to put my clothes back on.

"What time is it?" I asked the room of beautiful ladies.

Sharon looked around the room until she spotted the clock on the wall. "It's late and you need to be getting home so you can get some rest. Do you want me to come with you to your place, or are you coming home with me?"

"Sharon, just get me out of here." I replied. I sluggishly tried to get out of the small ass bed.

"Alright then, I guess I'll just stay with you and leave your house in the morning," she said. A half-ass smile crept on her face.

I could tell Nicole was upset about Sharon going home with us, but hell, I just wanted to get out of there. I was tired, and most of all, I wanted to put the day behind me as fast as possible.

Michael Gallon

.   .   .

CHAPTER TWENTY
LET'S GO HOME!

Now that I had seen her face for the last time, I could get on with what I had to do. By the time we had all walked outside to get into our different vehicles, it was around 12:30 a.m. I looked over at the ladies I had with me and said, "Wow, what a fucking day!"

"Yeah, I just want to get back home and take off these clothes Nicole threw her pizza all up on. Then I'ma get in my bed and eat a big ass bowl of Frosted Flakes," Strawberry declared.

"Girl, Mike just getting out of the hospital and your ass is *still* talking about some damn cereal," Entyce said, as the two of them headed toward Richard's truck.

"It's okay, Entyce. But why is she talking about eating some damn Frosted Flakes, corn flakes?" I asked with a concerned look on my face.

"Because Entyce long-faced ass ate up everybody's leftovers from earlier so we had to order pizza," Nicole rolled her eyes at Entyce.

Everybody laughed at the comment but I sensed that Richard was a bit shaken up. I looked over at Mignon and uttered, "Hey, you might wanna drive for my boy Richard. I don't think he needs to drive after just hearing the news about his kid's mother."

"Yeah, I can tell. I'll make sure everybody gets back home safely."

Sharon had already walked up ahead to get my car when fast ass Nicole pulled me by my shirt tail and whispered, "Don't forget, Michael. You still owe me for saving your ass the other night at the Caribbean. As soon as your precious boo thang lets you up for air, it's gonna be me and you."

"Oh, y-yeah," I stuttered out and chuckled.

"I'm not playing with you, Michael. I'm dead ass serious. I want some more of that D."

"Whatever, Nicole," I barked. She walked away making sure I saw her nice ass and round hips swaying from side to side.

As I stood there waiting on Sharon to pull up with my car, my phone began to vibrate inside my pants pocket. Passively, I looked down at the caller I.D. and realized it was none other than Sexy Redd calling. I hadn't heard from her since she'd left earlier that day.

"Hello."

"Michael."

"Yes, Rhynyia, what's good?"

"I should be asking your ass that question Mr. Are you okay?" she asked. She sounded concerned.

"Yes, wait a minute ... How did you know?" I asked. I quickly looked around to see if anyone was following me.

"Know what, silly?"

"Know I was at the hospital," I replied.

"I didn't. Now why are you at the hospital, Mr.?" she angrily asked.

"How about, I was still seeing her face, and for some reason I blacked out."

"You what? And *whose* face?" I could hear the worry and fear in her voice as she asked me what happened.

"Do-Dirty—I could still see her face. For some odd reason, this time when I saw her face, I blacked out and had to be rushed to the hospital immediately."

"I'm sorry to hear that, Michael. Is everything okay now?"

"Yeah. They just released me about thirty minutes ago. But how about lil ass Do-Dirty has kids by the cousin I just hired to help me with the girls."

"What?"

"Yes, and when I tell you I feel awful ..."

"I know you do, baby."

"I kept seeing her face every time I blacked out. It was like she was trying to tell me something. When they got me to the hospital I finally spoke to her ghost or something."

"Her *spirit*, Michael," she replied.

"Whatever, Rhynyia. Her *ghost*!" I shouted back.

"Okay, go on, what happened next?"

"She forgave me for taking her life and then asked me to help look after her kids. Then the grim reaper snatched her lil thieving ass away!"

"Well, Michael, you do know when you kill someone and they see you before they die, their soul cannot rest until it's at peace with those it offended."

"Thanks, Princess Rhynyia. I will definitely remember that next time I have to take someone's life," I replied sarcastically. "Now how was the flight back home?"

"It was okay. I just wish you were here with me so I could take care of you."

"Yeah, me too. You know how I don't like sleeping without you."

"Michael, you do know since we've been together this is our first time being away from one another."

"Yeah, I do realize we've always been by each other's side." Just as I had uttered those words, I looked up to see Sharon with my damn two-way pager in the palm of her hand as she eased up in my car.

Oh shit! If she opens up that pager all hell is going to break loose! I thought. I ran at top speed toward my car, trying to get the pager out of her hand. I briskly snatched open my car door as she leaned her head over towards me.

"I was trying to tell you your pager was going off, silly," she said nonchalantly.

"Thank you," I replied, and quickly took the pager from her.

I could hear Rhynyia in the background. "Is everything alright, Michael?"

"Yes, everything is fine. Someone was paging me about a show this weekend."

"Okay, well it's late and I know you probably want to get home and get yourself some rest. So, let me say goodnight, and remember I love you." I quickly pushed my door closed and turned away from Sharon.

"I love you too," I told her. We ended the call just as Sharon rolled down my passenger window.

"Do you want to stay here, or do you want to go home so I can give your handsome, black ass some of this good, tight-ass pussy?"

I smiled deviously and winked at her. "Say no more, baby girl. Let's go home."

CHAPTER TWENTY-ONE
BERNARD FATS WALKER

"Wow, Michael, your house is beautiful—no, it's amazing," Sharon said. It was her first time entering my new home. "I've dreamed about living in a house like this many of nights," she added, as she admired the layout.

"Why thank you, Sharon. It's okay. Honestly, sometimes, I still can't believe I live here myself."

"It must cost you a fortune to live here, and look at how big your damn pool is," she said. Pure excitement showed on her radiant face.

"Nice, huh?"

"Yes, *that*, it is, Michael. You have to give me a personal tour of this big ass house."

"Sure, Sharon, anything you want. And to answer your question, I wouldn't be staying here if I couldn't afford it. With what the girls and I make in a week's time, we manage to get by."

"So they pay rent for staying here too?"

"You damn right, they ain't about to stay here rent-free. Where they do that at?" I said. I watched as she took in her surroundings.

"Boy, you're a trip. You sure have come a long way since the days of working at the wages office," she replied and smiled back at me.

"Yeah, something like that. Would you like me to cook you something to eat?"

"That would be nice, Michael, but since you had such a rough day, I'll cook you something really quick. Where are the girls?" she asked. She waltzed those nice ass hips of hers into the kitchen.

"That was the girls paging me earlier. They're gonna stop by the Waffle House and pick up something to eat. Let me call them and have them pick us something as well."

"Sounds good to me, Michael. I'll have eggs, grits, bacon, and orange juice. Oh, make sure they get me some raisin toast too."

"I have some orange juice in the fridge. Let me get you a glass before I walk you upstairs." I quickly poured her a glass of juice and then made the call to have the girls pick us up some breakfast. We reached the door to my bedroom and I slung open the door. Sharon's eyes grew and she screamed at the size of my double-king size bed.

"Damn, son, this bed is huge! At least five people can fit in there at one time," she screamed, and threw her lil short ass across the bed. The bed seemed to swallow her up as soon as she leaped into it.

"I know. It's just in case I wanted to have a sleep over."

"Whatever, Michael!" She rolled around and marveled at the humongous size of the room.

My phone began to vibrate again. "Go ahead and make yourself comfortable while I take this call."

"Damn, Michael, it's after one in the morning. Who could be calling you at this time of morning?"

"I have no idea, but let me take this while you do you," I said and stepped out of the room.

"Hello," I said in an irritated tone, as if the person on the other end knew they were calling me at a bad time.

"Mike?"

"Yeah, who the hell is this calling me this fuckin' early in the morning?"

"Nigga, shut the fuck up and listen closely, my nigga. I know you had something to do with my niece and her crew of friends being killed. If you don't want me to go to them crackers, I suggest you listen to my demands."

"Hold on," I said. I could feel the wrinkles growing across my forehead and my temple began to bulge. "Who in the hell is this?" I screamed into the phone.

"Shut up and listen to what I have to say! Interrupt me one more time and I'ma send them crackers to your muthafuckin' doorstep to pick yo' black ass up!"

"Speak, nigga!"

"Alright, like I was saying before yo' black ass rudely interrupted me, I'ma need two hundred fifty thousand dollars by Monday morning. If I don't get it, I'ma let them bitches know who killed them folks at the paper mill."

Damn! I thought to myself, as I leaned up against the wall that aligned my hallway. It could only be one person with that kind of information —Bernard Fats Walker.

"So this is how you gonna play this, huh, Fats?"

"Yep, you leave me with no other choice, partner! When you fuckin' fired me, I lost everything I had, nigga—my house, my car, and my fuckin' ugly ass wife. So you either gonna break bread with me, or yo' cool ass is going to jail!"

"Okay, man, listen, it's gonna be hard for me to touch that kind of money that fast."

"I don't care how you get it. But you either get it or them folks gonna get you. I already contacted detective Protho and his crooked ass partner."

"C'mon, man, give me some time. I'll call you back tomorrow around noon to let you know when and where I can drop off the money."

"Listen, Mike, I ain't playin" with yo' punk ass. You got a few days to come up with my money so stop stalling and make it happen. Oh, and by the way, since you had my niece and her crew taken out, your black ass is going to pay for her funeral!" *Click!*

"Bernard, B! That black ass bitch hung the fuck up," I said to myself. I placed my phone back in my pocket. Where was I going to get that type of money from that fucking fast? And even if I could, I sure as hell wasn't going to give it to his black ass. There was only one other person who could help me besides Sexy Redd. But I had made a vow to never get the Valentino family involved in my personnel business. If I called my cousin Eric Valentino, he would most definitely want to know why I needed that type of money. And knowing him, he would want to go digging into my business and find out exactly what it was I was doing.

For a minute or two, I thought about asking him for the money. I had said to myself, that it was his brother Edward, who had actually introduced me to the stripping business in the first place. So maybe he would help me with my lil dilemma. I quickly shook the notion off and walked back inside of my room. Sharon was laying in my bed with no panties on, wearing one of my Jerseys. She tried to cover up her sensuous looking vagina. She stared at me as I made my way back through the door.

"Damn, Michael, the phone call took you so long I thought you had blacked out again."

"Funny, Sharon. Nah, that was one of my ex-employees talking about he needed to borrow some money."

She took a small sip of her orange juice and replied, "That sounds just like my Uncle Bernard."

"What? You have an uncle named Bernard?"

"Yeah, he was over at my aunt's house when we went over there earlier today. He claims he lost his job, so he has no money coming in. He wanted me to loan his fat, nasty ass some money."

I sat on the edge of my bed thinking to myself. *Damn, it looks like I'ma have to kill half of Sharon's family in order for me to go on with my life.* It was bad enough that lil ass Do-Dirty was her cousin, now I was finding out that Fats was her fucking uncle.

CHAPTER TWENTY-TWO
BABY DADDY

I was deep in thought when Sharon eased up behind me and placed her hands on my back. "Damn, Mike, what time are the girls coming with our food? I might be asleep by the time they get here."

"They should be here in a few minutes. It's late and they have a very big weekend ahead of them. They're going to need all the rest they can get, so I know they're not trying to stay out too late."

"I'm fuckin' starving. I hope the food ain't too cold by the time they get here."

I turned around to watch her ease back against the silk pillows on my bed. "If it is, boo, we do have a microwave downstairs," I replied sarcastically and smiled. She sucked her teeth as she continued to lay there in the Jersey and no panties.

I sat motionless, thinking to myself of how I couldn't believe Bernard was Sharon's fuckin' uncle and how he was trying to extort money from me. Now that I knew his ass was dead broke, I knew there was no way he would go to the police. Since I was his only meal ticket, he needed me to stay out of jail so he could eat. The only problem I had now was I didn't need him to fuck up what I had started, so his time on earth was about to be cut short.

All I had to do was make that dreaded phone call to my dear friend who specialized in the removal of people who got in the way. I had talked to my girl, Yani, a few weeks earlier about my situation. At the time, I hadn't realized I'd need her in town so soon to make someone disappear. Now that Sexy Redd was gone, she was the only person besides my brother who could do the job and get away with it. *Maybe it would be good if I had both of them in town to dispose of my problem,* I thought to myself. As I contemplated, I heard the alarm beeping alerting me that the girls had just walked back into the house.

"Michael! ... foods here," Mignon shouted upstairs. I turned around, looked back at my boo, and said, "You happy now? Let me go down stairs and get your food."

"Yeah, and make sure you hurry up," she replied with a smile covering her face, "your baby and I are starving."

"Whatever, girl, you not about to turn me into no house maid," I turned and told her right before I walked out of the room.

"Boy, hurry your ass up so I can eat and then give you some of this tight ass pussy," she uttered, while smiling at me.

Damn, I knew she'd been wanting to make love ever since we'd left the hospital, but there was only one problem. And the problem was: there was no way that I was about to have sex with her in the bed Sexy Redd and I had slept in. And besides, Sexy Redd hadn't been gone a good twenty-four hours yet. It was entirely too soon for that, and I couldn't disrespect my baby that fast.

So, as I walked down the stairs, I tried to think of a way I wouldn't have to give her what she wanted so early that midmorning. Just as I had got into the kitchen, Mignon hit me with, "Hey, Mike, the food for you and Sharon is right here."

"Thanks, Mignon, what took you guys so long?"

"Richard wanted to stop by his place and pick up some clothes." I quickly looked over to see Richard at the end of bar area. "Oh, Rich, my bad homie. Are you okay?"

"Yeah, Mike, I'm good, but I'm still trippin' about the death of my lil lady."

"I hear you, man, and it's fucked up that someone would take her out like that," I said, while putting Sharon's food together.

"I feel you. Don't get me wrong, Mike, she may have led a foul ass life but our kids are going to need their mother in their precious young ass lives."

"I agree with you wholeheartedly, cousin. Hell, I didn't even know you and her were in a relationship."

"Yeah, her two oldest daughters are mine. We broke up after she had my second child."

The girls sat around the countertop and listened to me and Richard's entire conversation. Minutes later, Sharon's hungry ass stomped down the stairs and found me sitting at the bar area talking to Richard.

"No wonder your big-headed ass ain't brought me my food yet. You down here running your damn mouth," she said, loudly grilling me in front of everyone. "I thought I told you me and your child was hungry!" Just as soon as she blurted the words out, Nicole spat out her drink. She quickly tried to wipe away the juice from around her mouth.

"Damn, Mike, you about to be a baby daddy?"

Michael Gallon

CHAPTER TWENTY-THREE
DICK OFF OF THE BONE

Sharon stood firm as she looked back over at Nicole and said, "Yes, girl, he is. His black ass put a bun in the oven."

"Damn, cuz, how many kids you got now?" Richard asked.

"Well, there is the baby girl, Aerial, in Lakeland, and my oldest daughter, Shakina, who lives in Haines City.

"Mike, I didn't know you had kids."

"Yeah, Nicole, I have some children too. Why? Is it a sin to have kids?" I asked a baffled looking Nicole.

"No, I'm just shocked to just now find out you have some."

"Hell, as whorish as his black ass is I'm surprised he ain't got a whole squad of kids," Sharon mumbled, as she turned to walk away.

"I'll see you guys in the morning. Let me get back up there with her cranky ass."

"Alright, Mike, I'll see you in the morning. Is it okay if I come with you all this weekend?"

"Sure thing, Richard, then you can get the feel for the job and meet some of the girls who'll be working with you."

"Sounds good, Mike," he said.

I turned back to the ladies. "And ladies, please make sure you guys get some rest. It's going to be a very long weekend."

"What time is the limo arriving?"

"The limo will be here around one, Mignon, so please be packed and ready. That goes for the rest of you ladies as well."

"Good night, daddy."

"Whatever, Nicole … goodnight to you also."

I left them downstairs eating and talking amongst one another, while I hurriedly got back to my room.

Upon entering my room, I found Sharon sitting on my bed busy eating her food like she hadn't eaten all day. I stood and stared at her for a minute or two. "Slow down, boo, you gonna choke."

"Shut up, Mike. When I told you I was hungry I wasn't lying. I haven't ate since earlier today."

"My bad, lil mama. Go ahead and do your thing."

She held her head up for a second as she replied, "If you not careful, I might just eat your food along with mine. Can I please have some more juice?"

"Yeah, I'll be right back." I quickly jumped out of bed and headed back downstairs to get her some juice.

"Come right back, Michael! I'm really thirsty."

"Girl, hush. I'll be right back," I yelled back.

On the way out the door, I caught my cousin Richard as he tiptoed into Strawberry's room.

Well, I guess his ass is alright since he was about to knock the bottom out of Strawberry. I hope he straps up 'cause I would hate for another one of my girls to turn another guy's private stock into bacon, I thought and laughed lightly. I got to the fridge and poured a glass of juice for Sharon. "Nah, I can't let her do my cousin like that," I mumbled. So before I went back to my room, I knocked on the door of Strawberry's room. Richard opened the door wearing nothing but a pair of white, Fruit of the Loom underwear. Strawberry on the other hand, was already bent over the bed with her pussy lips spread open for entrance.

"Damn cuz, you don't waste no time, do you?"

"Nah, cuz, this lil freak been beggin' for this dick ever since I got here," Richard replied, with a great big Kool-Aid smile covering his wide ass face.

"I see," I said, returning his smile, "well, take these two Magnum condoms—make sure you strap up."

Even though she was still bent over and ready to be fucked, Strawberry turned her big-headed ass around and said, "Damn, Mike, I want a baby from your fine ass cousin too!"

"Whatever, Strawberry," I sarcastically replied. I closed the door and went back toward my room.

Before I could turn the knob on my own room door, I heard Strawberry say to my cousin, "Damn, wait a minute before you put that condom on. Let me show you how I eat the dick off of the bone. …"

***

STRAWBERRY WAS A REAL FREAK. I walked back into my room and found Sharon with one of my pork chops hanging from her mouth. I stood in the doorway with the glass of orange juice and watched her devour the meat off my breakfast platter.

"I told you I was hungry. I should've ordered the pork chop breakfast too."

I was so in love with her and stricken by her beauty, I simply replied, "No problem, boo, go ahead and enjoy my breakfast for me. While you at it though, let me ask you something?"

"Go ahead, Mike, what is it now?" She never stopped chewing on the tender piece of swine as she looked up at me

"Have you ever heard someone say: "eat the dick off of the bone?"

She laughed and picked up the glass of juice. After washing down the pork chop, she slowly put the glass down and replied, "Mike, you so damn silly. No, I haven't heard that one before, why?"

"Well, that's what I just heard Strawberry tell my cousin."

"Well, I guess she's about to eat her some dick off of the bone. At least someone around this big ass house is getting some dick this morning," she uttered, while trying to hold back her girlish smile.

***

I TRIED TO EXPLAIN TO SHARON that I was tired from all of the excitement I'd endured throughout the day. As much as I would've loved to, I just wouldn't be able to perform to my fullest potential.

With her legs wide open, she revealed her shaven, soaking-wet pussy. "Shhh, no problem, Michael, let me get that dick hard and I'll do all the work."

All I could do was look at her with those pretty ass eyes of hers. "Damn, Sharon, you really want some dick? It's like, three-fifteen in the morning," I said. I tried to look tired.

She looked back at me and said, "Yep, that's the best time of the morning to get some hard ass dick."

Before I could put up an argument, she placed her soft lips around my erect manhood. She looked up at me with just the head of my penis dangling from her warm mouth. "See, Michael, I knew you already wanted me. Hell, John Boy is already hard as a rock." She started sucking on my manhood as if it was one of the pork chops she'd just eaten.

Minutes later, I was turning her ass around so I could place her in the sixty-nine position. After another ten minutes of slurping and sucking on one another, she rolled my chiseled frame over on my back and got on top of me. She slowly, and very gently, slid down the shaft of my hardened erection. Her face displayed a slight grimace of pain as if it was too much for her to handle.

I looked her directly in her eyes. "Alright now, if you can't handle it just get up and I'll get on top of you."

"No, it isn't that baby. I just want to make sure you don't cum before I do. I haven't had any of my dick in a very long time. So I'm gonna make sure I enjoy every minute of all mine," she said back to me. She took her time going up and down on my shaft.

Moments later, she was riding me like she was riding a wild stallion. We had to be making love for at least forty-five minutes before she finally fell off of me after having her fourth or fifth orgasm.

I looked over at her. "You okay?" I asked.

She just lay there, stretched out and trying to catch her breath. She wiped away the perspiration of the full-fledged workout she'd just put in. Sluggishly, she rolled over on her side and looked back at me.

"Yes, baby. I think I had five orgasms at once." Her breathing was hard and fast, as if she had just run ten, full-speed wind sprints.

I looked back at her and whispered, "Damn, already?"

"Yes," she answered seductively.

"Well, that's too bad, sweetheart," I replied with a devilish grin across my face.

With her head partially tilted to one side, and her eyebrows slightly raised, she looked up at me curiously. "Why?" she questioned.

"Because I ain't got mine yet." I smiled though I was serious. She tried to roll out of bed but I caught her by her arm. "Oh no, baby!"

"Oh yeah, baby," I countered, "you woke his ass up, so you gonna have to deal with him. Now turn that fat ass around so I can hit it from the back."

She looked back at me with that gorgeous frown on her face and said, "See, now you playing, Michael. While I was putting in all the work, your ass was just laying there holding back."

I was carefully turning her ass over as I looked at her and said, "No, I wasn't, I was enjoying every minute of your fine red ass. I can't help it if I don't cum as fast as you do."

"Whatever, Mr.-Take-So-Long-To-Cum. Yo' ass got five minutes up inside this good ass pussy, and if your ass ain't came by then, you just gonna have to cum when I get back."

"Say no more, baby."

"Alright, Michael, I'm serious."

"So you gonna time my nut but you can get as many as you want?"

"Yep," she replied, as she turned around and stared at me. I stood up to place my erect penis deep inside her wet ass pussy. As soon as I was balls-deep inside her, she reached for one of the silk pillows and began to scream into it.

"Oh shit, Michael. Wait a minute. You're too fuckin' deep inside me. I can feel your dick all up in my stomach. Baby wait, you gonna hit the baby in his head!"

I laughed out loud as she tried to laugh with me. At the same time, she threw her arm back and tried to keep me from pushing even deeper inside of her stomach. I quickly pushed her arm out of the way and continued long-stroking her fine ass.

"Girl, who in the hell told you some dumb ass shit like that?"

"My cousin, Loretta. She said that's why her baby's head is all knotted up!"

"Sharon, bend your fine ass over and take this dick," I said, as I continued pounding her ass.

She was still trying to talk and throw her arm in an attempt to make me to ease up. However, I wasn't having it since I was still trying to get that one nut off.

"Mike, you better not hit my baby in the head!"

"Fuck that, I'm about to show your ass who runs this mutha-fucka!" Two minutes later, I was cummin' all up inside of that tight ass pussy.

"Damn, that's it?" she said, as she slowly slid off of me.

"Yep. Why?"

"'Cause I thought you would be a little longer than that Mr.-All-Day-and-Night!" She lay across from me holding her legs trying to prevent them from shaking.

"Sorry to disappoint you," I replied, while trying to catch my breath.

"I can't believe you came that fast."

"Well, like they say: 'pregnant pussy is the best pussy to get'."

"Whatever, Michael. Go get us a bath cloth so you can clean us up."

"I'm tired, Sharon, you go get it."

Ten minutes later, she had wiped both of us off and was lying next to me fast asleep.

CHAPTER TWENTY-FOUR
MONEY AND GREED

Damn, I had just made love to someone else, right there in the bed Sexy Redd and I had shared. I didn't know if I should feel bad, or just shrug off the disrespect I'd displayed behind her back. I had a serious problem, and the problem was that I was deeply in love with two beautiful looking women at the same time. And to make matters even worse, they were both pregnant at the same time. The most important factor of the whole ordeal was that they looked as if they could be sisters. *Nah,* I thought, as I eased out of bed, *no way.*

I got up and sent a message to my dear friend, Yani. After texting her, I lay in bed and thought long and hard. ... *All the while I was thinking I was tired and sleepy from all the work I was putting in, but it wasn't the work at all. It was the fact that I was about to add two more kids to my resume of life. Two more kids that my two, beautiful daughters wouldn't know about until they read this portion of the book.*

The very next morning, I was up around eight thirty. I had to get my day started so I could be ahead of the game. Sharon woke up about thirty minutes after and looked like she'd been through hell and back.

"Michael, I can't believe you beat my cootie cat up like that earlier this morning."

"Sorry, bae, but you got what you asked for, remember?" I replied, as I continued fleetly moving about the room.

"Yes, I did. Don't worry though, I won't ever bother you again when you tell me you tired," she uttered, as she fell back onto my bed, with her arms loosely hanging off the side.

"Whatever," I replied. I walked toward the bathroom so I could take a quick morning shower.

"Bae, I have to be home before ten. My mom and aunt have to start getting things prepared so we can bury Do- Dirty," she voiced, as she screamed into my bathroom.

"Okay, do you want me to take you home so you can get your day started?" I shouted back from beyond the door.

"Yes. I would love to stay here and go on the road with you guys, but I know you be busy as hell when you with all those females. And besides, we're trying to have her funeral next Saturday, so that means I have to help with the preparations."

"Are you going to be okay?" I shouted.

"Yes!"

"Okay, if your family needs anything don't hesitate to ask," I yelled, as she walked her naked body into the shower with me. "Oh no you don't. Let me get out of here before you go through what you went through this morning," I said. I quickly flushed my eyes to rinse the soap out that had gotten in them.

"Thank you." She smiled shyly.

While Sharon showered, I dried off and got dressed in something casual. Once I had that done, I was off to my den to make a few important phone calls. The first person I dialed was my wild-and-crazy ass brother. We had different mothers but the same father due to a prior relationship our father had with his mother. Eventually, a few years later, our father married my mother, and the rest was history.

His phone rang one time before he answered. "What's up, Baby Boy?" He greeted me in his deep, heavy-baritone voice.

"Nothing that the Firstborn can't handle," I replied.

"Talk to me. What's on your mind this early Friday morning?"

"Hey, listen, you remember the lil situation you took care of a few days ago?"

"You talking about the fireworks right?"

"Yeah, the fireworks. Well, how about someone else needs to be set up for a party as well."

"So do they want to be the guest of honor or a participant?"

"He needs to be the guest of honor!"

"Damn, that serious, huh?"

"Yeah, man, my ex-security guard called me earlier this morning and demanded two hundred fifty thousand dollars in order to keep quiet about the firework display you put on for his thieving ass friends."

"No problem. Let me make some arrangements and I'll be in route shortly."

"Fine. I was thinking about having someone help assist you with the setup."

"Who did you have in mind, Baby Boy?"

"This lil female I know from Lil Haiti. She goes by the name of Yani."

"Sounds like a plan. Other than that, how is the family?" he asked, before hanging up.

"Dad is fine as usual. My dear mom is still set in her own lil way."

"What about Baby Girl?"

"Well, you know how Cynthia is. She's always going to be doing something for Cynthia."

"How about your side of the family? How is your fine ass sister, Sophia, doing?"

"Last time I spoke with her she was doing fine."

"Alright, give everyone my love and I shall see you soon. Love you, Firstborn."

"Love you too, Baby Boy."

When I hung up my phone, I placed my head down on the desk and thought to myself. *How did things get so far out of hand like this so soon.* And to think ... it was all because of money and greed.

Prestige Limo Service ...

I HAD JUST LAID BACK IN THE soft, black, leather seat inside of my den. I looked out of the window and wondered was this the life I wanted to be in, or was it fate. Then just like a bolt of lightning, the answer hit me dead in the center of my bewildered face. I hadn't chosen this life, this life had chosen me. I was locked into the occupation for the rest of my life, or until fate stepped in and stopped me.

No matter what I did or tried to do, I was never going to be able to get away from it. It was as if I was born to be the type of person I had turned into. As I continued to stare out of the window of my den, the thought of my life being inherited by my kids crossed my mind. I quickly shrugged the thought out of my head as I stood up and walked closer to the window.

"Only time would tell whether or not they grew up to be just like me," I said out loud.

Then, I heard her voice standing behind me. "What was that?" I quickly turned around to see.

"Sharon, girl you startled me, what were you doing standing behind me?"

"Nothing, crazy ass man. Now what were you just saying to yourself about your kids?"

"Nothing, just talking to myself," I said, as she stood with her hands around my waist.

"Alright, Mr., Yesterday you were blacking out and now you're talking to yourself. Are you sure you alright?" she asked.

"Listen, I'm okay. Who says a man can't talk to himself sometimes?" I asked. She acted as though my sheer presence made her the happiest girl in the world.

"Yeah, I guess they can, 'cause I've been standing here for five minutes listening to you think out loud."

"Okay, you should have said something. Now are you hungry?"

"A little bit. I was thinking we could pick up something on the way to my house."

"That's fine. Let me wrap up in here and I'll take you home."

She continued staring at me. "No problem, baby. I'll just stay in here with you, if you don't mind?"

"No problem, you. That's fine."

She searched the room with her eyes. "So this is where you handle all your important business, I see," she muttered.

"Yes, this is my office and also my quiet room where I come to get away from everyone else."

Minutes later, Richard walked into my den. "Good morning, Sharon," he spoke when he noticed Sharon and me talking.

"Good morning, Richard. What's up with you this beautiful Friday morning?" she asked, as she stood up to give him a hug.

"Nothing. This house is huge isn't it?" he asked, as he looked over at me. "Good morning to you as well, cousin."

"What's up, Rich?"

"Yes, it is. I was telling Michael that this morning when I walked in here for the very first time."

I looked back at my timid looking cousin and cut into his conversation with Sharon. "So Richard, how long have you known my lil boo thang here?"

"I think we met one day at one of their family cookouts about five years ago."

"Nah, Richard, we met that day you and Do-Dirty was arguing about her mom's light bill she wanted you to pay."

"Oh yeah! You absolutely right. I remember that day as if it was yesterday. We did meet that day because you butted in and said, 'Man if you puttin' that dick to my lil cousin, you should at least help with some of the damn bills.' That was probably like six years ago, because my oldest girl is six and a half right about now."

"Yep, that was me," Sharon said, as they continued their little family reunion. I walked by them and headed to the garage so I could warm up my car.

While inside of the garage, my pager went off. I hastily flipped it open to see that it was a message from Yani:

✆Michael, I received your message this morning. I jumped on the first flight to Orlando. I will be there by eleven thirty this morning. I look forward to seeing you again, and remember, no worries my friend.✆

Damn, Yani was good. I had to really move fast. I checked my watch and saw it was 10:10 a.m. I had to get Sharon home and then somehow have Yani picked up from the airport. I pulled out my cell phone and placed a call. I would've made it earlier that morning had I known she would be arriving that fast. The phone rang two times before the bright voice answered. "Good morning, Prestige Limo Service. How can I help you?"

"This is Michael Valentino. Is Preston available?"

"Hello, Mr. Valentino. Yes, one minute please."

Michael Gallon

CHAPTER TWENTY-FIVE
THE DISCUSSION

I had just got off the phone with the limo company. I was on my way upstairs to get Sharon, when I overheard her and Richard talking about Do-Dirty's death.

"You know Dirty used to work with Mike before she got fired," Richard said, as they were walking out of my den.

"Yeah I know, my aunt was telling my mom about that," Sharon replied.

"When we were at the Waffle House, the girls told me she got caught trying to steal Nicole's money bag one night after a show. That's what got her ass fired." Richard shook his head in dismay.

"Yep, sounds like Dirty. She was always trying to steal something."

"Yeah, but it seems like there could be more to the story though," Richard replied. He was still having his doubts about what had actually led to the death of his children's mother.

"Why do you say that, Richard?" Sharon asked with her arms folded across her stomach.

"Because, when I brought her name up, the girls started acting a bit skeptical as if they knew what really happened to her. Matter of fact, she had just told me she was about to hit a big lick, something about robbing some nigga in some nice ass subdivision."

"You don't say?" Sharon replied. Now she, too, seemed to have her doubts as to what had happened to her cousin, and who might've been behind the horrific ordeal.

"What?"

"Nothing, Richard I was just saying something under my breath. You don't think she was talking about hitting Mike and his girls, do you?"

"I have no idea. I would hope not. That would be so fucked up if my own cousin had something to do with the death of my kids' mother."

"It's probably nothing, Richard. Hell, Michael said he would even help pay for the burial if we needed any financial help. And the way things are looking, we're gonna need all the help we can get since her mother didn't have any life insurance on her lil grown ass," Sharon replied. She put her head down.

"Oh well, I guess you're right. Why would Mike do something like that in the first place, huh?"

Right. Because if I know Mike, and I do, if he knew anything about the murder he would've let the police know so they could find the people responsible for her death and the others she was with."

After hearing enough of Sharon and Richard trying to be homicide detectives, I loutishly walked around the corner and caught them both by surprise.

"Hey, you, are you ready?"

Sharon hesitated for a brief minute as Richard turned around with a shy hint of suspicion in his eyes. Sternly, I held my ground as I stood there looking back in his eyes. *If this nigga even think about asking me if I killed his peeps, I'ma push his ass down that staircase so damn fast, his neck gonna pop before he hit the first step!* I thought to myself.

The two of them looked at me as if I had caught them making out with one another.

Sharon spoke up first when she looked at me and answered, "Yes, boo." She turned to look back at Richard and uttered, "I'll talk at'cha later, Richard, enjoy your weekend, and make sure you keep Michael out of trouble."

"I will and thanks once again, Sharon. I'll see you when we get back in town. Please keep me posted on any news you find out in regard to Do-Dirty," Richard said, as I whisked her away. We were halfway down the stairs when I looked back up to see Richard watching us as we walked down the stairs together.

"Hey, Rich, make sure the girls get up in time so they can get their things together for the weekend. Some of the girls may need to be picked up before the limo gets here at one. If so, I'll call you to let you know."

"Alright, Mike, I'm right here waiting on you to get back."

By the time I reached the garage, Sharon was already inside the car looking as cute as ever. She was rocking a pair of Versace shades and listening to music and bobbing her head up and down, back and forth.

When I opened the door, she had my Boise system playing some Trick Daddy, the song was 10-20-Life. She turned to me with that pretty smile of hers. "Mike, please turn that shit up and let these rich white people out here hear how good that shit sounds"

"Damn, Sharon, what you know 'bout Trick Daddy?"

"Whatever, nigga, turn that shit up!" she said, as she turned to me and slid her shades down.

We struck out for her house and she continued to vibe and bob her head to the music. *Damn, she can be hood too, all while looking just as good as the next female,* I thought.

Now that Redd was gone, it was evident I was gonna make lil Ms. Sharon my priority. I must admit I was feeling some type of way while driving her back home that morning. I was bumping my head to the music as well, and I was feeling myself as I bent the curve heading out of MetroWest.

I had just got to the light to make a left when I looked up and into my rearview mirror and noticed someone following me out of the nice high-rise subdivision.

I somberly adjusted the mirror and mumbled to myself so Sharon wouldn't hear me, "Damn, where was Sexy Redd, when I needed her the most."

Michael Gallon

CHAPTER TWENTY-SIX
WHITE SMOKE

After I dropped Sharon back off at her house, I headed back home to get ready so me and the girls could hurry up and get out of town for the weekend. As I sat at the red light waiting for it to change to green, I looked down to check the time on my watch. Eleven fifteen. *Yani should be landing soon, I hope the limo got there on time because I would surely hate for her to have to sit around and wait on her ride.* I made a right turn and decided to take the long way home so I could shake whoever it was following me.

After a quick peek in my rearview, I no longer saw the white smoke from the car that had been following me earlier. So, I eased up a bit and relaxed as I pushed the pedal to the medal trying to get home. I had just got onto Highway 50 when my phone rang.

"Hello."

"Hey, Mike, this is Seneavu."

"I know, Seneavu, I do have caller I.D."

"My bad, Mike. Damn, you don't have to be such a smart ass."

"Sorry, it's just been a long morning. What's up wit' cha?"

"Is there enough room for me and two new girls this weekend?" she asked, as I pulled my phone down from my ear and stared at it. Then I shook my head from side to side, displaying the hell no sign.

"Nope, it's all full this weekend. You should've told me you wanted to go earlier and I would've made room for your ass," I replied. It was always like that with the girls in the group—there were some days they wanted to go to work, and then there were the days they didn't want to go.

Money and girls were coming in so fast, I couldn't even keep a roster of all the fine females I had in the group. By now, I had so many girls that when one girl didn't come to work, someone else was usually sitting in her place. Most of the time the girl who had missed a trip wouldn't get her spot back unless another chick decided she wanted to take an unexpected vacation. Females were actually fighting over a spot in whatever vehicle I had on the road that particular weekend. In other words, if you weren't with us, you would be home chilling—you *and* your broke ass boyfriend. What was even funnier was that the females who thought they'd made enough money earlier in the week, were usually the ones who stayed home, then by Saturday, they would be calling me.

The conversation would go something like this:

"Hey, Mike, where y'all at?"

I would always reply back with, *"Why?"*

Then whatever girl it was would say in her saddest baby voice, *"Because I really needed to make some money. Can I catch the Greyhound to where y'all at?"*

You know what I would say next? Yep, you guessed it.

"Nope! Your silly ass should've been ready when we left. I'm already packed with females."

The truth was there were always other females in the group who didn't want that particular female with us. Hell, it wasn't me. The more females I had with me out of town, the more money I could be making. I didn't care if they had to sit on top of one another to get there. My motto was: *the more girls, the more money!*

Years later, I would be driving up and down Florida highways with a car load of females. Usually, whenever I went to do a show, there would always be females there who had changed their confused minds by the time we got to our destination. Nowadays, I always made sure I had girls for backup. Sometimes, I would actually meet girls in whatever town we were in for that weekend, and they would wanna go so they could shake their ass for a lil cash.

***

BY THE TIME I'D GOT BACK HOME, Richard and the females at the house were getting themselves together so we could leave. It was around 12:15 p.m. when I walked in. I had just walked through the front door when my phone started ringing off the hook. I thought it might've been Yani calling to let me know she had landed, but just as I started to answer, I remembered I was supposed to call Fats. I answered and it was him on the line.

"Hello."

"Nigga, what's up? You forgot to call me."

"Man, I was just about to call you."

"Nigga, stop lying. You just dropped my fucking niece off at her house. So I see you been fuckin' both of my nieces and shit!"

"Nah, Fats," I replied. "I'm only fucking one of your nieces. My cousin Richard is the one fuckin' the other one," I slyly said, letting him know I was the muthafuckin' man in them streets.

"So I see you fuckin' niggas think y'all got it like that, huh? Well the price just went the fuck up!"

"C'mon, man, you fuckin' trippin'!"

"Five hundred thousand dollars, nigga."

"Fats, that's half a million dollars—who you think I am? Hugh fuckin' Heffner, nigga?"

"You might as well be, nigga. Yo' ass walking 'round your brand new crib with all them fine ass, butt-naked hoes and shit. You never even once asked me if I wanted to fuck of any of them bad ass bitches, with your cool muthafuckin' ass. But you didn't mind asking me to help you move that big ass fuckin' safe inside that fat ass crib of yours!"

Bingo, he had just said what I'd been waiting to hear from the start. He was the one behind them fools coming to my house that night trying to rob me and my girls for the loot. That's how he had put the idea together about me being the one who had disposed of them fools. I was furious as I stood there speaking with him on the phone.

"So this is what this shit is all about, nigga? Some butt-naked hoes and a few dollars?"

"Hell yeah, lil ass nigga. Have you ever seen my fuckin' wife? If you haven't, let me be the first to tell you she looks like a fuckin' pig in the face! You think I liked fuckin' her ugly, fat, nasty ass?"

"Damn, nigga, I never even knew yo' fat, ugly ass was married." *Who would want to marry your ass 'cause you not too handsome yourself,* I thought but didn't voice my opinion.

"That's because I got her pregnant right out of high school."

"Oh, I see. And now you want me to pay for your mistakes."

"Nigga, you paying me for causing me so much stress and strife after you fired me the first night yo' ass did a show. And then you let them hoes walk right by me butt-ass naked and you wouldn't even let me lick one of them hoes ass, or even suck on one of their long ass clits I know them fine ass bitches got."

I had to admit, Fats wasn't too nice on the eyes but I never knew he was fucked up like that over my females. I could tell he wanted one of the females more than he actually wanted the money.

"Okay, listen Fats … I got a bad ass female coming in from Miami later today. She's a light skin, lil Haitian chick. Let me tell her about yo' ass and we'll go from there." I could hear that fat ass nigga breathing hard through the phone.

"M-Mike, sh-she fine, dawg?" he stuttered out.

"B, she's fine as hell."

"You think she'll let me fuck her in the ass while she stand up on her tippy toes?"

"Damn, sick ass nigga! Now you wanna fuck bitches all in their ass and shit while they on their tippy toes?"

"Hell yeah, that's the shit, nigga."

"Yeah, you right," I replied shaking my head, "that's how you get the *shit* on your dick, dumb ass, nigga."

"Man, fuck that. How she look?"

"She's about five-nine and weighs around a hundred and forty five pounds, and she got hazel-brown eyes."

"Man, stop playing. If her ass looked that damn good, yo' ass would be fuckin' her! I know how your cool ass work. You must'a forgot, nigga. I used to work for you."

"Listen, man, she's bad as hell, and she look a lot like Jada Pinkett."

"You talking about the chick in that movie Set It Off?"

"Yep, she looks just like her."

"Man, I got to have her and that cash."

"Damn, man, you not gonna give me a pass since I'ma hook your fat ass up with her?"

"Hell nah, nigga! I'll take her and the cash. Hell, I'ma need some money to trick with, my nigga."

As I continued listening to Fats' stupid ass, I heard Triston, the limo driver, pulling up in the driveway. When I heard the limo door slam followed by the sound of two voices, I realized it was Yani and the driver. As the two approached the door, I eased the phone down and slid to the door. I opened it and couldn't believe my eyes. Yani, a sleek, five foot nine, light-skin goddess, stood in the doorway looking as beautiful as ever.

"Bonjour, Michael," she said in her Haitian accent, which sounded like 'Bon-shore, Mee-kul'.

"Well hello, Yani, you look as beautiful as ever." While I complimented her, I could hear Fats breathing even harder in the background.

"Mike, is that her dawg?"

"Yeah, Fats—hold on for a minute while I escort her in the house."

"You ain't even gotta take her in your house, dawg," he said, "I'm already outside watching her fine ass. I'm at your fuckin' crib."

"Nigga, say what?"

"Man, I'm outside. I been the following your ass all morning. I know you seen the white smoke coming from the tailpipe of my raggedy ass Granada."

Here I was thinking it might've been those two crooked ass cops following me and come to find out it was his fat, nasty black ass.

"So, you've been the muthafucka following me all morning?" I asked him with a unit covering my face.

"Hell yeah, how you think I knew you had just took my niece home? See, nigga, you my meal ticket out of here, so do you think I'ma let something happen to my investment plan? Shit, the loot I'm 'bout to get from your cool wannabe ass gonna allow me to retire and move to Miami. I'ma live out the rest of my natural born life in paradise."

Yani was still looking around my home when I placed my hand over the phone and whispered to her, "This is the mark on the phone with me now." She immediately grabbed the phone out of my hand.

As if we'd rehearsed it, she started talking to his ass all sexy and nasty just like his perverted ass liked it. She began to tell him how she wanted to see him and how she wanted him to suck out of her ass and lick her pussy. Then she told him she was going to suck his dick and massage his balls at the same time. But the worst part of her diabolical plan was when she told his black ass she was going to roll his big nasty ass over and suck out of *his* ass. I almost threw up my breakfast, as I listened to all the nasty, disgusting things she pretended she was going to do to him.

Like I said, Bernard Fats Walker wasn't that nice on the eyes. He stood around six foot even and weighed somewhere in the neighborhood of two hundred eighty pounds. His skin was the color of the actor's, Wesley Snipes— in other words, he was a very dark skin brother. Even worse, he had the nerve to adorn three gold teeth inside his mouth, and the rest were somewhere other than his mouth because they were missing in action. His thick, crusted, black-and-pink lips were always chapped due to him smoking crack ever since the tender age of nine. He'd had a very painful childhood, as he told me during his interview for the job of being my security guard.

Unfortunately, he had watched his father take a bullet to the back for trying to steal two live chickens out of Miss Ethel Williams' yard on the fourth of July. He went on to inform me that he'd grown up hating the July holiday. His father had died on that very same day because he'd been trying to steal the damn chickens so he could barbecue for the fourth.

It was a very sad story considering that while his father lay bleeding from his back, his food stamp card slid out of his back pocket. When I asked him why his father didn't just go to the store and buy the chickens, he looked at me with those crusted ass black-and-pink lips of his and uttered, "I don't know, he died before I could ask him." Like I said, the brother had a very distasteful upbringing.

He then went on to say that his mother dropped him and his brothers off at her sister's house one day and told them she was going Christmas shopping. The only thing wrong with that was the fact that it was the month of January when she dropped them off. Now, some thirty-two years later, and she still hadn't returned, so he hated that day as well. When I asked him what happened to his brothers, he stated that they were so bad, one hot sunny day they ran away from his aunt's house and she never even reported them missing.

Years later, he found out they were living a few houses down the road. He claimed his brothers said they went there because the people had a lot of food and cable television. *Wow!*

Some would even go as far to say, he was so hard on the natural eye, if you saw him walking toward you in a very dark alley, you would actually turn around and swiftly walk in the opposite direction of the huge man.

But for the strangest reason, he always felt as though he had what all the women in Orlando, Florida, wanted. Whatever that was, only heaven knows. Not to mention, the constant smell of sour milk that resonated around his massive body frame, which I really believe came from him not fully washing his big nasty ass.

I was trying very hard to keep myself from laughing as I stood there listening to Yani and Fats on my phone. Then Nicole came from down stairs and saw Yani with Triston.

She quickly yelled to me when she got to the last stair, "So Mike, who is the new chick? She's sexy as fuck!"

"Nicole, chill, baby girl, she's here to handle some important business. Are you guys ready and packed?"

"So she's not dancing with us?"

"Nah, not this weekend, beautiful."

"Okay, well to answer your question, yes I'm packed. Now the rest of them hoes say they'll be ready in about ten minutes or less."

"Fine. Have Triston grab all the bags and load them inside the limo."

"Yes, sir, boss. Will do."

"Nicole, I'm not your boss. We all work together!"

"Whatever, Mike, you give the orders around here, so that makes you the boss. And please don't forget you still owe me for that favor the other night," she said, while turning around so I could see her fat red ass.

Michael Gallon

CHAPTER TWENTY-SEVEN
TAKE-OUT

Nicole had just made it to the front door of the house when I asked, "How much is it going to cost me?" My lips curled into a crooked smile.

She turned around with a mischievous smile of her own and countered. "It's not going to cost you anything. Just know, I'm sleeping in your room this weekend when we get to Jacksonville. That dick of yours belongs to me!"

I smiled and replied, "Girl, you're a trip."

"I'm going to show you how much of a *trip* I am once I eat that dick off of the bone." *There goes that phrase again.*

"Hey, what does that mean anyway? I heard Strawberry say that to my cousin earlier this morning." Before she could answer, Richard came from around the corner of the living room grabbing and pulling at his dick.

"Maaaan, that Strawberry really knows how to eat the dick off of the bone!" His eyes were about to pop out of his head as he stood there describing how well her head game was. *I hope your cool ass used a condom, or your ass might be around here talking about your dick look likes bacon too!* I thought to myself, as I laughed and ran up to my room to get my bags.

Minutes later, Yani came into my room with my phone in her outstretched hand. She couldn't help but look at me with those pretty hazel-brown eyes of hers.

"Here you go, Mike. That fool is already downstairs talking about he wants to chill with me for the rest of the day."

"Damn, girl, I thought you would at least get a chance to chill here at the crib before you had to put in work on that fat ass nigga!"

"Yeah, I hear you, but 'da quicker I put his fat ass to sleep, da quicker I can be back home to look after me very sick muda," she replied as she stood there in my doorway looking nice as ever.

"So what about my brother because he was going to help you with the disposal of his ass?"

"Dat's fine. Give he me number and I can have him to meet me at da hotel."

"Cool, he should be on his way down here from Madison, Florida. I'll call him from the limo and give him your number."

"Fine," she said. As she turned to walk out of my room, I stopped her in mid-stride and asked, "So how long you think it's going to take for you all to have him out of the way?"

"Dat depends on how fast you can fill me in on a few dings and den let me get out of here. Me still want to get to de hotel so me can change me wig and clothes. I hab to make sure know one remembers seeing me ass in town, me bruda."

By the time I had finished giving her the lowdown on Fats, everyone was standing down stairs in the living room—even Fats' ugly black ass.

While walking downstairs with Yani closely by my side, I happened to glance over at Fats and sputtered, "Well, how are you doing, Bernard?"

He looked up at me standing on the staircase and replied, "I'm doing fine, Mike. I ain't been up in this big ass house since the day I helped you install that big ass safe you got up in here."

He stood in my foyer looking around as if he was scoping out my house. Me on the other hand, wanted to take him out right there in the center of my foyer. But I knew it wasn't the right place nor time, nor was I the right man to do that to another person—even if his ass *was* trying to extort me for half a million dollars I *didn't* have.

"Yeah, hell yeah! I like this big muthafucka. When this lil ass nigga pay me my fuckin' money, I might just buy me two of these big ass houses," he blurted out, loud enough for everyone to hear him.

An obscured looking Richard looked over at me and asked, "What money? And what the hell is he talking about a safe for cousin?"

"Nothing, Richard. I meant the safe your cousin got up in here!" Fats replied, before I could answer his question.

"*Safe?* What you got a safe up in this muthafucker for, cuz?" Richard asked me. I didn't know what to say since I still didn't want him to put two and two together and conclude that maybe I was the one Do-Dirty had been talking about robbing.

"Yeah, Rich, I got a safe in here somewhere."

"Man, dawg, yo' cousin know exactly where his fuckin' safe at. I don't know why he tryna act like he don't know what the fuck I'm talkin' 'bout," Bernard grumbled. Yani saw that I was about to go off on his fat ass and decided to step in and defuse what was about to blow up.

"Bernard, bring your fat sexy black ass so I can put me mouth on dem little ass nuts of yours."

"Damn, B, yo' balls little and shit?" I joked, and caused everyone in the room to burst out into laughter.

"When yo' black ass get back in town, they gonna be just as big as yours," he grimaced, "and we'll see who gonna be laughing then, pretty ass nigga," Bernard replied. I stared at him and noticed how the pink on his lips began to crack, and tried to contain my laughter. *I guess he didn't find my question funny*, I thought.

He slid his right hand inside the pocket of his high-water pants—which were obviously too tight for his ass—they were squeezing his nuts so tight, you could see the print of his nuts from the back. After struggling to get his hand in his pocket, he pulled out a tube of Chapstick. He slowly rubbed it along the huge things on his face that he called lips, and smiled at me.

"What-the-fuck-ever! Yani take care of his ass, I'm gone!"

"So you not coming with us?" Strawberry asked Yani, as we headed out the front door.

"No, I'm not going to be able to make it wit' you guys dis time, maybe another time," she replied. The way her words rolled off her tongue made her native accent even sexier. I kindly took out a wad of bills that were nestled inside my money clip. I slid out four crisp hundred dollar bills and placed them in her small hand.

"Here, pay for the room, and grab you something to eat."

She placed her arms around my neck and whispered into my ear. "Your problem will be handled before da end of de night. As soon as yo' bruda get here, we will take he fat nasty ass out!"

***

I COULD SMELL THE NICE AROMA of the Red Essence perfume that lingered from her body as we embraced.

"Excuse me, playa, don't you have to be going so you can make my money?" Fats rudely cut in. I slowly pulled away from Yani. Staring at this heavenly creature sent from above, I didn't want to let her go and felt as if I had been momentarily lost in another world.

"Hey thanks, Yani. I'll talk with you later." She looked back at me with that lovely smile of hers.

"Be good, my bruda, and yes, we will talk soon!"

I walked up to the limo where Triston stood near the rear passenger door waiting for me. He was dressed just like one of those high-priced chauffeurs you only see in the movies or driving for someone with a lot of money.

"Are we ready, sir?" he asked with a genuine smile adorned across his masculine face.

"Yes, my good man. The first stop will be at some apartments located over in Eatonville."

"Yes sir, right away sir," he said, as he briskly closed the door and walked around to the driver side of the limo.

Just as soon as my ass hit the soft, plush-leather seat, Nicole slid her tender-to-the-touch ass all up under me. She grabbed me by the arm and interlocked her arm with mines. Once she felt like she had me all to herself, she looked over into my eyes and smiled.

"Like I told your ass earlier, Mr.," she mumbled, "your ass belongs to me all weekend."

"Alright, we'll see," I replied. I cut an evil grin back at her.

She made herself comfortable. "I'm not playing with your ass, Michael Valentino," she replied.

As the driver drove away, I looked out of the window and saw Yani and Bernard getting inside of his beat-up '82 blue-and-silver Granada with the white rag top. The car was so old, the tailpipe rattled and emitted white and black smoke as he bent the curve and headed out of the MetroWest area. I had forgot to tell Yani the windows on his car didn't roll down and he didn't have any air in his whip. I observed her facial expression as we passed right by them headed to Eatonville. She looked mad as hell and beads of sweat rained down her gorgeous face. Bernard turned off while the limo continued straight. Once out of range, I texted my brother the info Yani had told me to give to him.

Minutes later, he was texted me back:

℗Perfect, I'm outside of Ocala right now. Be safe and I'll talk with you later.℗

Michael Gallon

CHAPTER TWENTY-EIGHT
GREYHOUND BUS STATION

We picked up the last female and were just about to merge onto I-4 headed toward Daytona Beach, Florida. As the limo found its way into the right lane, you could feel the acceleration of the nice, plush automobile. I had just leaned back and got myself comfortable. I sensed a few eyes fixated on me, seemingly because Nicole was holding on to me so tightly.

"Mike, where in the hell is Sexy Redd?" Ms. JK asked. Everyone stopped talking and waited anxiously for my reply. Me, always being the cool one and never being put under pressure, calmly cleared my throat.

"She had to go back home for an emergency," I told her honestly. "She said it had something to do with her family, but hopefully, she'll be back soon," I added.

"The way she was talking yesterday at the meeting, I would've thought you and her were leaving together," Tiny voiced.

Again, JK just had to open her mouth and respond. "Girl, y'all must be crazy if y'all think Mike gonna stop doing shows. Don't y'all get it by now? He would replace one of us with a new chick and keep right on moving before he would even think about stopping the Florida Hot Girls from dancing."

"Damn, Mike ... so you would just replace us like that?"

"No, Charlie B. I would at least ask you why you didn't want to work the particular show you're missing before I replace you. You all are the ones who control your destiny and fate in the group. Now relax and enjoy the ride. And please, ladies, no more questions about my precious Sexy Redd not being here amongst us, or when she's coming back."

With that being said, silence filled the air and everyone focused on the upcoming show. It wasn't long before everyone laid back and dozed off to sleep.

Relaxed and made for comfort, the luxurious, white-stretch limo floated past the Sanford exit and headed to Daytona, and from there Jacksonville, Florida.

***

A FEW HOURS LATER, we arrived in Jacksonville and cruised a route to the Golf Fair Flea Market. The girls wanted to do some last minute shopping and also let the guys know what club they would be performing at for the weekend.

After they had been spotted in Frank's club, I had been approached by several club owners in the area who wanted my ladies at their club. There was one specific club that stuck out from the rest, so I'd decided to take my ladies there—the infamous Black Magic Club located off of Beaver Street.

After we finished shopping, we grabbed a bite to eat and headed to the hotel. The ladies decided to pair up so there would be two ladies to a room. Almost as soon as their heads hit their pillows, they were fast asleep, getting the needed rest for the weekend.

Now, me, on the other hand, I had other plans up my sleeve. I got myself situated in my room, made my way back outside to the limo, and headed downtown to the Greyhound Bus Station.

The limo drove up just in time to see her bus arriving—she was actually the third person to get off the bus. She seemed to glide down the steps of the bus and she was still as fine as had been the first time I'd met her. She casually slid her Channel shades down the bridge of her cute nose, and when she looked up, she spotted me standing by the limo with open arms. Her name was Diva, a cutie I'd met a while back in Gainesville. Her name said it all becauseDiva that's exactly what she was: a beautiful caramel-skin complexioned Diva.

Diva stood around five foot seven weighing around a hundred and thirty five pounds with a nice soft tender, soft ass. Along with her gorgeous body was her adorable country smile that would cause any man to melt upon laying eyes on her and those heavenly brown eyes of hers.

***

I HAD MET DIVI WHILE RIDING through some apartments in Gainesville, Florida known as Village Green. The girls and I were out doing some recruiting the day I spotted her walking through the complex working out. At first, she told me her boyfriend, Jerome Cleophus Lundy, wouldn't approve of her dancing, so I respected that but still gave her my number, and I left it at that.

Of course, everyone knows how guys can be. So, one day, when she'd gotten home early from work, she witnessed an awful surprise when she caught Jerome, her estranged boyfriend of two months, in bed with her niece. *Dirty Muthafucka.* When it happened, she'd told me that he tried to blame it on the alcohol since he'd been drinking all morning. So his excuse was that he was drunk and didn't know how he'd ended up in her bed, with another woman, butt-ass naked. Strange thing about it was, when she found him, there were no signs of alcohol anywhere in the house and he was wide awake. After she put his black-as-night having ass out of her apartment, she didn't hesitate to phone me and let me know she was ready for a new career. The rest is history.

I greeted her after she'd walked up to me with her bags in her hand. "Hello, beautiful."

"Hello to you as well, Mr. Michael."

"It's nice to finally get to see you."

"Same here, Michael. I've been thinking about you since the day we met. By the way, thanks for paying for my ticket," she said sincerely. "I'll pay you back right after I make some money tonight!"

"Hey, listen, you don't owe me anything. It's the least I could do since it was all last minute," I said. We climbed back in the limo and the driver hopped on I-95 and headed back to the hotel off Baymeadows.

During the ride back, Diva and I chopped it up a bit before we got to the room. Just hearing the way she talked, I could tell she was a real down to earth young lady. Country as hell, but what the heck? I was country too. The only difference between her and I was that I was raised in the city so I had lost all my country ways when I adapted to city life.

Michael Gallon

I wonder how good her sex game is and if she knows how to eat the dick off of the bone ... I thought as I allowed my eyes to roam her body.

Little did I know, Diva had some questions of her own about me wandering around in her head. *I sure hope this sexy, fine, black ass brother knows how to put it down in the bedroom. The way that bulge is sticking out of his pants, it looks like I'm gonna have a mouthful to deal with* ... she thought to herself. She smiled at me all the way back to the hotel room.

When we got back to the lavish and luxurious living quarters, Ms. Diva took control of the situation at hand. Slowly, she undressed by removing one item at a time. When she finally got to her thong, I was ready and waiting to dig off inside of her. Even though she'd given birth to two children, you couldn't tell judging by her firm, flat abs. Her ass was wide and round, and her breasts were a plump 34B. I was mystified, maybe even shocked to see how nice she looked naked. It only took me a minute or two and before I knew it, she had my erect manhood in her mouth, and worked her jaws like she was eating smoked turkey necks. I had to stop her before I nutted all up in her mouth. I must admit, the chick really had some skillful techniques. She massaged my balls while her neck simultaneously bobbed back and forth as if she was a chicken at feeding time.

While doing the chicken on my manhood, she played with her clit at the same time. I reached for her head while looking directly in her brown eyes.

"Stop, I'm about to cum," I said, halting her, "just let me have some of that soaking wet pussy of yours," I told her.

She paused and eased her gorgeous body across the bed ever so gently and easily. I began sucking on her perky titties, and then worked my way down to her wet pussy. Seconds later, I pulled her clit into my mouth and sucked on it as if it was a piece of hickory smoked bacon.

"Michael, Michael, Michael!" she called out, while running her hands through my hair.

I stood up and gazed intensely in her eyes. Holding the base of my penis in my hand, I whispered, "I'm about to fuck the shit out of your ass."

***

I SLOWLY EASED UP INSIDE OF HER and she grabbed my ass cheeks with force. Then, as if she were in a tug-of-war, she pulled me deep inside of her vagina walls. *Damn, I sure hope she don't want it rough and shit. The last time I had a female who wanted rough sex, I ended up breaking my dick, and I ain't about to go through that painful ordeal again,* I thought, as I continued to beat her walls. So instead of me doing the rough stuff, I started long-dickin' her ass— like a surgeon, I strategically pulled my manhood until just the head of my shaft was inside her, then I slowly pushed it back deep inside of her. She gasped for air as if she couldn't breathe. I could see the emotion and tension building up in her.

"Are you alright?"

"Yeah, just keep going," she panted out, like a dog in heat. "I ain't never had a man long dick me before." She continued to breathe hard and acted as if she was about to have a stroke.

While still putting her through the festivities, I had to turn my head to the side so she wouldn't see me laughing at the expression on her face. I was pounding the shit out of her fine country ass. I believed I had pushed so hard and deep inside of her, she actually farted. I didn't know if it was her pussy or her ass.

She quickly turned her head to the side of me and whispered into my ear, "Oh, I'm so sorry. Please excuse me, Michael."

Her passing gas caused me to remember something my uncle had told me about a time my dad was making love to a woman. It seems as though my dad had just come home from the Army and he was out with one of his female friends. Apparently, they were in the middle of having sex when she farted. *She looked over at my dad and uttered, "Excuse me, Buck, I'm sorry."*

My dad in return replied, "Nah, that's my fault. I was supposed to make you shit!"

Diva"Michael, have you busted yet?" poor ole Diva whispered in my ear, as I continued to drill her.

"Nah, not yet. I'm about to get there right about now."

Man, I bust a nut so damn hard, I caught a cramp in my back that went directly down to my leg. I was so fucked up, I started rolling around on the floor. She stood over me butt ass naked with semen streaming down her caramel-colored legs.

"What's wrong?" she asked me in a panic, "are you having a seizure or something?" Due to the pain of the cramp, I couldn't answer her right away. I guess it scared her because she yelled out, "Oh lord, please don't let this man die on me before I can make me some money. I have to pay rent when I get back home."

I finally rolled over and frantically yelled in pain. "Get me a hot rag out of the bathroom. I seem to have caught a cramp in my leg!" She hurried away, and within seconds she was back with the hot rag as if it was going to save my life. The pain subsided minutes later. It was a technique my dear dad had taught me when I played high school football.

"Are you okay, Michael?" she asked, as I made an attempt to sit on the edge of the bed.

"Yes, thank you for being so fast on your feet," I looked up into her face and replied.

"I had to be. I didn't know what was going on with you. And besides, how would I pay my rent if you had died on me?" We laughed as she helped me up.

"There was nothing to worry about, sweetheart. I wasn't about to die," I said to her. I glared at how fine she looked butt ass naked.

"Thank goodness," she replied. We walked into the bathroom to take a shower together.

***

WE STOOD IN THE SHOWER and let the pulsating water beat against our heated bodies. She looked at me with those cute, brown eyes of hers and asked, "Do you mind washing my back?"

I simply smiled back at her and uttered, "Not at all, beautiful. Turn around." She turned her elegant body around. I gently placed a hot, soapy rag up against her back and began washing her back in circular motion, as if she was a newborn baby.

"Okay, now you turn around so I can wash yours," she said softly.

"Yes, ma'am, right away, ma'am," I replied. I turned around and placed my hands against the tile of the shower and waited for her to place the rag against my skin.

We must have been in the shower for about twenty minutes before I stepped out and watched her lather her body all over again.

"I'll be out in a few," she yelled, as I dried off and walked back to the bedroom.

"No problem, baby girl, take your time," I replied, just as I had ventured back into the bedroom.

As soon as I sat on the bed and reached for my deodorant, my door began to rattle. Someone was on the other side knocking really hard. Diva was still in the shower so I closed the bathroom door and looked out the peephole to see who it could be.

"Hell, I know I ain't order no room service," I said to myself, as I looked through the tiny hole. I wasn't the least bit surprised when I realized it was Nicole's fine, fast ass. I quickly snatched the door open and wrapped my towel around me. "What's up? What you want? I asked.

She slid the strawberry-flavored lollipop out of her mouth and looked at me. "Your black ass know what I want, and what I want is wrapped up and hiding behind that damn towel you got on," she replied. Slowly, she looked me up in down. "You must have thought I was playing with you when I told you I wanted to be rewarded for what I did for your ass the other night," she snapped, as she did the ghetto-girl neck roll.

"Damn, Nicole." I scratched my head, somewhat annoyed. "I'm kinda in the middle of something," I told her, while trying to keep her from finding out I already had company.

She reached for the doorknob and pushed the door open wide. Now, she was standing directly in my room looking at me perpendicularly and then in my eyes.

"Michael, I don't know who you think you fooling. You know damn well you want some more of this good ass pussy and tight ass." Just as soon as the words left her mouth, Diva walked out of the bathroom and she also had a towel wrapped around her naked body. Nicole's mouth fell wide open and she looked as if she'd seen a ghost.

Diva looked at us with a shitty ass grin over her face and said, "Oh, I'm sorry. I didn't know we had company, Michael."

Nicole looked back at Divaher and then gave me the same nasty ass look minus the grin. "Oh, no worries, I was just leaving. I just wanted to see what time we were leaving for the club tonight." She turned her nose up at me and hastily walked out of the room.

"I hope she ain't mad at you, Michael," Diva mumbled, as she walked over to the vanity mirror.

"Only dogs and wild animals get mad," I replied.

"What was that, bae?"

"Nah, she ain't mad, she is about to get even."

***

ON THE WAY TO THE CLUB THAT NIGHT, the ride was somewhat quiet and smooth. Some of the ladies were a bit surprised when they saw Diva sitting up under me as if she was the new chick in my life.

The ladies hadn't seen me with any other female since Sexy Redd had been by my side. But now that Diva was sitting in her place, their facial expressions reflected their jealousy. The tension in the atmosphere was as thick as the London Fog.

"So, is this one of the new managers for the group, Mike?" Lil Kitty opened her small ass mouth and asked.

All eyes immediately focused on me as I sat there thinking of what to say. You know me, so I sat there for a brief minute and looked back at her thin ass with a smile on my face. "Did anyone say she was the new manager, Lil Kitty?" I answered her in a sarcastic tone.

"No, but you know how you do things around here," she debated, "one minute we have this girl for a manager and the next minute we got that one," she added. A smile spread over her small ass face.

"Whatever, Lil Kitty," I replied and waved her off with my hand.

Diva just sat there patiently waiting to say something on her own behalf.

"Excuse me, it's Lil Kitty right?" Lil Kitty turned her attention to Diva, and then she looked around at the girls. "Oh, I see you can talk!" Now all the attention focused on Diva as the other ladies waited for her comeback.

"There's no need to get your little panties in a rut, lil one," Diva said in a tone that matched Lil' Kitty's. She slid up in the seat and added, "I'm only here to make my money and get back home to my kids."

The girls centered their attention back on the smallest female in the group, Lil Kitty. She looked back at them and then stared at me.

"Ump, I see you got yourself a spunky one, Mr. Mike."

"Lil Kitty, please. Not tonight and not right now. Let's just focus on what we all came here to do tonight, please," I answered.

"Yeah, Lil Kitty, just let Mike enjoy his new plaything for right now," Nicole cut in. She sat at the end of the seat next to the rear passenger door with her nose turned up at me.

"Damn, I see Lil Kitty ain't the only one upset by her presence here tonight!" Tiny laughed.

"Mind your business, Tiny 'cause you don't wanna fuck with me tonight."

"My bad, Nicole. I just see how her being here got you all upset. Matter of fact, since you found out she was here you ain't said nothing all day!"

"Whatever, Tiny, just leave it alone," Nicole uttered.

Richard, who'd been sitting up near the front of the limo, looked at me and said, "Damn cuz, I didn't even realize we had another chick riding with us. When did she get here, Mike?"

"The first rule in this ever-growing business, Richard, is to always be mindful of your surroundings. When you guys were all chilling back at your rooms earlier today, me and the limo driver took off for the Greyhound Bus Station. Now, can everyone welcome the new female to the group? Florida Hot Girls, meet Ms. Diva. Ms. Diva, meet the world-famous Florida Hot Girls."

CHAPTER TWENTY-NINE
MALIK

Black Magic was a small lowkey hole-in-the-wall type of club. It was located off of Beaver Street, right down the road from another strip club known as The Silver Fox. My females had attempted to dance at the Fox a few times, but the club rules were too strict for my ladies to adhere to. So after a few times there, they decided they'd rather not dance there any longer.

Truth be told, I believe my girls just didn't like the competition they had to contend with at the Fox. You see, The Fox wasn't called *The Fox* for just any type of wild animal. The Fox was called *The Fox* for all the fine ass women they had inside the establishment. When I tell you they had some fire ass females all up and around in there, believe me, they did!

The ladies inside The Fox had to be the finest females Duval County, and any other surrounding county, had to offer—every female in that club had to be a ten or better. Not one of the Florida Hot Girls could compete with the females who danced at The Silver Fox during my tenure as the owner of the world famous Florida Hot Girls while living in Orlando, Florida.

Now, Sexy Redd, Mignon, Nicole and a few of the other females I would meet later on down the road could compete, but as far as the rest, my answer would always be, "Naaaaaaaaaaah."

The night I happened to step off inside The Fox, I didn't see one ugly chick in the building. Every female I saw in there had a banging body and was as attractive as can be.

Now, Black Magic on the other hand, had some nice girls inside of their lowkey establishment as well. However, those girls were your average, local, around-the-way type of females. They weren't bad looking or nothing like that. It's just that you could tell those girls weren't trying to further their dancing skills or careers anywhere besides Black Magic. The girls were cute, nice looking women who knew how to get their money and then get the hell out of dodge. The owner was this lil slim, very dark skin brother who went by the name of Malik.

Malik stood around the same height as me. He was five foot ten, and probably weighed around one hundred sixty-five pounds. He ran a very strict club when it came to the girls who worked in his company, especially when it was time to pay him what you owed him. It was as if he ran his club like a very well-oiled machine. Every one of his immediate associates controlled a different part of the small business while he sat back and reaped the benefits of his small empire.

For example, the guy who ran the door also sold anything you could put your mouth around and smoke. Him and my girl Chazz would become very close friends after that first night of the girls dancing there. Another guy who worked at the bar, also lived in the club after the club closed. I would find out later that a lot of the clubs in Duval county were set up like that.

Malik's third associate worked the floor area, meaning he watched and maintained the cash flow the girls made. Then there was this other guy who was the quiet, laid-back type; he would sign the girls in so he could keep track of how many females had to pay a tip-out fee at the end of the night. Malik would eventually send his ass off to school to become a Bails Bondsman and name the bond service "Black Magic Bails Bonds".

Like I said, Malik was a smooth ass brother who had his shit together. Last but not least, was this big ass guy who stood at the door of the club's VIP rooms. He made sure anyone who went through the door, paid the small fee required to get back their alone with one of his fine females. He enforced the rules to a tee. If you were one of them slow, hard-headed niggas who couldn't comprehend the rules, he didn't have a problem beating them into you until your head popped off. Basically, all Malik did was sit back and collect money from every associate working for him.

***

FRIDAY NIGHTS WERE USUALLY good nights inside club Black Magic, except this Friday night would be entirely different. As we all know, it was the very first night the world famous Florida Hot Girls would actually be dancing inside the club.

Even though we'd danced at several other clubs in the Jacksonville area, I decided we needed a place to spread our wings. You know how it was when the girls started off inside of club Apollo South in Tampa and then relocated to Hollywood Nites? Exactly. Just like that! Black Magic was about to get a taste of the Florida women who were considered premier when it came to the stripping business.

As the girls were walking through the club mingling, flirting, and making their tips, my girl, Nicole, was barely speaking to me. She was still upset that I hadn't spent any quality time with her. Mignon was over in the corner doing her thing, dancing, and smiling in her customer's face as he threw big faces at her adorable little feet.

Meanwhile, JK and her group of ladies were sitting off on a couch that was located to the left side of the club. She was laughing and picking at the girls who weren't making any money.

In the meantime, Charlie B and her newfound waitress partner were busy making their rounds. And, Chazz, well, by now you know where she was and what she was doing. Wherever there was weed smoke in the air, that's where your girl Chazz was. As far as Richard and I, we were standing next to the dressing room area. I looked over at him standing next to me with his mouth wide open.

"Yo', Rich, snap out of it man." I pulled on his shirt sleeve. "Have you seen my girl Diva?" I asked.

After three minutes of me yanking and pulling at him, he looked over at me with glassy eyes. Then he pointed in her direction and mumbled, "Man, that's who my ass is watching up there on the stage. Your girl Diva is fine as hell!"

I slowly turned my head towards the stage to witness her ass up on the stage all by herself. Half the guys in attendance were around her, and they were throwing money everywhere.

"Do your thing, Diva," I shouted at her. I smiled and turned toward the DJ booth. Lil Kitty's lil narrow booty ass was inside of the booth trying to seduce the DJ.

Lil Red, who was now a pro when it came to dancing inside the club, was on top of a group of guys' table getting broke off something proper. Tiny had her short and fine red ass over by the VIP door dancing with two local pro football players.

I was still standing near the door surveying the club when I asked myself the million-dollar question ... *Now where in the hell is my girl Strawberry?* After minutes of scanning the perimeter for her, I spotted her off to the side, over on the floor, with her pussy spread wide open.

"Hey, Ms. Tight Coochie, come here for a minute, please," I yelled.

"Yes, Mike," she replied. She moved in close enough so my arm could wrap around her.

"Go over there and tell Strawberry to get her ass up off the damn floor! By the time the night is over, she's gonna have carpet burns all over her wide, flat ass."

"Yes, Mike, is there anything else?" she asked.

"No, I'm good," I replied. Then I looked around while standing there looking for Step and Peekachu.

"Hey, you two, come here right now!"

"Yeah, Mike, what is it now?" Step asked. Something was in her right hand and she tried to hide it.

"What's that shit inside of your hand, Step?"

"What? I just swallowed it. It wasn't nothing but a little pill to help me stay awake."

"Well, whatever it was, I hope you didn't give one to your friend Bobby Brown here!"

Peekachu rolled her beady eyes at me and quickly snapped back. "Shut up, Mike! Real fucking funny."

"By the way, Peekachu, you look real nice tonight."

"Thanks, Mike. You still ain't getting none of this good ass pussy though."

"Damn, well at least I tried, Peekachu!" Richard started laughing.

"Mike, you couldn't get none of this good ass pussy if I was on five of them Bobby Brown pills," she replied, then her and Step both laughed at the remark.

"Peekachu, to tell you the truth, if you *was* on five of them fuckin' pills, *nobody* would be getting none of that good-good between them red ass thighs of yours!"

Richard and I were still standing there watching the crew of fine, nice looking ladies working for me, when he leaned over toward me.

"Hey, Mike, why you call ole girl Ms. Tight Coochie?" he asked.

I leaned back over and smiled at him and simply replied, "The name says it all homie!"

"So let me ask you something, Mike. Have you ever been with her?" The way he asked, it was as if he was working for the police or something.

"Who you think gave her the name Ms. Tight Coochie?"

***

AFTER ABOUT TWO HOURS of the girls dancing and doing what they did best, me and Richard stood off to the side of the small night spot. We stood and watched them along with the other females who were in attendance.

I soberly wandered over in a corner, away from the all the noise and attention of the crowded night atmosphere. Before I knew it, I had found myself sitting over in a corner in the darkest area of the club possible. At that very moment, Sexy Redd was on my clouded mind. *Should I call her? Or better yet, what was she doing and when would I see her again?* I thought to myself.

I placed my head down on the table and tried to get her off my mind. But more importantly, I wondered if we could be having a little baby boy or beautiful baby girl. Honestly, I didn't care what she was having, just as long as it was a healthy baby.

While sitting there all alone I decided to do something very unusual for me, which was break one of my number one rules. I saw the first waitress of the night and quickly snagged her by her arm.

"Excuse me, Miss? What do y'all have to drink around here in these neck of the woods?"

She looked down at me sitting there at that dingy, dirty ass table. "What kind of question is that sir?" she asked with a slight unit on her face. "You see how small this lil raggedy ass club is. The only drinksl we serve up in here is beer!"

I looked at her and smiled slightly at her witty attitude. "I guess I'll have what everyone else is drinking."

"Fine, one Corona coming up," she said. She hastily walked away to retrieve my cold bottle of Corona.

"Damn, so this is the life huh, cousin?" Richard blurted out, as soon he found me sitting over in the dark corner of the club.

"Something like that, cousin. How you like your new job choice?" I asked. At the same time, I continued observing my girls take over the kush night spot.

He spun his head around as if it was on a swivel, and then returned it back as if he was the Exorcist.

"Oh, yeah, a nigga can really get used to this type of life style."

"I see. But you know the most important aspect of the job is being very mindful of everything around you at all times."

"I see," he replied. Trust me, I already have that part down pat," he assured me, just as the waitress came back with my drink order.

"Here you are, sir. Will there be anything else?" I looked up at her, and then over at Richard.

"Do you want something to drink, cousin?"

"Nah, cousin, I don't drink," he replied. However, his answer would change drastically before the cool midwinter night ended.

"No, ma'am, thank you, and keep the change."

The slim-figured waitress looked inside her small hand and her eyes grew wide at the amount of money I'd given her. "You sure you want me to keep the change?" she asked, as her face shined brightly as ever.

"Why? I didn't give you enough?"

She smiled at my cousin and me and answered, "Yes sir, you gave me a fifty dollar bill. The beer is only two dollars and fifty cents," she surprisingly replied.

"No problem, boo," I told her, "get your nails or hair done. It's on me and the Florida Hot Girls." I winked at her modestly.

She looked down at me with gratitude. "Thank you. What's your name if you don't mind me asking?"

I took a sip from the beer and frowned from the taste as I sat the cold bottle down on the table.

"Michael Valentino. And, no, thank *you*." I gave her my Prince smile again, and watched her walk away quickly. She was probably hoping I wouldn't come to my senses and take my money back.

By the time she reached the bar, I could tell by the look on her that she still couldn't believe I had tipped her that much money.

Richard saw the frown on my face and quickly asked, "What? Something wrong with the cold one, cuz?"

"Yeah, it's very bitter. I don't know why I ordered it. Here," I told him and held the bottle out, "dispose of it for me before the girls catch me with a beer in front of me."

Richard abruptly scooped up the beer and departed from my table just as quickly as he'd walked up on me. I leaned forward to see what he'd done with the beer and realized he was walking through the crowd with the bottle tipped up to this mouth, gulping it down as if it was a cold ass Pepsi.

Michael Gallon

CHAPTER THIRTY
NOT CHYNA

The night at Black Magic dragged along like a long, hot, boring Sunday morning similar to sitting in church. You know how it is when you're listening to the preacher but wishing you were somewhere else.

As the years dragged on, I eventually got to the point that I just didn't like being caught up in anyone's strip club any longer. I would either become restless, or just plain bored.

The only reason I would stay was due to the fact that if I left the ladies alone in the club, anything was bound to happen. they would either stop dancing, or try to sneak out of the club with some strange guy. I wasn't about to have that because if something were to happen to either of them, I would be the one held solely responsible. And if that wasn't the case, I also had to worry about the ladies who would try to get over by telling me they hadn't made any money for the night. Of course, that would mean they couldn't pay their tip-out fee or buy their own food after the club closed. So, to prevent any of those things from happening, I had to stay in the club with them in order to stay on top of my game.

That night, as the time slowly crept by, a few of the girls were busy making plans for after the club. Lil Kitty was the first one to come up to me.

"Mike, what's up, homeboy?"

I quickly turned to her petite frame and replied, "Nothing, Lil Kitty."

"Listen, me and a few of the girls are going to leave with the DJ and his homies after the club." She held out her hand to give me the money she held. "Here is our tip-out fee," she said. "We'll see you tomorrow around noon." She placed each girls' bar fee in of my hand then went back to dancing.

Just as abruptly had she walked away, Chyna approached me next. "I'm about to get dressed-in, Mike. These lame ass brothers ain't got no damn money. I would have stayed my red ass home if I knew it was going to be like this!"

"So what, you don't like the club?"

"Nah, I'm just not feeling this spot like the rest of the girls are."

"Alright then, boo, go ahead and get dressed." When she walked away I couldn't keep myself from lusting for the chance encounter to be intimate with her fine red ass. Don't get me wrong, I was still a lil sour with her ass for letting me put Innocence in a bad situation, but it was just something about Chyna that wouldn't let me get rid of her so fast. She was right about one thing though ... You see, Black Magic was an entirely different club from all the rest. The difference was, anybody who wanted to get their freak on inside of a club, Black Magic was the one to do it in.

The problem was, Chyna wasn't gonna be the girl you were gonna do it with. The very day she started working with the group she'd made it very clear that she wasn't going to be the kind of female who fucked in someone's club—and that's what I liked about her. Her motto was no fuckin' while on duty with the Florida Hot Girls. And besides, she had a man she was madly in love with at home. Plain and simple, my girl Chyna wasn't having it.

At least, that's what I thought. That is, until the very next night at Black Magic.

***

THAT NIGHT, BLACK MAGIC seemed as if it were going to be a nice night for the Girls and I. There was just one problem, and the problem was this ...

Contrary to what my Prosecutor and the Federal Judge deemed some thirteen years later, I was not a pimp! However, in their eyes, and from their perspectives, the rules inside the Black Magic club were what had put me in the elite category of pimping.

Like I explained before, if you wanted to get your freak on in a club, you could do just that at Black Magic and this is how it was told to me.

You see, inside Black Magic, the price to actually fuck one of the strippers inside the establishment was just fifty dollars. Yes, fifty measly fuckin' dollars, that's it. So if you had fifty dollars you could get yourself some head and pussy—all for that one low, low price. Now, my girls were forbidden to partake in anything of that nature. Let me repeat myself, *my girls were forbidden to partake in anything of that nature,* until my man, Malik, pulled me to the side and personally did the breakdown for me. I was standing off to the side, minding my business, and still observing my females work the floor.

He walked up beside me and said, "Hey, Mike, let me holla at'cha for a quick minute."

I looked at him with a strange and odd look on my face and quickly replied, "Yeah, what's up, my man? Did one of my girls break one of the rules of the elaborate establishment you have here?" I asked, sarcastically.

"Nah, let me show you something. See how your girls are just standing around, trying to make a hundred dollars?"

I had a confused look on my face as I carefully answered. "Yeah."

"Okay, you see my girl, Money, over there paying her bar fee?"

Yeah, you talking about the cute, short red one right?"

"Yes," he answered, "now she just made a quick hundred and fifty dollars in forty-five minutes."

"Damn, how did she do that, Malik?" I asked him as if I didn't already know.

He quickly articulated. "Well, shit, she went in the VIP room with three different guys and charged each one of them fifty dollars each, for a piece of her tantalizing ass!"

"Oh really? Wow that's it huh? Just fifty dollars?" I replied. I acted as if I had actually driven the short bus to his club with my females as my passengers.

"All them pretty ass bitches you got here from Orlando gotta do is the same thing. It's just that fucking simple, my man."

"Damn, so what you saying, Malik, is that if my girls let those same lame ass brothers fuck the shit out of their fine asses, they could make the same thing?"

"Yep," he said with the whites of his eyes protruding from out of the eye sockets.

"Okay, Malik, let me make a mental note of what you just broke down for me and then get back with you." He walked away smiling as he waved and dapped hands with several of the locals at his establishment.

Now if you ask me, I'm not a pimp, that's for damn sho. Nor am I a fan of any young lady fuckin' for money, especially up in no fuckin' hole in the wall strip club. But try telling that to a female who needs to pay her bills and you know what she's going to ask you? *"Well are you going to pay my fuckin' bills?"* and most likely your answer would be something like this: *"Hell nah, I didn't make them did I?"* That's why some of them do what they do.

Years later, a Federal Judge would see it the way the Prosecutor and a handful of agents with a mere Associates degree saw it. As a result, they deemed me public enemy number one, and then they slapped me across the face with an enormous amount of time for taking a few females throughout the state of Florida to shake their ass for a lil amount of cash.

In the end, it would be so much damn time, father time himself couldn't do it all.

CHAPTER THIRTY-ONE
DAMN, STRAWBERRY

The club was closing in about forty minutes and I had to be the happiest guy in there. I was bored as hell. It was nice to see my girls making money and having fun, but for some odd reason, that club always left me with an eerie feeling.

The girls had walked right past Richard and I, headed to the dressing room so they could change back into their street clothes.

"Hey, Mike, I got this guy who wants me to leave with him when the club shuts down," one of the girls ran up to me and said. I looked back at her with my mouth twisted sideways. She knew how I felt about them leaving with anyone after the club, especially since we were out of town in unfamiliar territory.

"Strawberry, that's totally up to you. You know I don't make decisions like that for you girls."

"No, Mike, I was just letting you know what I was doing, that's all."

"That's fine, Strawberry. Pay your bar fee and fine for leaving the club."

"No problem, Mike, thanks." She walked away as I spotted Ms. Peekachu and her partner, off to the side of the club talking with a few young gents.

"I hope y'all made enough money since y'all over there acting like y'all own the fuckin' club!"

Peekachu looked back at me and shouted, "C'mon, Mike! We got enough money between both of us to buy your black ass!" They both started laughing and turned their backs on me before slapping their ass cheeks in unison.

Meanwhile, the rest of the ladies were busy getting dressed-in so we could leave and go enjoy our morning ritual of breakfast after the club. Malik saw me walking outside the club with Richard and yelled out to me from across the bar as he was counting up his take for the night.

"Hey, Mike, where y'all going for breakfast?"

I took a minute or two and paused as if I was actually thinking of a nice place to eat. "I haven't decided yet," I lied.

"When you find out, let me know," he told me.

"Yeah, will do, Malik," I replied, as I continued to walk outside. I really wasn't in the mood for his company or anybody else's for that matter. All I wanted to do was pick me up something to eat and get back to my room. I knew exactly what Malik's intentions were from the minute I walked inside his club with my ladies. All he wanted to do was follow us to where we were eating and then try to persuade one, or a few, of my girls to leave with him and his entourage of horny ass guys.

I laughed the thought off as I stood outside the club with Richard counting up my bar fee.

It wasn't until he nudged me and said, "Hey cuz, ain't that everyone's girl in that raggedy ass car with all them fuckin' dudes?"

I instantly turned my head to see her leaving with a car load of guys. "Damn, girl, you just don't get it, do you?" I said out loud as the car made a right onto Beaver Street and then headed to only God knows where. I had no problem with her leaving, it's just *how* she was leaving and *with whom*. She was riding in a beat up bucket with eight guys and her ass was the only female in the car, all by herself.

I yelled at her and the lil bucket at the tops of my lungs.

"Hey, Strawberry, hey wait!" She couldn't hear me as the driver sped away. I could see her head bobbing up and down like the guy had a booming sound system inside of that lil piece of shit car he was driving. Come to think of it, I don't even know how all of those people fit in that small ass piece of shit car.

"Do you want me to go get her, cuz?" Richard asked, as he, too, watched the car speed away.

"Nah man, I guess she knows what she's doing," I replied, as Suga Bear walked by us.

"You know them young ass niggas are about to knock the bottom out of her lil ass! I hope her dingy ass knows what hotel we're staying at. If not, her ass is out of fuckin' gas!"

I put my head down and thought, *why didn't she just take somebody with her ass?*

By the time we all got to the limo, Triston was already standing outside the door with the same expression he'd had earlier. Everyone stepped inside and got comfortable.

"Where to, sir?" he asked, as he looked me directly in my eyes.

,"Denny's my good man. The one right next to the hotel on Baymeadows," I replied, as I gingerly stepped off inside the limo.

Just as soon as I sat my black ass down next to the lovely looking Ms. Diva, Triston sped off from the club. We arrived at Denny's within twenty minutes. As fast as he was driving I guess he was just as hungry as we were.

When we entered inside, I looked for an open booth for Diva and me to sit, to make sure we were far away from everyone else. I usually sat with the ladies so we could chop it up about whatever had transpired inside the club. But that morning I was feeling a bit uneasy, so instead, Ms. Diva and I sat at a booth and enjoyed each other's company.

There wasn't too much conversation between us due to her excitement about all the money she'd made. She was counting up her money when she looked over at me sitting across from her.

"Michael, I've never made this much money at one time in my entire life!" I smiled back at her as she continued counting up her ones.

"Yeah, you keep dancing like that at the club and you'll make way more than that."

She motioned me to lean across the table so she could give me a kiss, she then whispered, "Thank you for letting me come get this money. If I keep making money like this, I might not ever want to go back home," she uttered, as she fell back in her seat.

When I heard the last part of her statement about not wanting to go back home, I quickly responded.

"Damn, so you made that much money?"

"Yes and I'm going to make a whole lot more tomorrow night!" I smiled back at her and then looked over at the rest of my ladies sitting at their tables talking and having a good ole time.

You see, that's how it was each and every morning after a show. Whatever town we were in or wherever we'd just done a bachelor party, we had to have a nice place to go and have our breakfast. That's when the ladies got a chance to sit back and brag to one another about who they'd met and how much money they'd made that night.

I happened to glance over at my lil special boo, Chyna. She still had a mad unit on her beautiful face because her night had been fucked up. She saw me looking at her and shyly smiled. I smiled back at her as her face gradually went back to displaying her anger. My heart went out to her because Chyna was gorgeous in every way, shape, form, and fashion. Her beauty was going to be her downfall in the stripping business. Because she was so damn fine, guys didn't want her dancing on them, they would rather be inside of her. If they could accomplish that, they would gain bragging rights and be able to boast and gloat to their homies about fuckin' someone as superb looking as she was.

I paid for our breakfast and we exited Denny's. I instructed all the ladies to meet in Nicole's room around twelve that afternoon for the daily meeting. At that time, I would go over the day's agenda.

On my way to the limo, Richard walked up behind me. "I really hope ole girl is alright," he said, referring to Strawberry.

I turned to look at him as I placed my money clip back in my pocket. "Who, Rich?" He placed his head down and uttered, "Strawberry."

"Yeah, me too, Rich, me too."

CHAPTER THIRTY-TWO
JEALOUS GIRL

We had just pulled into the hotel parking lot when I looked over at all the ladies sitting inside the limo.

"Alright, ladies, twelve o'clock pronto—don't be late! Because I would hate to have to place a fine on that ass! Now have a nice and pleasant morning."

Nicole was the first one to look over at me. Of course, she didn't say anything. She just mean-mugged me and rolled her Chinese-looking eyes at me.

"Damn, Mike, if looks could kill, Nicole would have already killed you by now," Mignon divulged, as we ventured outside of the limo.

The early morning air was very cool that brisk, winter morning. I looked back at Mignon, standing opposite of me, and noticed her nipples protruding through the skimpy, black silk shirt she'd worn.

"I know," I concurred. "Hey, do me a favor." Mignon shivered from the coldness while the rest of the girls grabbed their bags from the trunk and hurriedly ran inside to keep from catching a cold.

"Yeah, Mike, what's up?" she asked as her bottom lip trembled.

"It's Nicole. Can you—"

"Don't worry, I'll speak with her once we get upstairs to our room. Is that it?" she asked, trying to urgently get inside.

"Yeah, that's it. Thanks," I replied.

"Don't mention it, Mike." She grabbed the bag Richard was holding for her and quickly darted away.

"You better slow down, girl! You don't wanna bust your ass running in those heels," Richard yelled as he ran behind her.

"Whatever, Richard. If you know like I do, yo ass better keep up," Mignon yelled, as she held the door for him to enter into the hotel.

"Is everything alright, Michael?" Diva asked as she walked up behind me. She snuggled her warm body up closer to mine, trying to keep herself from being cold.

"Why of course, young lady? What would make you think something was wrong?"

"I guess it's the way that your lil friend Nicky, or is it Nicole?" she asked, as she politely smiled at me.

"It's Nicole, baby. Yeah, she, and everything else, is fine," I replied. I kissed her on her thin lips and placed my arm around her voluptuous hips. "Now let's get out of the cold and up to our warm, comfortable room so we can get some sleep. I think tomorrow is going to be a very long animated day."

She looked up at me with those eyes of hers and quickly replied, "Forget about the day ahead of us. Just as soon as I get through taking a hot shower I'm gonna show your black ass just how the ladies from Gainesville, Florida, put it down."

"Damn, I can't wait," I replied, sounding like the lil squirrel on the cartoon *Over The Hedge.*

We made out way towards the elevator door smiling at one another.

"Yeah, just keep playing with my emotions, Mr. Michael Valentino. You won't be laughing when your precious Sexy Redd gets a copy of the video I'll be sending her ass over in Puerto Rico," my very jealous female friend mumbled before she vacated the lobby of the hotel.

12:00 p.m. sharp …

DIVIA AND I HAD JUST WALKED over to Nicole's room. As we walked in the room, I couldn't help but notice a bright yellow cab parked out front of the hotel still running. I looked over at Diva.

"That seems odd, don't you think?"

She looked back at me. "And what's that, bae?"

"That cab right there is still running and the driver is sitting inside the cab looking very agitated about something."

Diva leaned her head forward to see what I was referring to.

"Yep, he does look like he's a little angry about something, don't he? I hope he ain't mad at one of the girls."

We got upstairs to the room, and as I had requested, all the girls were there, even Strawberry.

But something seemed odd and out of place. Something just didn't feel right. It caught my attention as soon as Diva and I hit the door of the hotel room. The vibe was slightly off and everyone in the room was off to themselves doing their own thing— everyone except Strawberry.

For example, Lil Kitty was in the mirror doing her hair while Chyna Doll was sitting on the edge of the bed with the same mad unit on her face from the previous night. JK and her crew of women were standing over in the corner of Nicole's room looking fine as hell like they were ready to film a music video. Charlie B and her waitress friend were still getting dressed for the mall and Nicole was standing beside Lil Kitty, at the mirror applying makeup.

Sexy ass Mignon made her way out of the bathroom, checking to make sure her outfit clung to her elegant body and all its curves. Entyce had just come from the downstairs lobby with a bucket of ice to ensure we had cold drinks for the meeting. Chief-smoking-head Chazz stood outside the room to spark up a blunt. And even though Strawberry had made it back, she was the only one who seemed out of place. She was sitting down in one of the chairs but her legs shook uncontrollably and her hands moved back and forth recklessly.

Nicole finally broke the silence. "Mike, we seem to have a our-selves a slight problem." Looking like a million bucks, she turned around to face me.

I calmly questioned her. "And what might that *slight problem* be, beautiful?"

She held her gaze on me and then turned it toward Diva. Divia stood next to me and she looked like brand new money. The red Prada Jeans hugged her ass like a glove. She was the sight of a lovely vixen, and capturing her beauty would be a photographer's dream.

Nicole paused for a brief minute before she spoke again. Then she eyed me and said, "Well, it's like this, Mike"— she placed her hands on her nicely-proportioned hips— "see that cab downstairs with the motor running?"

I turned to look back down at the cab, and then back at Nicole. "Yeah, I see it. So what? What the hell does it have to do with me? What I want to know is why the hell is it out there?" By now I had gotten irritated with Nicole's mind games. "Did one of you guys call for a cab?" She rolled her eyes at me and then at Strawberry.

"No, but it seems as though that's how Ms. Thang got here and the trick ain't even got no damn money to pay for it," she informed me and concurrently threw Strawberry under the bus.

"Not the damn hot girl who left the club with a gang of niggas this morning!" Suga Bear stood up and shouted out loud. Bitch, yo dumb ass was with so many niggas in that piece of a car, I thought y'all was some damn Mexicans piled up in that lil' shitty ass bucket!"

I had to admit, the shit was so damn funny, I burst out laughing so hard, I started choking. It was one of those bend-over-and-hold-your-knees kind laughs. My eyes watered from laughter. "Shut the hell up, Step!" I shouted, as I tried to contain my laughter and catch my balance at the same damn time.

The entire room had burst into laughter. Nicole laughed so hard she started crying. I ended up tripping over Diva's foot and stumbled right out of the partially-opened door. Before I realized it, I had bumped into an Arabian looking guy. Without my having noticed, he had walked up and stood in the doorway of the room. A pissed off look was etched on his black face.

"Where de el es mi money, de cab es already at one hundurd and twenty dollar," he yelled out, in broken and badly-spoken English.

The loud tone of the Arabian man's voice resonated throughout the room. I knew things were about to get serious, so I looked over at Strawberry.

"Damn, Strawberry, where did he bring your ass from? The fucking moon?" I asked. She stayed silent with her head hung low in shame. Her legs continued to shake back and forth as if she was about to run. She looked up at Diva and me. Her eyes were blood-shot red and she remained mute.

In the entire time of knowing her, I had never seen the expression, she had that day, on her face.

Minutes later, Charlie B stepped up and yelled across the room at the cab driver. "Don't worry, she'll have your money in a few minutes. Now step your ass back outside of our room!"

The driver looked shocked when the beautiful, Nubian Princess ordered his ass out of the room.

"No problem," he said, clearer than anything he'd said thus far. "I wait right here outside of de door."

Bam!

Charlie B slammed the door in his dark colored face. The door slammed right before Diva and I hurried back inside the room.

"Okay ladies, we see one of our sisters here has a problem." Charlie B looked from one girl to another at the room full of gorgeous women. "I don't have to ask you all what to do, so let's make it happen!" With the announcement embedded in their heads, I assumed they must have felt sorry for ole Strawberry. So, without any hesitation, they each took out portions of money and paid the cab for her.

Charlie B then left the room and went outside to pay the cab fee.

"I hope yo' ass make enough money tonight so you can pay us back," Lil Kitty snapped at Strawberry, "'cause I don't know about the rest of the girls in this group, but I needs mine back!"

"Oh, she definitely gonna pay us back or I'ma be the first one to dig off in that ass," Nicole included.

Charlie B had just walked back in and I guess felt sorry for ole (Berry) and shouted. "Ladies listen, if she doesn't have it, I'll pay it for her!"

"Well if it's like that, you should of paid it for her then, instead of us paying out of our own pockets."

"You're right Chyna, well if any of you guys want your money back now, I'll give it to you before we leave for the Golf Fair Flea market."

"No, keep your money Charlie B, I'll pay all of you guys back tonight after the club, I promise." Strawberry recited as she stood up and hastily walked into the bathroom.

"Okay, now that we got that lil dilemma out of the way, can we get on with the agenda for today?" I asked the women, as they all settled in for another one of my interesting meetings.

CHAPTER THIRTY-THREE
BY MY SIDE

12:30 a.m. ...

MY HOTEL PHONE RANG around twelve thirty, just after midnight. I answered to a female voice, on the other end yelling at me.

"Mike, wake your punk ass up!" the voice shouted, without the usual greeting formalities. "It's way past club time and your black ass is still in the damn bed sleep! We're gonna be late on account of your black ass," Chyna yelled, as I laid still trying to wake up.

I rolled over with the phone in my hand and whispered to Diva. "Hey, what time is it anyway?"

She rolled over half-naked and groggy, and replied, "It's twelve thirty-five, we're late for the club."

"Oh shit, I'm up! I'll be ready in like ten minutes," I yelled back into the phone.

Diva was awake as soon as she heard the phone ring. "Man, I'm still tired from all that fun earlier today. I'm so sorry," I told herDiva. I yawned and stumbled over my shoes as I tried to make it to the bathroom.

"No problem, Mike. Just take your time. This is your group," she said. She walked out of the bathroom and pulled the red thong onto that nice ass of hers. I watched her tentatively as she walked past me.

"Thanks, Diva, I'll be ready in another five minutes."

By the time we arrived at the limo, the girls were patiently sitting inside, dressed and ready to go.

Lil Kitty was the first one to comment of our lateness. "Yo' black ass get a muthafuckin' fine for being late and causing the rest of us to be late as well!"

"Whatever, Lil Kitty," I replied. I turned my focus toward the tinted window as Triston pulled away from the hotel.

"Yo' black ass was probably upstairs in your room long dickin' a bitch and shit," Nicole voiced, as the limo made a right turn at the light, headed for the interstate.

"Damn, lil homie, you were up there fuckin' and shit putting us all behind schedule? Yeah, your black ass has a muthafuckin' fine for being the fuck late. Get us to the damn club and make it fast," Suga Bear yelled. The other girls just looked at Diva and me and rolled their eyesDiva.

"Shut the hell up, Suga Bear. No, I wasn't upstairs fuckin'! For your information, I was fuckin' sleep," I replied as the rest of the girls kept their eyes on Diva, waiting on her to say something.

Triston had us at the club within twenty minutes. The girls forgot all about being late when we pulled up in the parking lot and they saw all the cars in attendance.

"Looks like it's thicker tonight than it was last night," Mignon said to the girls. They looked around and tried to scope out the number of cars in the parking lot.

"Hey, chick, make sure you have my bread on deck after the club!"

"Lil Kitty, I got you girl. Just chill," Strawberry replied. She stepped outside of the limo and right into a pile of fresh dog shit.

"Damn, what a way to start the night off, Strawberry," Suga Bear said as she walked right past her. Strawberry bent over nearly in tears because of her bad luck.

"Fuck!" she griped, as she stood on one foot. She looked around for something to wipe her shoe off on.

"Triston, help with that while I get the ladies inside."

"No problem, Mike," he replied.

The rest of the females were already at the entrance of the club waiting on me. When we entered, I noticed Malik standing behind the bar.

"Yo', Mike, let me holler at you, dawg," he quickly shouted out when he saw us. I knew right then what his dark skin ass was gonna say. I slowly walked behind the damn bar..

" While I handle this, get the girls inside the dressing room so they can get dressed," I told Mignon.

"No problem, Mike, see you in a few," she replied. When she walked away, some random guy pulled at her waist.

"Hey, Mike, my man. Rick said your girls didn't pay their bar fee last night."

Hell, it was bad enough they had to pay me thirty-five dollars, now they had to pay his damn bar fee too.

Shit, by the end of the night, they ain't gonna have no damn money after paying all these damn fees and shit, I thought to myself. I stood behind the bar and listened to him while I watched his crew of girls work the large crowd in the club.

I looked back over to him and said, "Oh yeah, I'll make sure they handle it tonight."

After speaking with him for about ten minutes or so, I was back on the floor standing by the dressing room waiting on my girls to come out and take over the club.

"Everything alright, cousin?" Richard asked, as he stood guard at the door of the dressing room. I casually looked back over at him.

"Everything is everything," I replied, "as long as I have the Florida Hot Girls by my side."

***

THE LADIES WERE COMING out of the dressing room one by one when Suga Bear came up to me with the news.

"Hey, lil playa, ole girl didn't bring the right shoes to dance in tonight."

"Who didn't bring the right shoes?" I asked, while looking like Morris Day in Purple Rain—in the movie, Jerome had gone up to him at the bar and said the password *what,* which was their code word for when Apollonia walked into the club.

"Strawberry, she's over in the corner of the club just chilling," she stated, with a genuine smile on her face as if something was funny.

"Okay, let Charlie B know what's going on with her ass!"

Five minutes later, Strawberry was up and moving and dancing like there was no tomorrow. Now I don't know what it was Charlie B had told her red ass, but whatever it was, she had a different attitude for the rest of the evening.

Hours later, the night was going well. Richard and I were looking over my nice stable of beautiful women work the crowd at Black Magic. Tips were flowing in, and on top of that, all the girls were happy—even my favorite girl, Chyna. She had a giant smile across her gorgeous face.

The DJ had the club jumping to Boosie Bad Ass, Better Believe It, and he was dancing with Lil Kitty and Entyce.

Chazz was all over some ugly ass guy, who *yes*, you guessed it, had some killer ass weed. And she had the biggest fuckin' blunt I had ever seen hanging from her skinny ass lips. The ugly ass guy was kissing her all inside her ear. Chazz smoked so much damn weed, I think she smoked in her sleep.

Her lil sister, Suga Bear, was over by the bar dancing with two niggas, taking both of the dudes' money.

"You go, Suga Bear, get that paper!" I yelled from across the floor.

She just looked back at me smiling and shouted, "Fuck you, Mike, I don't look like no fucking, Suga Bear!"

You see, Suga Bear was a lil nick name I had given her when she first came to the group since she looked so much like the lil bear from the cereal commercial "HoneyCombs". Every one of my girls had a brother up in their ass that night and all of 'em collected that money.

Mignon and Nicole were up on stage when some brothers they'd met at the mall went up by the stage and made it thunderstorm on them. Diva was over at some other guy's table, and she had her ass buried so deep in his wide ass face, if she had farted, he would've actually ate it—that's just how far his face was in her ass as he threw a stack full of dollars at her thighs. JK and her girls were in those same damn seats they had sat in the night before. They were still laughing at the other females in the club who didn't look to be making any money.

Strawberry was busy trying to get her money so she could pay all the girls back after the club. My cousin Richard just stood beside me looking like he couldn't believe he was actually up in a strip club with his cool ass cousin while collecting so much fuckin' money, all at the same damn time.

Michael Gallon

CHAPTER THIRTY-FOUR
SLAY SOMETHING NEW

Standing there beside Richard, I caught a glimpse of Malik coming toward us out of the corner of my eye.

"Yo' girls looking good tonight, boy," he said, as soon as he was within arm's reach, "I mean, you got them hoes in check."

"Yeah, but they called dancers, *not hoes,*" I looked back at the brother and replied.

"Oh my bad, Mike, I mean strippers," he replied. He smiled back at me.

Richard nudged me and uttered, "The girls are really doing their thing up on stage tonight, ain't they?"

"Yeah, they tryna get they bar fees," I said out loud and sarcastically. I wanted Malik to hear me so things would be cool between Malik and me.

Malik abruptly turned towards me. "Yo', Mike, I ain't tripping about that lil bar fee, dawg. I just wanna make sure you making your bread."

"Yeah, I appreciate you for letting my ladies come up in your spot and make it too."

He smiled at both of us before he opened his mouth. "No problem, my nigga, always." We dapped each other up and he slid his midnight-colored ass right back inside of his office to smoke on some melodious smelling kush.

Now when Malik walked away, Richard and I stood there silently watching all the ladies inside the club. I didn't know about Richard, but I had my eyes locked on this one slim chick Malik had pointed out to me earlier by the name of Money.

Money had to be the cutest, lil jazzy ass female I had ever seen. She stood around five foot six and weighed around a cool hundred and twenty pounds. She had the cutest lil perky ass which hung out of the red thong that clung so tightly around her firm, lil ass. Her skin complexion was a slight shade of light-brown and she had a small pair of tits. The more I stared at her the more difficult it was for me to watch her and not want to take her into the VIP room and do something personal with her fine and sexy ass.

There was only one problem to what my heart desired. The mere fact that I never played while I was at work meant taking her inside the VIP room would have to wait until another time and place.

At that point and time of my career, I was about getting my money—not only that night, but any night I was up in the small ass club.

By 2 a.m., the club was at capacity and there was no room anywhere in that damn hot box. Richard and me had to stand inside of the ladies' dressing room just so we could watch the ladies continue making their money.

While standing there doing me and watching the ladies, Diva walked up to me talking about her coming back with me for a few days, possibly weeks. Just as soon as she offered her sentiments in my ear, it was as if my ears closed but my mind wondered... *I hope she don't get too fuckin' comfortable to the point that she don't wanna go back home.* A few days would be fine, but after a while I would get tired of fuckin' the same chick. With all the females I had coming in and out of my house, I was trying to slay something new every day.

***

I was still standing there in total bliss as I listened to what Divawas coming out of Diva's mouth. Suddenly, she pushed her soft ass back, and up against me.

"Mike, do you hear me talking to you?" she whispered softly, and pulled my head around to face her. She'd caught me by surprise as I looked down at her. Having all that ass up against Johnboy made it hard to comprehend.

"Oh yeah, whatever you say, Diva."

"Whatever, Mike, let me go make some more money. I'll be right back," she voiced, as she walked away swiftly. She looked back at me momentarily then continued her stride.

"Damn, I sure as hell can't have that," I said out loud.

Rich turned to me with a puzzled stare. "What's that, cuz?"

"Man, ole girl tripping. How 'bout she talking 'bout coming back home with us? Talking 'bout if it's cool she might wanna stay a while."

Richard threw his head back and laughed and asked, "So what your girl Sharon gonna say about that one?" He chuckled again and grabbed his groin like men do when they're hyped and deep in conversation.

"I know, right. Shiiit, it's bad enough I gotta deal with the ones I already got at the house," I replied.

"Tell me about it, cuz, and not only that," he said and pointed discreetly, "what you gonna do with the one walking this way right now?"

I looked in the direction in which he'd pointed his index finger. It was just in time to see Nicole walking up. She stopped dead in front of me and stared me right in the face.

At first, I had to search for the words I wanted to speak. Thinking fast on my feet, I said, "Hey, Nicole, do me a favor?" I didn't give her a chance to reply before I added, "Tell all the girls to be dressed in by three thirty so we can be out of here by four."

She held her stare on me without saying a word.

"Nicole, did you hear what I asked you?"

"Yeah, I heard you. Is there anything else, baby?"

"No, Nicole." I chuckled. "Girl, you keep playing with me and I'ma do something serious to your fine lil ass."

"That's what I want you to do, daddy. I want you to make love to me like you did that day you and Ms. Kitty both had something in one of my tight holes." She smiled and placed a nice, wet kiss on my lips. Walking away, she made sure I saw how nice her ass looked swaying from side to side.

Gotdamn! I thought. *She gon' make me tear that ass up for real!* I reached down and adjusted Johnboy when he tried to stand at attention. *Down, boy.*

"Damn, cuz. Boy, you got all these little females sweating your ass!" Richard shouted over the music. The smile on my face said it all.

"Yeah, I don't know what it is about her sexy ass, but whatever it is, I sure as hell want some!"

A few minutes later, Nicole was back in my face. "Hey, Mike, I relayed your message. Most of the girls are coming back with us, but Chyna said her and White Chocolate got a date with some guys after the club."

I hastily turned to her. "She has what? Not Chyna! I know you must be talking about the wrong chick."

"For real, Mike, she said they got a date and they'll see you later. Now let me go make me some more money before we leave, please."

I was stunned as I looked at Nicole still standing in front of me smiling about the bad news she had just delivered. It felt as though a horse had just kicked me in the nuts.

"Go ahead. Nicole, I'll get with you after the club," I mumbled. She briskly walked away.

The next thing I knew, I noticed Strawberry. She tried to walk past me and into the girls' dressing room without me noticing her apple headed ass.

"Strawberry, come here for a quick minute, please?"

"Yes, Mike," she said once she was within inches of my face.

"Hey, do you see the guys you left with last night in here tonight?" Her eyes scanned the vicinity of the club.

"Ummm, yeah," she answered, "that's them sitting over there at that table. Shoot, they been trying to get me to go with them again tonight. Why? What's up?"

I looked at the simple look on her face and replied. "Nothing, excuse me and Richard for one minute, please. Somebody needs to pay they tab. Ain't shit free from the Florida Hot Girls," I said with conviction.

I walked off and motioned Richard to follow.

CHAPTER THIRTY-FIVE
WET ASS AND PUSSY

With pep in our step, we strode over to the table where the guys who'd had their way with Strawberry the night before, sat.

Richard pulled me by my shirt and grumbled, "Hey, Mike, what you about to do? I ain't got my piece on me right now, man." I looked back at him with a look in my eye that hadn't been there since my days of fighting for my country over in Desert Storm. Over there, I had led a squad of five soldiers under heavy fire and distress into a remote, undisclosed site. and I'd rescued two dozen soldiers from captivity. So, approaching these niggas was small things to a giant.

"No problem, cuz. Shiit, I can't shoot 'em all up in the club anyway. I ain't tryna go to prison for murder."

With that being said, we kept right on stepping until we'd reached their table. I cleared my throat to get their attention.

"Excuse me, young fellas," I greeted politely. "How y'all boys doing tonight?"

"We doing fine, Mr. Who the fuck are you, the club manager?" a tall slim brother asked. He turned and stared at me with a dirty scowl on his flat face. I looked over at Richard and then back at the slim brother.

"Nah, lil playa, I'm glad you asked though. You see all those cute ass females standing over there by the dressing room door?" I quizzed him.

"Yeah. So. What's up?" the short thug of the crew asked with a smirk scattered over his skinny face.

"I'm glad you asked that too. Well, to answer your questions as simple as possible, it seems that last night you guys took one of my young ladies back with you. But, see, that's not the problem," I explained, "my problem is based on the fact that you had your way with her and didn't bother to pay her no money," I probed. The tall, slim brother took a good look at the girls. He must have seen Strawberry standing amongst the girls.

Michael Gallon

"Yeah, I see ole girl, and nah, we sure as hell didn't give her ass no bread," he said smugly. "But we fucked that bitch 'til the sun came up, nigga," he replied, as he grabbed his crotch and scowled at Richard.

"Yeah, I fucked the lil bitty so hard, the bitch started crying and begging me to take my dick out of that tight ass hole of hers," the other guy bragged. He smirked and took a long sip from the beer he'd been babysitting.

These lil niggas got the game fucked up! I thought.

"Wait a minute, lil ass nigga. You all up in our face questioning us about a bitch who didn't get paid," he went on. Him and his comrades must've had me confused with one of them BoBo-the-Clown ass niggas. But they would soon find out otherwise.

"Well, see, it's like this," I said, still trying to keep my cool, "me and my cousin wouldn't even be over here bothering you if y'all had just paid her what you owed her. But when you guys didn't pay *her*, you didn't pay *us*! You young brothers wouldn't like it if my cousin and me fucked y'all's sorry ass mommas and didn't pay them, now would you?"

The tall, slim brother snapped his head around so fast, I thought the nigga had broke his neck.

"Say what, my nigga?" he said in loud tone.

"You heard me, fuck nigga!" I shouted and matched his tone. He took a swing at my head. I ducked his swing and snatched the other guy's beer bottle right out of his mouth while he was drinking it, then smacked the tall guy right across his face with it.

Richard followed suit and hit another one right up under his chin. The tall guy I'd smashed in the face with the beer bottle, grabbed his face as it split and dribbled blood like water dripping from a faucet. He looked at his hands which were covered in with his own blood and summoned his flunkies.

"Aww shit, this crazy ass, wannabe pimp, done hit me in my fuckin' mouth with a fuckin' Corona bottle! Hell nah, y'all get that nigga," he shouted to the rest of his gang.

A few of his homies just sat there with shocked expressions on their faces. They were stunned, and they looked as if they had frozen in place.

The short thug of the bunch blinked his eyes rapidly and wondered ... *What the hell just happened?* The nigga looked at me as if I had horns on my head and a tail coming from my ass.

"If one of you young punk ass niggas make another wrong move, me and my cousin gonna wet y'all punk assess the fuck up, one-by-one in this raggedy muthafuckin' club! It's gonna be so much blood up in this muthafucka, everybody in this bitch gon' think we over here slaughtering pigs! Now get yo' homie and put something on his face before he bleeds to death." I ordered. "Oh, and teach that nigga how to keep his fuckin' mouth closed so he won't keep gettin' hit in." I grinned a sly smile, and as if nothing had ever happened, I popped my collar, turned, and proceeded to walk away with the same pep I'd approached with.

"Hey man," one of them called out to me. I paused my steps and looked back over my shoulder. "We don't want no trouble. We just tryna have a good time," the lil homie confessed.

"Yeah, I know," I agreed honestly, "we all are, including my girl you guys sent home this morning without paying her. Y'all fucked the shit out of her, and then put her ass in a fuckin' cab and sent her back to me with a wet ass and pussy!" *About To Get Real ...*

Blood, sweat, and tears dripped down the slim guy's face. He sat foolhardy, and waited on someone to speak on his ignorant behavior. After a few seconds of waiting and deliberating on what to do next, the shy, innocent-looking guy spoke up.

"Damn, we didn't think about it like that, sir."

"I know y'all didn't," I said, as I made a U-turn and walked back over to them. "Y'all were too busy thinking with your little heads instead of your big heads. So now, y'all asses 'bout to pay for what yo' little head fucked up," and took a seat.

By now, Nicole, Mignon, and Entyce had noticed us going back and forth, and one-by-one, the girls strutted over. They had already taken off the club attire they'd danced in, and now they stood behind me waiting for whatever was about to jump off..

"Ladies, I think I got these guys' attention now," I said smoothly. I looked back, and over to my right at Mignon. "Could one of you please go tell Strawberry to come and sit with us please?"

"Yes, Mike. I'll be right back," Nicole replied, as she walked away in search of Strawberry.

The people in the club continued partying as if nothing had happened since they wanted no parts of it. While waiting for Nicole and Strawberry, one of the security guards came over to the table.

"Hey, Mike, is everything alright over here?" he asked.

I looked up at the large man and quickly voiced, "Yes, my good man, everything is all good. We're just trying to get to know one another, that's all."

"Okay, you alright young fella?" He looked down, and the brother I had hit tried to conceal the cut the bottle had left on his mouth. "Do you need anything for that nasty cut you got there on your face?"

His young partner, who seemed to be the scariest, looked up and quickly replied. "Yeah, he does. Could you get him a towel or something, please? His mouth is full of blood."

"Yeah, I saw the way he took that Corona bottle to the mouth. Let me get something for that before he gets blood all over our damn table," the large security guard recited, as he walked away from the table laughing to himself.

As soon as he vanished around the corner, Strawberry came over to the table and placed her hand on my shoulder before sitting down. Still seated, I stared directly into the eyes of the young man sitting in front of me crying.

"Yeah, Mike," she said.

I slowly looked over at her. "So are these the young men who had their way with you early this morning and sent you back to me without any money for the services you rendered them?"

Strawberry broke the tension with her slow minded ass. "Yeah, Mike, these are the gentlemen who had their way with me earlier this morning. Hi fellas, did y'all enjoy the awful way you treated me this morning?"

Not one of them responded. Time seemed to move in slow motion as I gazed over at the short thug who'd been silent the entire time we'd been at the table. For some reason he seemed nervous. He looked like he was about to go for the weapon which was tucked away in his trousers.

I guess Mignon must've seen the same thing I saw because she quickly intervened and sat down next to the guy. She poked him in his side with a gold-plated .380 and quietly whispered into his ear.

"Now I know yo' soft, bitch-made ass don't want me to fill you up with holes do you?" The feel of the gun placed against his ribs caused his bottom lip to quiver.

"Nah," he said, then abruptly turned to her, "I was just making sure I had it tucked away so this nigga y'all with won't shoot us," he replied.

Damn, this shit just got real for me and the Florida Hot Girls, I thought to myself.

Michael Gallon

CHAPTER THIRTY-SIX
THE DEED IS DONE

The tension at that table was so intense you could've cut the atmosphere with a butter knife. I could tell that the individuals who sat on the opposite side of the girls and I were at a crossroad.

"Now what makes you young fellas think I was going to shoot you nice fellas?"

The ring leader looked at me with his eyes slightly open and replied, "Because you said if we made one false move, you were gonna wet us up right here in this raggedy ass club!"

I reached my hand out across the table and laughed. "No, you must have misunderstood what I had said, young man. I wasn't going to wet you guys up, these fine ass ladies behind me were going to wet you guys up. You see, every one of these beautiful, Nubian princesses carry something serious inside of her bag.

Me and my cousin were simply gonna beat the shit out y'all if you were lucky enough not to get hit by the array of hollow-point bullets. And fellas, it looks like my ladies are gonna take it from here," I said and pointed to the girls. "If you guys will excuse my cousin and me, I have to take this important phone call from my dear friend, Yani," I said, as I got up from the table.

Cool and collective, I looked over at Richard. "Yo', cuz, follow me," I told him. When we walked away from the table. I heard Mignon giving orders to the guys.

"Okay, we gonna do it like this ... all you young ass niggas who look like you ain't old enough to even be up in here, empty dem damn pockets right the fuck now! If I don't see the lint inside yo' pocket, you young ass niggas gonna see my .380!"

"So y'all just gonna jack us while we up in the club?" I heard the ring leader ask.

"Nah, we just taking back what you guys already owe us for not looking out for Strawberry earlier.

"Yeah, since you broke ass brothers didn't pay her, we all had to chip in for that expensive ass cab," Nicole replied, as she began collecting money out of the pockets of the five young men. I let out a brief chuckle and answered my phone.

"Hello."

"Mike."

"Yes, Yani." She sounded so luscious.

"The deed is done!" I stood there for a brief moment as I offered a moment of silence for my dear friend, Fats.

"So what happened?" I asked. I was relieved since I no longer had to deal with his fat, black ass.

"Well, right now, we at de sabage yard. We need to dispose of he ass and he raggedy ass car wit' he and gay ass Leroy in the trunk."

I pulled the phone down from my face and whispered, "Gay ass Leroy?"

"Who in the hell is gay ass Leroy?" She then replied in her Haitian accent. "I'll explain 'bout yo gay ass boy later."

"Okay, did everything go as planned?"

"Yeah, without a hitch."

"Cool, I'll be back tomorrow sometime around two. When I get back I'll swing by your hotel room and take care of you."

"No problem, me bruda," she replied.

"Hey, where's my brother?"

"He taking care of da attendant at de lot."

"Cool, once again thanks and I'll talk with you tomorrow."

"Be safe, me bruda!"

We hung up and I immediately went searching for Chyna. Nicole had told me earlier that her and White Chocolate had dates with some brothers I had never seen before. Either I'd heard it wrong, or just didn't think she had the right girl.

I recklessly searched throughout the club for my girl.

HOW DOES IT FEEL?

I BUMPED INTO CHAZZ, as I placed my phone back in my pocket, still carelessly searching the club. "Hey, Chazz, have you seen Chyna?" I asked in a slight panic.

She turned to me with her eyes half closed and replied, "Nah, I haven't seen any of the girls since I've been smoking on this good ass Kush Malik let me try."

I angrily looked at her and said, "Damn, Chazz, you smoke so damn much, you sure you not part Indian?" She just laughed and kept right on blowing smoke in my face and in the stale air of the night club.

I then stood off to the side and began surveying the club. *Okay, she ain't over there with JK and her crew of girls... wait a minute, she might be outside waiting on me.*

I swiftly began walking towards the exit of the club when I passed right by Rick. He had been busy collecting the girls' bar fee before they walked out the door of the club.

"Hey, Rick, did any of my girls go outside?"

"Nah, Mike, all your girls are still inside trying to make those last few dollars."

"Okay, thanks, my brother." I quickly turned to walk back inside, and who was standing right behind me with a true smile wrapped around her beautiful face? Chyna.

Her bright, red face and smile did something to me as she looked up at me and asked, "You looking for me, Mike?"

I placed my hands on my hip as if I was about to scold her for almost causing me to have a heart attack on account of her missing or leaving with some guy.

"Yes, Chyna, what's this I hear about you and White Chocolate having a date?"

She looked up at me with a serious unit on her face as she replied, "Yes, we do, I'll explain everything when we get outside."

"What?" I angrily asked her.

"Mike, I'll explain everything when we all get outside. Now is there anything else?"

I couldn't fight her and I sure as hell couldn't stop her when she had her mind made up on whatever it was she wanted to do.

I just looked at her and said, "Okay, Chyna, go ahead and make sure the girls are all dressed. I'm about to pay the bar fee for the girls so Malik won't be tripping."

She ran off, eager to let the ladies know about getting ready. I looked over to the table where those guys were still sitting and they all looked beat down.

I had got a few feet away from their table when I asked, "Are you guys alright?"

The leader looked up at me with his eyes full of tears. "Yes, sir. We paid your girls for last night and also gave them some extra cash for being here tonight."

With a slight grin on my face. I looked over at Mignon and the crew and replied, "Why thank you, fellas. I hope we can still be friends now that we've taken care of that very small problem we had."

"Why of course, sir. Anytime you and the Florida Hot Girls are in town, me and my homies are going to make sure the girls are happy and getting their tips."

"Now that's the type of attitude you guys should've had last night. I like the way you guys are thinking. It's been a pleasure meeting you nice fellas. And please, make sure you guys get your boy here to the hospital so he can get that mouth of his fixed up."

Now while we were deep into our conversation, I hadn't noticed the song the DJ was playing in the background until Strawberry began to hum it out loud. The song was "How Does It Feel" by D'Angelo.

"Girl, you're a mess," I said, as she stood beside me counting all the money she and the other girls had taken from the guys who had did her dirty the previous night.

CHAPTER THIRTY-SEVEN
PLEASE DON'T GO

The guy with the deep laceration across his face still had the blood-stained towel wrapped around his face, as his younger brother looked up at me.

"Yes, sir, we're heading that way as soon as we leave. Come to think about it, we're about to take his ass there right now. C'mon, man get your ass up so we can get you fixed up," he yelled. He placed his hand under his brother's shoulders and helped lift him up from his seat.

I then turned to walk inside Malik's office and he greeted me as he was coming through his door. His voice met me before I could even look at his dark ass.

"Yo', Mike, what's up, partner?"

"Nothing, Malik. I got your bar fee from my ladies," I answered. I had been caught off guard by his use of the word *'partner'*.

He looked back at me with that evil grin he always seemed to have on his black ass face. "Oh, okay," he said and took the money, "now that's what I'm talking 'bout." He quickly started up a conversation on having my girls at his club every weekend. He told me if they came, they would have to pay a small tip-out fee.

"I'll think about it and let you know something before next weekend," I replied, while trying to walk away from the actual Devil himself.

The truth about the whole thing was that a few of the girls in the group really didn't like going to his club. So, if I agreed, I would have to find another spot in Jacksonville to accommodate the females who didn't like his club. I was still standing behind the bar deep in thought when Nicole walked up to me.

"Mike, all the girls are outside in the limo waiting on you."

"Is Richard outside too?"

"Yes, Mike, he's collecting your tip-out fee as we speak."

"Thanks, I'm right behind you." She grabbed me by the arm and looked up at me as we made our way outside of the club.

"Hey, Mike, these toy guns we picked up at the Flea Market today really came in handy tonight, didn't they?"

I looked down at the beauty and replied, "Yeah, they sure as hell did, lil one. If them niggas knew you guys had them fake ass guns pointed at them, they probably would've robbed us for playing like we had real ones."

"Yeah, you absolutely right about that!"

We had just made it to the limo, and noticed Chyna and White Chocolate standing outside of the limo waiting on me. Chyna stepped to the side and placed her right hand into my chest. She gently pushed me away so we could talk in private.

"Mike, listen ... me and slim right here got these two guys who wanna take us back with them and spend major money with us."

I was shocked by what I was hearing. Chyna was the one female I never thought would leave with a guy—no matter who he was or how much money he had in his pockets.

I looked her directly in the eyes and voiced my opinion. "Chyna not you. You're the one who never falls for the lame ass game these niggas play."

She placed her hands on her petite hips. She had her head down as if my remark had shamed her. She kicked some dirt on the ground as she searched her mind for an answer that would make it make sense.

"Yeah, I hear you, Mike," she said and paused... "But this nigga showed me two stacks, and he claims he's gonna give me eighteen hundred dollars," she explained with excitement written all over her face.

I grabbed her by the arms and looked her in face as I tried to convince her. "Okay, Chyna. Think about it for one minute. If he's gonna give you that much money, why don't you have him give you at least half of it up front and then give it to one of the girls to hold for you. Then, get the rest when you guys are done doing whatever it is you about to do. That way, if he changes his mind or tries anything slick with you guys, at least you'll already have half of the money."

She quickly looked back at me. "Hell nah, Mike, I don't trust none of these girls with my money. Trust me, Mike, I got this," she replied.

Realizing she was convinced, I placed my head down in disgust. "Okay, Chyna. Well, we'll be leaving in the morning at 10 a.m. If you and ole girl miss the ride, y'all just gonna be out of fuckin' gas."

She turned and slowly began to walk away as she yelled to White Chocolate. "Yo', slim, let's bounce!" The two walked away from the limo. As they did, smart ass Nicole began playing the song by KC and the Sunshine Band called "Please Don't Go".

***

THE PAIN AND THE HURT cut me deep as I watched Chyna and White Chocolate walk around the corner of the club that early mid-morning. It hurt even more as Nicole turned the music up and began singing along with the song.

I slid my weakened body into the limo as Diva looked at me and asked me, "Are you alright?"

"Yeah, Diva. I just hate to see the girls leave with total strangers."

"Damn, Mike, did you look like that when I left with them busta-ass niggas last night?" Strawberry asked. The group of women started laughing.

I began laughing too. "Fuck you, Strawberry. Triston take us to get something to eat, please!"

"Yes, sir! Right away, sir," he shouted.

I turned my focus toward the window and allowed my eyes to take in the scenery.

"Now where in the hell is Chyna and the lil White girl who came?" Lil Kitty asked. She had that simple smile across her face— a smile she always seemed to have no matter what came out of her mouth.

"To answer your question, Lil Kitty, she claimed she— wait a minute— Nicole, please turn that damn song off—now, back to you, Lil Kitty. She claimed she had some extra money to make, so who am I to stop her when it comes to her wanting to make extra money?"

"Well, I hope she didn't leave with that guy I saw her ass with earlier 'cause that same lame ass nigga told me he would give me two grand if I left with him," Charlie B said, while chewing on watermelon-flavored bubble gum. She laughed at Chyna's mistake.

"Talking about the guy who had on that Fubu Jersey?" Lil Red asked. She peeped out of the limo window and tried to see if they were leaving with the guy she had just described.

"Yes, him, child."

"He so full of shit. I hope she got her money upfront, Mike," Entyce chimed in.

"Let's just hope she knows what's she's doing," I told them.

"Damn, and she took the lil slim White chick with her too?" Lil Red stated, just as Triston merged onto Interstate 10.

"Yep, she claimed his homie wanted the White girl."

"Yo', Triston."

"Yes, Mr, Valentino."

"Denny's, please."

"Yes, sir. We should be there in about fifteen minutes."

"Man, I'm tired of Denny's. Can we go to Waffle House?" Lil Kitty asked, still smiling.

"I tell you what, Lil Kitty, the ladies who want to go to Waffle House can go after Triston drops us off at Denny's. Cool with you?"

"Yep, Mike. Thanks."

"Anything for you, Lil Kitty."

She looked back at me and uttered, "Whatever, Mike."

Ten minutes later we were all walking into Denny's, ready to eat, and Lil Kitty was right behind us. Seemed as though she was the only one who wanted to eat at Waffle House. She didn't feel like eating by herself so she changed her lil feeble mind.

While sitting down eating with the ladies, I informed the group to be at the limo at 10 a.m. sharp the following morning. We would be leaving around 10:15 and if their asses weren't there by that time, they would have to find another ride home.

"Did you tell Chyna what time to be back?" Suga Bear yelled across the table, with bacon and syrup dripping from her mouth.

Before I could answer, Peekachu who was sitting right beside her sidekick with pancakes and syrup dripping from her mouth answered for me. "Hell, Step, with all the money her ass is about to make, she just might buy her ass a car and drive her red ass back to Orlando!" The girls all began to chuckle.

Nicole stood up and added, "I know that's right!"

"Okay, enough jokes, ladies. Can we all just eat so we can get out of here and get back to our rooms so we can get some sleep."

"I hear you, Mike, 'cause I feel like eating me some dick off the bone," Strawberry voiced out loud, as she cut an inviting smile over at my cousin Richard.

Michael Gallon

CHAPTER THIRTY-EIGHT
RELOCATION

The laughter and camaraderie we shared that early, chilly, midwinter's morning, inside of Denny's, helped me ease the tension and stress I was going through. My mind and feelings were adrift, as the girls and I sat there eating and chopping it up.

The moment kept me occupied since my precious Chyna had decided to partake in some after-club entertainment with some fellas I didn't even know. I didn't even get a chance to see them leave with the niggas.

The girls and me sat at Denny's and laughed for at least ten minutes straight. Suga Bear wiped her mouth and stood up to go pay for her food. She had gotten just a few feet away from the booths we'd occupied before she stopped and yelled back at Strawberry.

"Damn, Strawberry, try giving your mouth a break sometimes. Girl, you keep eating dick off the bone like that, you gonna end up big as a house!"

"Shut up, Suga Bear," Strawberry shouted back.

While the ladies all went back and forth amongst each other, I couldn't help but think about Chyna and White Chocolate. I hoped and prayed they would be safe in the mean streets of Duval County. Especially, since there had been a wave of senseless killings throughout the city after certain night spots closed for business.

To be honest about the entire situation, Chyna meant a lot to me. Like I had stated before, I really felt some type of way about her, and I sure as hell didn't want to see anything bad happen to her on my watch. A major part of me really didn't want her leaving with any guys, but I couldn't stop her. She needed the extra money and I guess she figured the guy she'd left with was going to give it to her and her newfound friend. Sincerely speaking, between you and me, Chyna was the one female in the group I wanted to be with more than anyone else in the group at the time of my short-lived career. Even though she'd made it perfectly clear to me from the very start that I wasn't her type. She was truly wifey material. The sad thing about that was the fact that she wasn't going to be my wife anytime soon.

When we finally left Denny's that morning, none of us knew what to expect when we woke up later that chilly Sunday morning. Instead, we just hoped the girls who left with dates that morning made it back in time. If they didn't, they would have to take up new residency in Jacksonville, Florida.

BACK TO RICHARD ...

AFTER WE'D MADE IT BACK TO THE HOTEL, everyone went their separate ways and into their rooms. I hadn't been asleep for long when my hotel phone sang out loud. I was still somewhat sleep when I rolled over and asked Diva to answer the phone.

"Hello." she answered in her country voice. She waited as the caller on the other end spoke. "Yes, ma'am, thank you."

"Michael, that was the front desk with your morning wake up call," she told me, as soon as she hung up the phone.

I still had fresh, hot morning breath to tend to as I yawned and said, "Thank you, beautiful. Damn it's time to get up already?"

I sat up on the edge of the massive, king size bed and rubbed my eyes.

"Michael, do I have enough time to take a hot shower?" She walked her naked ass in front of me and headed towards the bathroom.

"Yes, Ms. Diva, go ahead. The limo won't leave without us. Let me call Nicole's room so she can have the rest of the girls up and ready for our departure."

"Alright, Michael. I'ma go ahead and get in the shower. You can join me if you like," she yelled from behind the bathroom door. At first I thought about joining her, but then I thought about my girls Chyna and White Chocolate. So, I decided to check on the girls instead.

Nicole's phone rang twice before she answered. Though it was first thing in the morning, she still managed to sound elegantly vibrant.

"Hello."

"Good morning Nicole."

"Hey, Mike."

"Hey, do me a favor and call all the girls' rooms and wake them up so that they won't be late."

"Sure thing, Michael. Is there anything else you want me to do for you?" she replied ever so softly.

"No, beautiful, and by the way, you're doing a great job for me since Sexy Redd had to leave us for a few weeks."

"Well since I'm doing such a great job, why can't I have her place in your big ass bed back at the house?"

I placed my head down and smirked at her remark. Slowly, lifting my head back up, I answered, "In time, Nicole ... in time."

She quickly snapped back at me. "Bye, Michael."

"Bye, Nicole," I casually said. I stretched my tired limbs and peered out of the hotel room window which was right by the bed. I looked down and saw Triston standing by the trunk of the limo, placing some of the girls' bags into the trunk one by one.

I suddenly thought about Chyna and White Chocolate, I rolled over in bed and dialed Strawberry's room to see if my cousin Richard had heard or seen the two of them. Strawberry answered the phone on the first ring. The poor girl sounded like she'd been up all morning, and she sounded out of breath.

"Hello."

"Strawberry, are you and Richard up yet?"

"Hell yeah, we never went to sleep. We been up all morning doing what grown folks do."

"Damn, so you just gonna fuck my dear cousin to death, huh?"

"Nah, I'm just trying to get into your family, Mike."

Damn, I knew what that meant. His dumb ass probably went up in ole Berry raw.

"Whatever, Strawberry. Just make sure y'all are at the limo in time. I would hate to have to leave both of you here. But have you guys heard from Chyna or White Chocolate?" I asked. I could hear Richard in the background laughing.

"Nope, hopefully they young, dumb assess are back by the time we leave. If they not, I guess you just gonna have to leave them."

"Thanks, Strawberry. Go ahead and get back to 'eating the dick off the bone'," I replied sarcastically.

"You better believe it, Mr. Mike," she replied, as she hurriedly hung up the phone and got back to doing what she did best.

CHAPTER THIRTY-NINE
WHAT'S WRONG WITH HER?

Now that I had checked on the girls, I was off to the shower to try and join Ms. Diva. I opened the door as she was just getting out of the shower. She was butt ass naked and drying her wet body off. She saw that I was already naked and my rock-hard erection stared her directly in her eyes. At first, she smiled at me, then she did the unthinkable and fell onto her knees as if I were a king and she was my servant. She placed my hard erection deep inside her warm mouth.

I leaned my head back and mumbled out loud. "Awww, nothing like some good ass head for breakfast..." For about ten, long minutes, she carefully and delicately sucked on Johnboy as though he was a smoked neck bone, fresh out of a hot steamy pot of Sunday Collard Greens.

She slurped and sucked, making damn sure she covered every inch of the sizable piece of meat as it plunged in and out of her mouth, from the base to the top of its candy apple-shaped head. I couldn't bear the attention he was receiving so I gently picked her up off of her knees and slowly turned her ass around.

"Stand up on your tippy toes so I can go as deep as possible," I whispered into her ear. She joyfully obliged and then turned her head back towards me and smiled. I inserted my rock-hard manhood up inside of her very wet vagina. Both of our emotions took center stage as I bent her over the bathtub and drilled into her like a jackhammer. We went at it as though we were making our very own porn flick, but of course with me being the star.

I was digging deeper and deeper when she turned her head around and mumbled, "Damn, Michael, what are you trying to do? Blow my back out or what?"

I looked down at her with perspiration rolling off of my forehead and replied while grinning. "Nah, baby girl, I'm just trying to make sure you never want to leave me!"

"Whatever, Michael. If you keep beating my coochie cat like this, I won't be able to leave this damn hotel room," she replied.

I stared at myself in the mirror. *Damn, she's right. I need to ease up on her before I knock a damn hole in her back*, I thought. "My bad, beautiful, I'm sorry. Follow me to the bedroom," I said, as I pulled out of her and walked into the bedroom area.

She followed my lead and pushed me down on the bed. Next, she climbed on top of me so she could ride me. Gently, she slid down the shaft of my manhood. Once she had all of it inside of her stomach, she began riding me like a wild pony trying to be broken in.

I looked up into her face and said, "Okay, young lady, don't start complaining when I start acting wild right along with your fine ass!"

She looked down at me and laughed. "Whatever, Michael, this is all my dick now," she replied.

Ten minutes later, I flipped her ass over and started hitting her from the back again. Together, we climaxed.

We lay in bed to calm our racing heartbeats. Divia rolled over and looked at the digital clock on the hotel nightstand.

"Bae, it's 10:20. We're going to be late!"

I was still out of breath and replied, "No problem, baby. Go ahead and get in the shower. Remember, the limo won't leave without us." For the second time that morning, we made our way in the bathroom, except this time, we both jumped into the shower. She was barely able to stand up.

I stood in front of her and washed over my body. She leaned up against my back and articulated into my ear. "Damn, Michael, you got a damn good sex game. I can't remember ever having a guy put it down on me the way you do. I can barely stand up." I looked back at her and gave her that Prince smile again. By now in my confused life, I had mastered it.

"I know, I see how your ass is bent over. Tell you what," I directed her, "just place your arms around my neck and hold yourself up. I'll wash your body for you," I said, as she rested on my back while I washed myself and then her.

***

WE MADE IT TO THE LIMO JUST as the last bag was placed inside the trunk. When we got inside, to my surprise, everyone was already there—even my girls, Chyna and White Chocolate.

As the limo pulled off a few of the girls started up some small conversation between them. But the look on Chyna's face said it all, she looked like she would've bitten the head off a Rattle snake if it had got in her way.

JK looked over at me and whispered, "What's wrong with her?"

I looked back at her fine ass and replied, "Hell, I don't fuckin' know."

Triston had just merged onto I-95 and headed south. While in between Diva and the door, I glanced over at White Chocolate, who had scratches all over her face and legs. She looked like she'd been in a fight with a fuckin' lion or some big ass ferocious cat. Whatever happened to her, Chyna wasn't saying anything and I wasn't about to ask her.

You see, one thing I could honestly say about ole Chyna, was that she was very nice with her hands. In other words, she could really throw them thangs. So, I wasn't about to get her ass crunk, neither was any other girl in the limo on that beautiful, nippy, Sunday morning.

Lil Kitty looked over at me and gave me one of her cute looking smiles. Suga Bear and Peekachu sat near the front of the limo exchanging laughter. It wasn't until Suga Bear came from left field and blurted out something so funny, it had her and Peekachu laughing even harder.

"Well, I be damned," she said, after looking at the marks covering White Chocolate's body. I had no idea what that meant, but I looked over to catch her sister, Chazz, over in the corner of the limo busy rolling up her morning blunt which was probably her fuckin' breakfast.

"I know you don't think you about to smoke that in here, especially with me inside this muthafucka," I said. She just looked back up at me and smiled with those big brown eyes of hers.

"No, Mike, I'm just getting it ready so I'll be prepared when we stop for gas,."

"Too bad Triston already gassed up which means we won't be stopping until we get to your house," I said, as I grinned at her.

"Damn, oh well, I guess I'll just have to smoke it when I get home."

"I guess so." I shook my head in disbelief at the sight of her rolling up the blunt.

After that, I snuggled closer to Ms. Diva so I could get comfortable for the two and a half hour drive back to Orlando.

On the way back to Orlando, everyone was off in their own little world. Some were fast asleep while a few were daydreaming about the past weekend. A few asked what time would I be by to pick them up that night for Apollo South.

"Nicole, take the names and numbers of the girls who want to go to Tampa tonight. Also, call a few of the other chicks who might want to go tonight because the ones who made money this weekend are probably gonna want tonight off."

"Okay, Michael, is there anything else?"

"Nah, I'm about to get me a nap. Wake me up once we get back to town."

By now, I had so many girls, Richard and I would have to split them up into two different teams of females. I would have team A and he would have team B. It was like sixty or more girls between both of us. I could call any one of them at any given time and let them know about a show.

Just as I went to put my head back to take my needed nap, my phone began to ring. *Damn, I can't ever get any rest. My damn phone never stops ringing*, I thought to myself, as I snatched the phone out of my pocket to see my brother calling.

"Hello."

"Baby Boy."

"Yeah, Firstborn, what's up?"

"We have a slight problem," he said into the phone. I raised up in my seat to hear what he had to say.

"What do you mean we have a problem?"

"That fat muthafucker took some pics of Yani, before we laid his fat ass to rest.

I was furious as I listened to what he had to say. I slowly pulled the phone down from my ear and stared at it as if it could see my facial expression.

Then I slowly uttered, "James, what in the hell do you mean *his ass took some pics*? I thought that you guys took care of his ass without a hitch."

"Mike listen, he took some pics of your girl and sent them to some fuckin' cops!"

"How do you know this?"

"Because some cop by the name of Protho called her phone wanting to know who she was and where Bernard was."

"Damn," I said in the phone, as I placed my head down into my chest.

Michael Gallon

CHAPTER FORTY
THE MURDER QUEENS

I plummeted back into my seat which caused my shoulder to hit Diva who, by now, was half asleep. My head spun as my brother waited for me to ask him the next question.

"So what did she say to his ass?"

"She acted as if he had the wrong phone number and hung up the phone."

"Okay. We should be okay if that's all that transpired," I said to him.

"I don't think so, bro-bro."

"What makes you say that, Firstborn?"

"Because Fats sent them a text message also."

"How do you know that?"

"Because his fat ass sent the same message to her phone as well. You might want to check your phone for the same message as well," he said. I quickly looked at my phone to see if I had any missed messages.

As soon as I pulled the phone down from my ear, the message flashed across my screen:

Yo, Detective Protho, this is Bernard Fats Walker. If for some reason I come up missing, I was with this fine ass female when it happened.

"Well, I be damned. I just got the message. Shit, where is Yani right now?" I asked him. Now I was under distress.

"We're both back at the hotel. What do we do now, Mike?"

"Listen, stay calm, big bro. Let me quarterback this thing out."

"Yeah. You used to be a nice lil QB at one time," he said back into the phone. He smiled at the memories of my quarterback days.

"Whatever, bro. I did my thing. Now listen and listen close. I'm on the way back home as we speak. When I get back in town I'm coming straight to the hotel. Stay there until I get there. Don't move or leave, cool?"

"Why don't we just come over to your place, Mike?"

"Hell nah, I don't need that added attention at my fuckin' crib right now."

"Just chill the fuck out, Firstborn. Get some coffee and calm your nerves, young ass nigga!"

"Man, I'm good. Shiit, they ain't got my pics, they got hers."

"Do you wanna speak to her?"

"Hell nah, just let me plan my next move before we all do slip up and do something careless."

"Do you know the police officer he sent the pics to?" he asked, while sounding a bit nervous and on edge.

"Yeah, I know him. Him and his partner were by my apartment a few months ago inquiring about another homicide they thought my girls had something to do with."

"So what happened?"

"I'll talk with you when I see you. I can't really talk like I want to right now."

He must've got the hint 'cause his next words were, "Peace, Baby Boy."

"Yeah, peace to you as well, my brother. Hey!" I called out just before he could disconnect the call.

"Yeah, Mike."

"Stay your ass put and let me handle this."

"Alright, Baby Boy, I'm waiting on you *and* them bad ass Florida Hot Girls."

"Yeah, whatever," I said and hung up.

When I hung up with my brother some of the girls were looking at me as if wondering what I had going on.

Suga Bear gawked at me curiously. "Hey, Mike, you talkin' about them niggas they found dead out there off of Pine Crest Road?"

"Damn, Suga Bear, you all in my damn business, ain't you?"

"Nah, I was just asking, because rumor has it, the girls who did it were called the Murder Queens," she replied, and instigated the situation further.

***

The Murder Queens 2

I WAS POSITIVELY CAUGHT OFF guard when I heard the name *Murder Queens* come from her mouth. There had been talk around town about a group of females killing brothers, but I didn't know them, nor had I ever seen them. At least, that's what I thought. I stared at Suga Bear long and hard .

"*The Murder Queens?*" I repeated the name as if I'd heard wrong.

"Yes, Mr. They're called *The Murder Queens.*" To be certain I'd heard her, she reiterated the name loudly and clearly, as if deafness was the cause of my confusion.

"Oh yeah, I heard about them females," Chyna said, as she broke her silence. She acted as though she was eager to know more about the girls who were hired, professional killers.

"Yeah, they say it's like four or five of them bad ass hoes and that they go around killing niggas for that cash," Lil Kitty said, while rolling over trying to get herself comfortable.

I looked back over at her and Suga Bear. "Now how y'all know about them and I don't know about them?"

Lil Kitty looked back at me with that same lil half ass smile covering her small ass face and replied, "I don't know why you don't know. Hell, they say them hoes work for your black ass anyway!"

I jumped up in my seat as I shouted back in my defense. "What!"

"Yeah, Mike, rumor has it that the group of females wasn't formed until you brought out the Florida Hot Girls," JK said, while sitting straight up in her chair looking at me.

"Man, you guys got me fucked up. I don't know nothing about no damn Murder Queens," I said to everyone sitting inside that limo.

The girls who had fallen asleep were slowly starting to wake up. They had started ear hustling as they listened to what was being said.

"I heard them hoes were the ones who killed them bitches at the ole paper mill," Lil Redd said. She poured her something to drink from her Mountain Dew soda can.

Richard swiftly snapped his head over in my direction and impulsively asked me, "Mike, do you know who killed my kids' mother?"

Before I could even answer him, the girls had all sat up in their seats with shocked looks on their faces.

"Wait a minute. So, Richard, you had some kids by Do-Dirty?" Lil Kitty asked. Her expression had changed from shocked to surprised.

Richard, who was still waiting on an answer from me, lethargically turned his head in Lil Kitty's direction. "Yeah, we have two beautiful daughters together," he told her, "are there any other questions about my dead baby mamma and me," he replied with tears beginning to snake down his face.

"Damn, that's so fucked up," JK mumbled. Richard hung his head low with grief as he thought about Do-Dirty's death.

He nervously held his hand up near his eyes and began wiping away the tears. "Yeah, tell me about it," Richard replied. Again, he looked back at me and waited on my response to his question. His eyes were bloodshot red, as he gazed at me looking back at him.

I sat still as if frozen, and hoped a logical answer would somehow drop out of the sky. I was caught off guard because I knew who killed the individuals at the ole mill that day, but I sure as hell wasn't about to tell him or anyone else for that matter. So instead I lied to both him and my girls.

"Nah, Richard, I don't know who did it, and I sure as hell don't know nothin' about no fuckin' Murder Queens."

Now that I had reassured him that I didn't know anything, I was very curious myself as to who the group of females who called themselves the Murder Queens were. Although I would never say it out loud, I felt suspicious about the people I *assumed* I knew, and especially those I had working for me.

I was puzzled by all the new information I'd been given. Even more peculiar, was the mere fact that Nicole, Mignon, Entyce, or Strawberry, hadn't said a mumbling word during the entire conversation. It was as if they weren't even there. Their silence made me wonder if they knew something the rest of us didn't know. But, one thing was for certain, and two things were for sure, it wouldn't be a secret much longer because the truth was gonna come out, and when it did, it would blow my mind!

All eyes were still on me. I stared in the direction of the four ladies and each one remained mute. I couldn't shake the feeling that they were hiding a dark secret that they had buried deeply within their souls. Whatever it was, they would keep it between them until the end of time.

As I pondered what it could be, I recalled how they'd acted that night they walked up on the niggas who had taken advantage of Strawberry a few nights prior. All kinds of thoughts raced through my mind but I quickly shook the theory. I didn't snap out of my funk until I heard Peekachu's voice chime in.

"All I know is, the rumor is that you know who these females are. And the reason people think you know is because after it happened, Ms. Kitty left, and now another one of your main females are gone also."

"Hold on," I nearly snapped. I quickly jumped back at her with a response. "Ms. Kitty got fired before she even went on the photo shoot with the girls, and she was long gone before them folks at the paper mill got killed," I said defensively. "And since y'all must know, I found out she had fucked some nigga in my damn apartment, in my damn bed! So I had to dismiss her trifling ass, and that's why she's no longer with the group!" I said, raising my voice with each word.

"What about Sexy Redd, Michael?" Lil Kitty burst out and asked me. Her signature smile beamed across her face.

"Damn, y'all some nosey ass females," I said to the carload of females who were now all in my business.

"Nah, Mike, we just wanna make sure we ain't riding with real serious killers up in this muthafucker!" Lil Redd stated. Her eyes seemed to glare at me and the shitty ass grin on her face made me look at her sideways.

"Well, like I told y'all earlier, Sexy Redd had a family emergency and that's why she had to go back home."

"Mike, you might as well tell us the truth, my nigga, because we gonna find out sooner or later," Seneavu voiced as she sat her dark ass up in her seat.

"Hold on for one minute, ladies! Y'all can just get off my dawg, Sexy Redd. I don't know where the hell y'all been for the last few days, and I guess none of you guys read the paper or even watch the damn news," I assumed in angry tone. "Last week, Sexy Redd's brother, Prince Naheed, was brutality murdered on a small Island known as *Vieques*. That's where she's from, and when she left here, she was in total panic mode in fear for her royal family. *Princess Rhynyia Santiago was escorted back to her country for her safety*," I explained as I read a few words of an article. "Here's a picture of her before she left on her father's luxury, private jet."

The ladies in the limo couldn't wait to see the image and they all reached for the article on Sexy Redd and her prestigious family. Their mouths dropped as Charlie B continued to read them the rest of the article.

"Apparently, her wealthy, flamboyant, business mogul father, Pierre Santiago, has some type of deal with our country. Once his only son was found dead, her country went into high alert, fearing that whoever killed her brother may attempt to take her out on our soil. She had to be immediately removed from our country for her safety," Charlie B said, as she turned the article from the USA To-day paper around.

"It goes on to say that she's home safe with the royal family, so y'all hoes can just stop saying she's part of some group called the damn Murder Queens."

Lil Kitty's head snapped around quick as fuck. She turned to me and commented. "So, Mike, you knew about this all along and didn't tell your dawg?"

I had been listening to what Charlie B had just read and I rubbed my hands together as if I had a rash on them. I looked over at Lil Kitty.

"Listen, Rhynyia only told me a small fraction of what was going on back in her country. All I know is she's safe back home with her family. Yes, her brother was found murdered. But by who? Evidently, the authorities don't know as of yet. As to when she might return, I don't know that either. I thought I told you guys I didn't want to discuss anything concerning Sexy Redd." I leaned back and tried as best as I could to hide my anger.

"So, all this damn time we been around a bitch who's a Princess in another fuckin' country? And to think, this bitch was over here shaking her ass for a lil cash when she didn't even have to. The chick got money coming out of her ass!"

"Tell me about it. Not to mention, she's having our baby as well!"

Michael Gallon

CHAPTER FORTY-ONE
HIGH AS A FUCKING KITE

I slipped. I should've never uttered that sentiment out loud. Everyone in the car went nuts when they heard what I'd said.

"She's *what*, Michael?" Nicole yelled out.

I placed my hand on my head and sighed. "Yessssssssss, Rhynyia is having my child!"

"Damn, it ain't even been that long since y'all got together and you already got her knocked up, Michael?" Mignon asked, as she, too, leaned up for the first time since we'd been talking.

"Oh well, if it makes her happy, I love it," Nicole voiced as she rolled her eyes over at Diva. Diva had been as quiet as a mouse during the entire time the conversation.

"Damn, Mike, what about Sharon? Ain't she pregnant too?"

"Yes, Entyce. Thanks for reminding me," I replied.

"Damn, cuz, who is this Sexy Redd? Have I ever seen her?" Richard asked. I guess he finally felt like talking.

"No, Richard. She left before you got a chance to meet her, but you will if you stick around this wild and crazy group long enough," Strawberry said.

I was still shaken by all that had been said.

"Anyway, shut the hell up, Lil Kitty. So what if she wanted to make some money and be around her man at the same time?" Charlie B voiced.

"For real, y'all ... the chick is a fuckin' princess full of fuckin' money and power, and she's over here dancing for dollars! How did you find all this out about her ass any way Charlie B?"

"First of all, Lil Kitty, like I said earlier, I read the paper. But I knew something was up the night y'all came to Waffle House and had breakfast. She had pulled me to the side and gave me some money, but some of the money had a picture of her on it. When I went to the bank the next day to put some in my account, the bank teller questioned me. He was like 'excuse me, ma'am. Where did you get this money from?' "When I told him, he said, 'this money is from the island of Vieques and the face on this hundred dollar note belongs to Princess Rhynyia.' When I asked him how he knew, his reply was that he was from that island as well."

"Wow, do you still have it, and how much is worth in the states?"

"Just say it has some value to it, Lil Kitty," Charlie B replied. Now she had the attention of everyone in the group.

"C'mon, man, so y'all saying this bitch like Eddie Murphy in *Coming To America*?"

"Nah, Lil kitty, I thought the same thing until I looked up the country and found out that it's right outside of Puerto Rico. There were also pictures of her family in the encyclopedia that solidify her position in her country." Charlie B recited, as I listened to her talk."

"So, cuz, you saying you didn't know nothing about her being a princess?"

"Nah, not one thing. I'm still tripping how some off y'all talking about I know who the Murder Queens are."

"Well, we know now Sexy Redd ain't one, or should we call her *Princess Rhynyia*? And we know she ain't have nothing to do with none of the murders y'all spoke on either?" Richard stated. As he talked, he looked over at me at the same time.

The vibe in the car was mellowing out when Ms. Weed Head Chazz spoke up. "Hey, Mike, what was that lil scene I saw last night up in the club with you and some of the girls?"

"Yeah, when y'all three girls, Mike, and Richard had some lil young gents cornered off in the club?" White Chocolate asked, as she placed some type of ointment on her wounds.

"Ladies, once again, if you all must know, we we're helping Strawberry get her money back from the guys who had fucked the shit out of her the night before."

"But, Mike, I could've sworn I saw Nicole pointing a gun at one of them niggas!"

"Damn, Chazz, how you see all of that from across the damn dark-ass club? And besides that, your black ass was as high as a fuckin' kite last night!"

By now, I was beat, nah better yet, I was downright tired, dawg, tired from question after question, to mere speculation about knowing about the infamous Murder Queens. And I still had to finish answering Chazz before she got the entire car wondering about Nicole, Mignon, Entyce, and Strawberry.

"Nah, Chazz, it was a toy gun. Here it is right here. See!"

Nicole handed Chazz the toy gun that she'd showed me inside the club after we left the guys' table.

Chazz held the toy gun as if it was a real one. "Damn, I need one of these for myself."

"Hold on, let me see that," Suga Bear said, while reaching her hand out for the toy gun. No bullshit, the damn gun looked authentic.

"So where your gun, Mignon?" Peekachu asked her. She studied her movement.

Mignon began eagerly searching for her gun. After a few minutes of searching for something she knew she didn't have, she turned back to Peekachu and said, "I must have left it back at the hotel."

"Alright, ladies, enough of the questions. How much longer before we reach Orlando, Triston?"

He looked back at me from the rearview mirror and shouted, "Forty-five minutes, sir."

"Thanks, now, ladies, y'all get some rest. We have a meeting once we all get back home. Until then, everybody be the fuck quiet! I got a lot on my mind."

"Yeah, I would have too if I had the Murder Queens on my payroll!"

"Whatever, Suga Bear. I heard your ass!"

Before I could close my tired and dreary eyes, Diva whispered in my ear.

"So, Mike, who's Sexy Redd, and is everything alright?"

I looked at her like *really? Didn't I just tell everyone to please leave me alone.*

"Yes, Diva, everything is fine, I'll explain the rest when we get to my place."

She looked back at me as if she meant me well. "Okay, baby, if you need me to do anything for you, just let me know."

"Thanks, Diva," I replied, as I turned halfway in my seat and tried my best to get comfortable.

Upon resting my weary head on the headrest, I caught Mignon looking at me from the corner of my eye. She looked as if she was trying to hide, what looked like, a tattoo on the inner part of her thigh. I could barely make it out, but it looked like a picture of a girl with a gun in her hand. She saw me trying to see it and quickly covered it up. I gave her a quick nod of my head, and the next thing I knew, I was out like a light.

***

AN HOUR LATER, THE LIMO was pulling into Orlando. By now, everyone was wide awake. Everyone still wanted to know more about Sexy Redd and the Murder Queens. I don't know why they were all looking at me. Hell, I couldn't tell them anything if I didn't know anything. Whatever was on their minds sure as hell couldn't be as much as what was I had on mine. Yani and my brother were my main concern at the present time.

I had just stretched a bit and was now staring out of the window as the limo pulled into Eatonville. Chyna, who had been the most quiet the entire trip, leaned in to me.

"Hey, Mike."

I dreadfully turned to her and said, "Yes, Chyna."

She looked at me so innocently. "Hey, when you find out about them damn Murder Queens, can you please tell them that I may need their help with some awful mean, nasty ass brothers!"

"Damn, didn't I tell y'all I don't nothing about them females!"

***

CHYNA HAD EVERYONE'S ATTENTION as the stretch limo pulled up in front of the apartment Chazz and Suga Bear resided in.

"And why is that, Chyna?" I asked, as I leaned up to hear what her dilemma was.

She then looked over at me with that same mean ass unit spread along her face. "I may need them to handle a lil problem I got with some brothers who played me for my cash. That's why, pimp!"

At first I thought about snapping back at her for calling me a pimp. But after a quick flashback of how nice her hands were, I quickly abolished that from my ridiculous thought pattern.

So instead I came back at her. "So Chyna, what actually happened earlier this morning?"

The whole time we'd been riding in the limo, Nicole and her crew of vagabonds had kept quiet and to themselves. However, as soon as Chyna asked for help from a group of females known as the Murder Queens, everything seemed a lil bit different. They acted as if they wanted to know just as much as everyone else.

"Remember earlier this morning when White Chocolate and me left with those lame ass niggas?"

"Yes, I do."

"Well, they took us to an old, rundown warehouse, then the guy who was supposed to break me off said he didn't want to fuck and all he wanted was some head instead. I was like, "Nigga, I'm not about to suck nobody's dick!"

"So he was like 'if you not suckin', you and ole White girl can walk the fuck back!'"

"Damn, so y'all didn't make no money?" Nicole asked, as if she was doing a damn interview.

"No," Chyna replied.

"Well, how did y'all get back to the hotel?" Entyce asked, while acting as if she was taking a mental note of what had transpired.

"We had to catch a fuckin' cab," Chyna barked.

"That's so fucked up. So why is White Chocolate sitting over there all scratched the fuck up?" Nicole asked, as we all sat patiently waiting on an answer.

Chyna took her time as she looked over at White Chocolate as if she was asking for her permission to tell what happened to her. I guess White Chocolate saw the sincerity in her eyes and stepped in.

"I got it, Chyna! What happened is I decided to give his homie some head for seventy dollars. The lame placed the money in my hand and just as I had finished and went to step out of the car, the nigga snatched his money back. My damn I.D. and arm was inside the car as the driver drove off while dragging my ass down the street!"

"Damn!" we all said in unison.

The girls looked at one another and showed sympathy for the two females who hadn't took heed to the first rule of leaving with someone after the club: *always get the bread upfront! Always, no matter what!*

"Now that was some foul ass shit," Mignon voiced, as she stared at both of the victimized girls.

"Yeah, , and I swear, by the time we go back next week, I'm gonna have my people find them fools and fuck them up," Chyna said, as she balled her fists up in anger.

"See, that's why we need some bitches like them damn Murder Queens on our team, Mike!"

"What the fuck ever, Suga Bear!" I sputtered back at her.

"Mike, for real. So when these niggas get out of pocket, them bad ass hoes can murk they punk ass for us!"

"Like I said, Suga Bear, I don't know who they are and if I did, I wouldn't hire them, that's for damn sho!"

"Why not, Mike. We really need them?"

"Whatever, Suga Bear. We're at your apartment, so go ahead and get your Suga Bear looking ass out of the fuckin' limo." She saw the smirk on my face.

She turned around and shouted, "You didn't say that when you were trying to eat all up in this fat ass pussy!"

I remained cool, calm, and collective as I replied, "Whatever, Suga bear, we ain't never had no count of sexual encounter."

"We will, Mike. I see how you be watching this pussy up on stage."

"Suga Bear, his ass watches all of us like that," Lil Redd uttered and caused the entire limo of girls to laugh out loud.

CHAPTER FORTY-TWO
FINALLY HOME

The laughter had just died down as I looked over at my girl, Lil Redd. "Thanks Lil Redd, get her Suga Bear looking ass right!"

Suga Bear was standing outside of the limo waiting on Triston to get her bags. "But, Mike, I thought we were having a meeting at your house?"

I leaned forward. "Yeah, we are, but that's for the females who live with me, silly ass Suga Bear. The rest of you females will be at the meeting tonight when we head to Tampa."

"Well, count me in, and make sure you come back by and pick me up," Suga Bear uttered, as she threw her bag over her shoulder.

"Me too!"

"Yeah, Peekachu," I voiced.

"Hey, Chazz, are you and Lovely coming tonight also?" "Hell yeah, my nigga. We wanna find out about them Murder Queen bitches!"

I was already disgusted about my brother and Yani, so when Chazz screamed that out, I yelled to Triston. "Man, pull off, Triston!"

The next females to drop off were Charlie B and White Chocolate. I looked over at Diva. She held onto my arm as if I was going to jump out of a moving car. I leaned over and whispered, "Excuse me, Diva, while I help these girls with their bags, Diva."

I had just stepped to the back of the limo, when I thought about what Charlie B had done for me. "Hey, thank you once again for helping me out of that sticky situation earlier."

"Don't mention it, Mike, it's all good," she said and gave me a nice, pleasant smile, "maybe the girls should read the paper a little bit more." We laughed at her comment.

"Yeah, you do have a point. Once again thanks, and if you hear from Sexy Redd before I do, tell her I said hello."

She turned around as she was walking away from me. "Why don't you just call her, Mike?" she asked, as she gazed at me with that radiant face of hers.

"Because I really don't want to bother her like that," I replied.

"Well shoot, she's your girl, so you won't be bothering her. I'm pretty sure she wants to hear from you. Shit, if you were my man I would want you to call me every day," she replied. Then, she turned and walk away, shaking her fine ass.

I never knew she felt that type of way about me. She waved bye.

"Mike, there are others who want to go home, too," Lil Kitty yelled from inside the limo.

"Alright, Lil Kitty, hold on, please," I shouted before stepping back into the limo.

"Hey, Mike, I'll call you later if I do hear from her," Charlie B yelled as she got to her front door.

"Thanks, Charlie B. Oh, and are you coming with us tonight?"

"Hell yeah! Now that I'm back on the team, I ain't about to let no hoe take my spot," she yelled.

"Damn, Lil Kitty, yo' lil short ass couldn't wait?" I asked, as I sat back in the limo.

"Damn, Mike, I need to get home, too," she snapped back.

"Okay, well I guess you staying home tonight, right?"

"Hell nah. The Apollo is one of my biggest nights so you know ya girl is going."

"Whatever."

The limo was driving down Kirkman trying to get over to Rio Grande when Richard peered in the rearview. "Hey, Mike, do you need me tonight?"

"Yeah, it looks that way since several females wanna go tonight, Richard."

"Okay, no problem. I'm going to pick up my truck and then go home to get some fresh clothes," he told me.

"That's fine," I replied. "Get with Nicole and she'll give you a list of the females you'll be picking up later to take to the club tonight," I informed him. "Be back at the house by 8:30."

Forty-five minutes later, we were pulling up into my driveway. I couldn't wait to finally be home. If only I had known what was in store for me. If I had, maybe I would've opted to stay in Jacksonville instead.

***

RICHARD AND I HAD WALKED over to his truck so we could discuss the events for the night's show. He had just gone to sit down when I reached inside my pocket and pulled out some money. I handed him seven hundred dollars. He but his eyes at the nice sum of money. He was shocked by my gesture and his wide-eyed expression was evidence.

"Yo', cuz, what's this for?"

I smiled sincerely. "That's what you earned this week. Use it to get you a few pairs of nice, tailored-made slacks and a couple of silk Versace shirts." His lips spread into a smile and displayed his gratitude.

He shuffled through the large bills as if it were a deck of cards. He looked at me, and then back at the money, and then back at me again. "You sure you didn't make a mistake?" he asked quizzically.

I fumbled with my house key before peeping over my shoulder to face him. "What? You don't want it?" I chuckled out.

"Hell yeah!" he said. It was the loudest I'd heard him speak since he'd got there.

"Thanks, cuz. Man, I'll see you around eight tonight." He held his hand out and I met it with mine as I turned and dapped him up. "Peace," he said, and walked off.

By now, I was more than anxious to get in my own house so I could rest my mind and body.

"Alright, cuz, be safe and I'll see you in a bit," I yelled out seconds before finally entering. *Home sweet home,* I thought.

Seconds later, when I ventured inside and found Diva standing in my foyer, amazed at the large size of my humble abode.

"Michael, you live here in this big ass house?" she asked. She reminded me of a little child at Disney World for the very first time.

"Yes, my love. How do you like it?" I answered modestly.

"It's amazing. I only see houses like this on television," she replied, as she stood there with a huge smile across her face.

"Yeah, I said the same thing the day we moved in. Listen, I got a few calls to make. Nicole will give you a quick tour of the place. Is that cool?"

"Yeah, that's fine," she replied.

" Nicole!" I called out.

"Yeah, Michael, what's up?" she answered from the top of the stairs. "Is there something you need me to do?"

"As a matter of fact, there is. Would you mind giving Diva a tour of the house?" Her whole demeanor changed and she smacked her lips. I contained my laughter though.

"Sure, Mike, give me a quick minute and I'll be more than happy to show your precious Ms. Diva around."

While the two of them went to my room, I ran off to my den to find out what the hell had gone wrong with Bernard's untimely demise. As soon as I sat down in the plush, black leather seat, I lunged forward for the phone and dialed Yani's number. She answered on the second ring.

"Hello, me bruda," she said in her beautiful Haitian accent.

"Yani, what happened?"

"Dat fat mudafucker snapped me picture when I was not looking and he sent de copy to de nosey ass policeman!"

"Damn, are you and my brother okay?"

"Yes."

"Okay, listen. The limo is on the way to pick you up and then take you to the airport. Once you get back in Miami, give me a call to let me know you made it back home safe."

"Mike, ev'ryting should be okay."

"Why do you say that?"

"Because me had on different wig when he fat ass took de picture of me."

"Not really, sweetheart," I told her seriously, "them nosey ass crackers got what they call face recognition. Just let me handle them. You get on that plane and get yourself back home. By the way, when you get inside the limo there's a manilla envelope for you inside the left console. Thank you once again and I'll be in touch with you soon."

I heard her exhale as a brief sigh of relief came through the phone. "Mike dere is no need to worry as long as you have de bad ass Murda Queens wit' you! Ev'ryting will be alright."

I jumped up from my office chair in sheer disbelief. "Yani, what are you talking about?" I asked unknowingly.

She simply replied, "Bye, Michael."

"Hey, wait a minute. Where's my brother?"

"He say someting about he sister in de town."

"My sister?" I asked. Now I was completely confused.

Click!

Yani had hung up.

I placed the phone down and rolled my chair around and thought. *Why would my sister be in town?...* What did she and Firstborn have in mind? The thought of them together weighed heavy on my confused mind. I got up and made my way over to the doorway of my study.

"Okay, ladies, I need you all downstairs really quick—everyone except Diva!" I summoned.

Divia waltzed from my bedroom with her two-piece bathing suit on. "Michael, since you don't need me, is it okay if I take a dip in the pool?" she asked, as she placed her right hand on my chest lovingly.

"Of course, that's fine, Diva. I have to meet with the ladies for a quick minute anyway."

She made her exit and headed down the stairs and out of the foyer. I went towards the kitchen to grab something to drink out of the fridge.

By the time I returned to the dining room area, all the girls living with me had come down stairs and they were all waiting on me. Each one appeared to have her arms folded across her chest.

"Michael, I hope this meeting don't last all fuckin' day," Nicole blurted out. Shit, I do waann get a couple of laps in the pool too before we have to leave for Tampa."

"Whatever, Nicole, it won't be that long. If you guys would just answer a few questions concerning the females that call themselves the Murder Queens," I probed.

"Oh my stars, here we go with this bullshit again," she said, and at the same time rolled her eyes. She looked up toward the ceiling like the answers could be found up there.

"It might be bullshit to you, Nicole, but to others it's some real nasty shit going on around here. And if my name is in it, I, at least, wanna know what the fuck is going on. Entyce, pick your damn head up! You not sleepy 'cause your happy ass slept all the way home," I said. My tone was firm and stern. I needed answers and I wanted them now.

"And why in the hell is Strawberry sitting over there like she's from another fuckin' planet? Do you even know what's going around you, Strawberry?" I asked in an aggravated tone of voice.

Strawberry turned her chair around to face me and dropped a fuckin' bombshell on me. She stood her wide, flat ass up and started talking.

"Well, it seems as though some of the females in this group are going around killing bitches, and for some reason you don't have the slightest idea who they are! So, ladies, I think it's time that we let Mr. Michael here know what's really going on!"

At the same exact time, they all stood up at the table and pulled their panties down and each one revealed her vagina. I sat there and looked on with my mouth wide open. I was stunned.

"Okay, so we about to have an all-out orgy right here in the dining room?" I shouted. I was dumbfounded.

Mignon stared me down with an outlandish look on her face. "No Mr.-I-can't-fuckin'-see!" She pointed to that same small tattoo I'd seen a few hours earlier.

"Oh my, what in the hell?"

On each of their vaginas was a small tattoo of a female shooting a gun. Right inside of their inner thigh, next to their vagina was the words: The Murder Queens ...

The Murder Queens 2

To Be Continued ...
The Murder Queens 3

Coming Soon

Lock Down Publications and Ca$h Presents assisted publishing packages.

BASIC PACKAGE $499
Editing
Cover Design
Formatting

UPGRADED PACKAGE $800
Typing
Editing
Cover Design
Formatting

ADVANCE PACKAGE $1,200
Typing
Editing
Cover Design
Formatting
Copyright registration
Proofreading
Upload book to Amazon

LDP SUPREME PACKAGE $1,500
Typing
Editing
Cover Design
Formatting
Copyright registration
Proofreading
Set up Amazon account
Upload book to Amazon
Advertise on LDP Amazon and Facebook page

***Other services available upon request. Additional charges
may apply
Lock Down Publications
P.O. Box 944
Stockbridge, GA 30281-9998
Phone # 470 303-9761

Submission Guideline

Submit the first three chapters of your completed manuscript to ldpsubmissions@gmail.com, subject line: Your book's title. The manuscript must be in a .doc file and sent as an attachment. Document should be in Times New Roman, double spaced and in size 12 font. Also, provide your synopsis and full contact information. If sending multiple submissions, they must each be in a separate email.

Have a story but no way to send it electronically? You can still submit to LDP/Ca$h Presents. Send in the first three chapters, written or typed, of your completed manuscript to:

LDP: Submissions Dept
Po Box 944
Stockbridge, Ga 30281

DO NOT send original manuscript. Must be a duplicate.

Provide your synopsis and a cover letter containing your full contact information.

Thanks for considering LDP and Ca$h Presents.

<u>NEW RELEASES</u>

SOUL OF A HUSTLER, HEART OF A KILLER by SAYNO-MORE

THE STREETS NEVER LET GO 3 by ROBERT BAPTISTE

RICH $AVAGE 2 by MARTELL "TROUBLESOME" BOLDEN

A GANGSTA'S PARADISE by TRAI'QUAN

THE MURDER QUEENS 2 by MICHAEL GALLON

STRAIGHT BEAST MODE III

De'Kari

KINGPIN KILLAZ IV

STREET KINGS III

PAID IN BLOOD III

CARTEL KILLAZ IV

DOPE GODS III

Hood Rich

SINS OF A HUSTLA II

ASAD

RICH $AVAGE III

By Martell Troublesome Bolden

YAYO V

Bred In The Game 2

S. Allen

THE STREETS WILL TALK II

By Yolanda Moore

SON OF A DOPE FIEND III

HEAVEN GOT A GHETTO II

SKI MASK MONEY II

By Renta

LOYALTY AIN'T PROMISED III

By Keith Williams

I'M NOTHING WITHOUT HIS LOVE II

SINS OF A THUG II

TO THE THUG I LOVED BEFORE II

IN A HUSTLER I TRUST II

By Monet Dragun

QUIET MONEY IV

EXTENDED CLIP III

Michael Gallon

THUG LIFE IV

By **Trai'Quan**

THE STREETS MADE ME IV

By **Larry D. Wright**

IF YOU CROSS ME ONCE II

ANGEL IV

By **Anthony Fields**

THE STREETS WILL NEVER CLOSE IV

By **K'ajji**

HARD AND RUTHLESS III

KILLA KOUNTY III

By **Khufu**

MONEY GAME III

By **Smoove Dolla**

JACK BOYS VS DOPE BOYS II

A GANGSTA'S QUR'AN V

COKE GIRLZ II

COKE BOYS II

By **Romell Tukes**

MURDA WAS THE CASE II

Elijah R. Freeman

THE STREETS NEVER LET GO III

By **Robert Baptiste**

AN UNFORESEEN LOVE IV

By **Meesha**

KING OF THE TRENCHES III
by **GHOST & TRANAY ADAMS**

MONEY MAFIA II

By **Jibril Williams**

QUEEN OF THE ZOO III

The Murder Queens 2

By **Black Migo**
VICIOUS LOYALTY III
By Kingpen
A GANGSTA'S PAIN III
By J-Blunt
CONFESSIONS OF A JACKBOY III
By Nicholas Lock
GRIMEY WAYS III
By Ray Vinci
KING KILLA II
By Vincent "Vitto" Holloway
BETRAYAL OF A THUG II
By Fre$h
THE MURDER QUEENS III
By Michael Gallon
THE BIRTH OF A GANGSTER III
By Delmont Player
TREAL LOVE II
By Le'Monica Jackson
FOR THE LOVE OF BLOOD II
By Jamel Mitchell
RAN OFF ON DA PLUG II
By Paper Boi Rari
HOOD CONSIGLIERE II
By Keese
PRETTY GIRLS DO NASTY THINGS II
By Nicole Goosby
PROTÉGÉ OF A LEGEND II
By Corey Robinson
IT'S JUST ME AND YOU II

Michael Gallon

By Ah'Million
BORN IN THE GRAVE II
By Self Made Tay

<u>**Available Now**</u>

RESTRAINING ORDER **I & II**
By **CA$H & Coffee**
LOVE KNOWS NO BOUNDARIES **I II & III**
By **Coffee**
RAISED AS A GOON I, II, III & IV
BRED BY THE SLUMS I, II, III
BLAST FOR ME I & II
ROTTEN TO THE CORE I II III
A BRONX TALE I, II, III
DUFFLE BAG CARTEL I II III IV V VI
HEARTLESS GOON I II III IV V
A SAVAGE DOPEBOY I II
DRUG LORDS I II III
CUTTHROAT MAFIA I II
KING OF THE TRENCHES
By **Ghost**
LAY IT DOWN **I & II**
LAST OF A DYING BREED I II
BLOOD STAINS OF A SHOTTA I & II III
By **Jamaica**
LOYAL TO THE GAME I II III

LIFE OF SIN I, II III

By **TJ & Jelissa**

BLOODY COMMAS I & II

SKI MASK CARTEL I II & III

KING OF NEW YORK I II,III IV V

RISE TO POWER I II III

COKE KINGS I II III IV V

BORN HEARTLESS I II III IV

KING OF THE TRAP I II

By **T.J. Edwards**

IF LOVING HIM IS WRONG...I & II

LOVE ME EVEN WHEN IT HURTS I II III

By **Jelissa**

WHEN THE STREETS CLAP BACK I & II III

THE HEART OF A SAVAGE I II III IV

MONEY MAFIA

LOYAL TO THE SOIL I II III

By **Jibril Williams**

A DISTINGUISHED THUG STOLE MY HEART I II & III

LOVE SHOULDN'T HURT I II III IV

RENEGADE BOYS I II III IV

PAID IN KARMA I II III

SAVAGE STORMS I II III

AN UNFORESEEN LOVE I II III

By **Meesha**

A GANGSTER'S CODE I &, II III

A GANGSTER'S SYN I II III

THE SAVAGE LIFE I II III

CHAINED TO THE STREETS I II III

BLOOD ON THE MONEY I II III

Michael Gallon

A GANGSTA'S PAIN I II

By J-Blunt

PUSH IT TO THE LIMIT

By **Bre' Hayes**

BLOOD OF A BOSS **I, II, III, IV, V**

SHADOWS OF THE GAME

TRAP BASTARD

By **Askari**

THE STREETS BLEED MURDER **I, II & III**

THE HEART OF A GANGSTA I II& III

By **Jerry Jackson**

CUM FOR ME I II III IV V VI VII VIII

An **LDP Erotica Collaboration**

BRIDE OF A HUSTLA **I II & II**

THE FETTI GIRLS **I, II& III**

CORRUPTED BY A GANGSTA I, II III, IV

BLINDED BY HIS LOVE

THE PRICE YOU PAY FOR LOVE I, II ,III

DOPE GIRL MAGIC I II III

By **Destiny Skai**

WHEN A GOOD GIRL GOES BAD

By **Adrienne**

THE COST OF LOYALTY I II III

By Kweli

A GANGSTER'S REVENGE **I II III & IV**

THE BOSS MAN'S DAUGHTERS I II III IV V

A SAVAGE LOVE **I & II**

BAE BELONGS TO ME I II

A HUSTLER'S DECEIT I, II, III

WHAT BAD BITCHES DO I, II, III

The Murder Queens 2

SOUL OF A MONSTER I II III

KILL ZONE

A DOPE BOY'S QUEEN I II III

TIL DEATH

By **Aryanna**

A KINGPIN'S AMBITON

A KINGPIN'S AMBITION **II**

I MURDER FOR THE DOUGH

By **Ambitious**

TRUE SAVAGE I II III IV V VI VII

DOPE BOY MAGIC I, II, III

MIDNIGHT CARTEL I II III

CITY OF KINGZ I II

NIGHTMARE ON SILENT AVE

THE PLUG OF LIL MEXICO II

CLASSIC CITY

By **Chris Green**

A DOPEBOY'S PRAYER

By **Eddie "Wolf" Lee**

THE KING CARTEL **I, II & III**

By **Frank Gresham**

THESE NIGGAS AIN'T LOYAL **I, II & III**

By **Nikki Tee**

GANGSTA SHYT **I II &III**

By **CATO**

THE ULTIMATE BETRAYAL

By **Phoenix**

BOSS'N UP **I , II & III**

By **Royal Nicole**

I LOVE YOU TO DEATH

Michael Gallon

By **Destiny J**
I RIDE FOR MY HITTA
I STILL RIDE FOR MY HITTA
By **Misty Holt**
LOVE & CHASIN' PAPER
By **Qay Crockett**
TO DIE IN VAIN
SINS OF A HUSTLA
By **ASAD**
BROOKLYN HUSTLAZ
By **Boogsy Morina**
BROOKLYN ON LOCK I & II
By **Sonovia**
GANGSTA CITY
By **Teddy Duke**
A DRUG KING AND HIS DIAMOND I & II III
A DOPEMAN'S RICHES
HER MAN, MINE'S TOO I, II
CASH MONEY HO'S
THE WIFEY I USED TO BE I II
PRETTY GIRLS DO NASTY THINGS
By Nicole Goosby
TRAPHOUSE KING **I II & III**
KINGPIN KILLAZ I II III
STREET KINGS I II
PAID IN BLOOD **I II**
CARTEL KILLAZ I II III
DOPE GODS I II
By **Hood Rich**
LIPSTICK KILLAH **I, II, III**

CRIME OF PASSION I II & III

FRIEND OR FOE I II III

By **Mimi**

STEADY MOBBN' **I, II, III**

THE STREETS STAINED MY SOUL I II III

By **Marcellus Allen**

WHO SHOT YA **I, II, III**

SON OF A DOPE FIEND I II

HEAVEN GOT A GHETTO

SKI MASK MONEY

Renta

GORILLAZ IN THE BAY **I II III IV**

TEARS OF A GANGSTA I II

3X KRAZY I II

STRAIGHT BEAST MODE I II

DE'KARI

TRIGGADALE I II III

MURDAROBER WAS THE CASE

Elijah R. Freeman

GOD BLESS THE TRAPPERS I, II, III

THESE SCANDALOUS STREETS I, II, III

FEAR MY GANGSTA I, II, III IV, V

THESE STREETS DON'T LOVE NOBODY I, II

BURY ME A G I, II, III, IV, V

A GANGSTA'S EMPIRE I, II, III, IV

THE DOPEMAN'S BODYGAURD I II

THE REALEST KILLAZ I II III

THE LAST OF THE OGS I II III

Tranay Adams

THE STREETS ARE CALLING

Michael Gallon

Duquie Wilson
MARRIED TO A BOSS I II III
By Destiny Skai & Chris Green
KINGZ OF THE GAME I II III IV V VI
Playa Ray
SLAUGHTER GANG I II III
RUTHLESS HEART I II III
By Willie Slaughter
FUK SHYT
By Blakk Diamond
DON'T F#CK WITH MY HEART I II
By Linnea
ADDICTED TO THE DRAMA I II III
IN THE ARM OF HIS BOSS II
By Jamila
YAYO I II III IV
A SHOOTER'S AMBITION I II
BRED IN THE GAME
By S. Allen
TRAP GOD I II III
RICH $AVAGE I II
MONEY IN THE GRAVE I II III
By Martell Troublesome Bolden
FOREVER GANGSTA
GLOCKS ON SATIN SHEETS I II
By Adrian Dulan
TOE TAGZ I II III IV
LEVELS TO THIS SHYT I II
IT'S JUST ME AND YOU
By Ah'Million

306

KINGPIN DREAMS I II III

RAN OFF ON DA PLUG

By Paper Boi Rari

CONFESSIONS OF A GANGSTA I II III IV

CONFESSIONS OF A JACKBOY I II

By Nicholas Lock

I'M NOTHING WITHOUT HIS LOVE

SINS OF A THUG

TO THE THUG I LOVED BEFORE

A GANGSTA SAVED XMAS

IN A HUSTLER I TRUST

By Monet Dragun

CAUGHT UP IN THE LIFE I II III

THE STREETS NEVER LET GO I II

By Robert Baptiste

NEW TO THE GAME I II III

MONEY, MURDER & MEMORIES I II III

By **Malik D. Rice**

LIFE OF A SAVAGE I II III

A GANGSTA'S QUR'AN I II III IV

MURDA SEASON I II III

GANGLAND CARTEL I II III

CHI'RAQ GANGSTAS I II III

KILLERS ON ELM STREET I II III

JACK BOYZ N DA BRONX I II III

A DOPEBOY'S DREAM I II III

JACK BOYS VS DOPE BOYS

COKE GIRLZ

COKE BOYS

By Romell Tukes

Michael Gallon

LOYALTY AIN'T PROMISED I II

By Keith Williams

QUIET MONEY I II III

THUG LIFE I II III

EXTENDED CLIP I II

A GANGSTA'S PARADISE

By **Trai'Quan**

THE STREETS MADE ME I II III

By **Larry D. Wright**

THE ULTIMATE SACRIFICE I, II, III, IV, V, VI

KHADIFI

IF YOU CROSS ME ONCE

ANGEL I II III

IN THE BLINK OF AN EYE

By **Anthony Fields**

THE LIFE OF A HOOD STAR

By Ca$h & Rashia Wilson

THE STREETS WILL NEVER CLOSE I II III

By K'ajji

CREAM I II III

THE STREETS WILL TALK

By Yolanda Moore

NIGHTMARES OF A HUSTLA I II III

By King Dream

CONCRETE KILLA I II III

VICIOUS LOYALTY I II

By Kingpen

HARD AND RUTHLESS I II

MOB TOWN 251

THE BILLIONAIRE BENTLEYS I II III

The Murder Queens 2

By Von Diesel
GHOST MOB

Stilloan Robinson
MOB TIES I II III IV V VI
SOUL OF A HUSTLER, HEART OF A KILLER

By SayNoMore
BODYMORE MURDERLAND I II III
THE BIRTH OF A GANGSTER I II

By Delmont Player
FOR THE LOVE OF A BOSS

By C. D. Blue
MOBBED UP I II III IV
THE BRICK MAN I II III IV
THE COCAINE PRINCESS I II III IV V

By King Rio
KILLA KOUNTY I II III

By Khufu
MONEY GAME I II

By Smoove Dolla
A GANGSTA'S KARMA I II

By FLAME
KING OF THE TRENCHES I II

by **GHOST & TRANAY ADAMS**
QUEEN OF THE ZOO I II

By **Black Migo**
GRIMEY WAYS I II

By Ray Vinci
XMAS WITH AN ATL SHOOTER

By Ca$h & Destiny Skai
KING KILLA

Michael Gallon

By Vincent "Vitto" Holloway
BETRAYAL OF A THUG
By Fre$h
THE MURDER QUEENS I II
By Michael Gallon
TREAL LOVE
By Le'Monica Jackson
FOR THE LOVE OF BLOOD
By Jamel Mitchell
HOOD CONSIGLIERE
By Keese
PROTÉGÉ OF A LEGEND
By Corey Robinson
BORN IN THE GRAVE
By Self Made Tay
MOAN IN MY MOUTH
By XTASY

<u>BOOKS BY LDP'S CEO, CA$H</u>

TRUST IN NO MAN

TRUST IN NO MAN 2

TRUST IN NO MAN 3

BONDED BY BLOOD

SHORTY GOT A THUG

THUGS CRY

THUGS CRY 2

THUGS CRY 3

TRUST NO BITCH

TRUST NO BITCH 2

TRUST NO BITCH 3

TIL MY CASKET DROPS

RESTRAINING ORDER

RESTRAINING ORDER 2

IN LOVE WITH A CONVICT

LIFE OF A HOOD STAR

XMAS WITH AN ATL SHOOTER

Michael Gallon